
★

I headed for the parking lot. The sun was going down and it was getting a little chilly. I pulled my sweater together and hurried to my car. I paused as I put the key in the lock. There was a paper stuck under the windshield wiper.

"I hate those ads," I mumbled as I reached for it. "I bet they don't drum up much business, either."

I glanced at it and saw it wasn't an ad, after all. It was a message to me. I read it and my heart began to beat faster. The note said: You need to get out of Elva Kingfield's life. I don't care if you are a minister, if you keep putting your nose in her business, it may get chopped off—or worse!

★

Previously published Worldwide Mystery title by
LYNETTE HALL HAMPTON

JILTED BY DEATH

LYNETTE HALL HAMPTON

ECHOES
OF
MERCY

WORLDWIDE®

TORONTO • NEW YORK • LONDON
AMSTERDAM • PARIS • SYDNEY • HAMBURG
STOCKHOLM • ATHENS • TOKYO • MILAN
MADRID • WARSAW • BUDAPEST • AUCKLAND

Dedicated to:
Camilla "Kit" Hall
My sister, my supporter,
my confidant and my best friend.

Recycling programs
for this product may
not exist in your area.

ECHOES OF MERCY

A Worldwide Mystery/January 2011

First published by Alabaster Book Publishing

ISBN-13: 978-0-373-26736-1

Printed in U.S.A.

Acknowledgments

A big thanks to:

My friends and family
for all their support and encouragement

My readers and editors:
Elaine Walsh and Camilla Hall

My critique group, The Kernersville Writers
Roundtable—Dixie, Larry, Helen, Joanne,
Emogene, John, Chuck, Dave, Cheriess

Alabaster Books for their expertise in printer set up,
pre-publicity tips and helping with book sales.

And to all of you who kept asking,
"When is the next Willa book coming out?"
It kept me working until it was ready to publish.

ONE

THE FALL FESTIVAL WAS winding down at First United Methodist Church in Liverpool, North Carolina. The remaining children were climbing on the tractor-drawn trailer for a last-minute hayride around the block. A few adults were strolling among the rows of tables set up under the oak trees in the front yard to examine the already picked over, handmade bazaar items to see if there was anything left they wanted to buy. Another group of grown-ups were stuffing their faces with the leftover hot dogs and hamburgers as the volunteer cooks cleaned the grills which had been set up in the church parking lot. A number of teenagers were gathered in groups playing volleyball, shooting baskets or sitting with friends just laughing and talking as the young often do. The rest of the volunteer workers and vendors were closing their booths as they made preparations to go home. The reporter from the Winston-Salem television station had finished her interviews and had put away her microphone. She was now chatting with Myrtle Johnson. Someone told me earlier that the reporter was a niece of the Johnsons'.

"Well, Willa, it looks like this idea of yours turned out well," Philip Gallaway, the senior minister, said to me across the picnic table where we were sipping sodas and eating a sandwich. It was the first chance either of us had to sit down, much less eat anything.

"I'm glad," I said, wiping my mouth with a paper napkin. "You never know what will happen when you do something like this for the first time. You have to go with it and see if the congregation supports it."

"I think there was a nice turnout, not only from our church, but from the town as well."

I nodded. "With all the rain we had this week, I was beginning to worry."

He laughed. "But look at today. Not a cloud in the sky."

I smiled at my boss and went on. "Thanks for letting me try it."

"Thank you for presenting it to the administrative board." He smiled at me and added, "When you were appointed here, I told the staff-parish committee that you were one of the best qualified assistant ministers I'd ever seen. I knew you had the ability to help me get this church more active in community affairs. Today proves I was right."

"Thank you, Philip. It's been a pleasure being your assistant. I feel I've grown spiritually and mentally since coming to this church." I meant what I was saying. It had been a pleasure working with and for Dr. Philip Gallaway. He was a great church leader who didn't just "preach" at the people. Though his words were often profound, his greatest quality was the fact that he led the congregation by example. His motto was to show, not just tell, people what to do. Even Mrs. Gallaway's Alzheimer's disease hadn't slowed him down.

"It's too bad that your friend couldn't get here in time to see what you're capable of arranging."

"It would have been nice," I said. I didn't add that Jacob's job as a traveling correspondent for one of the animal networks afforded him so many exciting affairs to attend that this festival would be awfully tame to him.

Liverpool's mayor, Jesse Snow, a soft breeze tousling his white hair, came up to the table. "Well, folks, you did good. Not only was this a wonderful venture for our church, but it was also good for Liverpool. A lot of people who go to other churches and probably some that don't even go to church showed up and that's always a plus. And," he added, "the media did a good job. We're going to be featured on the eleven-o'clock news tonight."

"I'm glad you're pleased, Mayor," Philip said. "But the credit goes to Willa. She did all the planning and most of the work."

Jesse laughed. "I don't doubt that. When our preacher Willa decides to do something, she doesn't hold back, does she?"

"Not at all."

"Gentlemen—" I blushed "—I appreciate the compliments, but it takes a lot of cooperation to pull off an event like this."

"I wish you would come to some of our town council meetings and give our leaders a few pointers. It takes them forever to decide on something, then another forever to plan it and then act on it."

"Well, you can't have her, Mayor. We need Willa right here at First United Methodist."

Bill Draper, the editor of Liverpool's weekly paper, walked up, camera in hand. Though he was a member of Oak Street Baptist, where my friend Trent Freeman was pastor, Bill had spent most of the afternoon covering the festivities here for next week's edition.

"Let me get a couple of shots of the tired preachers before I leave," he said.

"That's a good idea." Jesse moved aside. "These two have worked like Trojans today."

"I can see that. Would you rate this festival a success, Reverend Gallaway?"

"Absolutely. I think it has been good for the church and the community."

"And you, Reverend Hinshaw? What do you think?"

"It seems that everyone who came enjoyed themselves. One of our goals was to bring the church and the community closer together in an informal setting. I feel we accomplished that."

Before he could ask another question a car that I would classify as a classic came roaring down the street which ran behind the church and the parking lot. With a squeal of the tires, it made a sharp turn into the graveyard driveway and came to a screeching halt.

Everyone laughed but me. I looked at the three of them, completely puzzled. "What's going on?"

"That's Elva Kingfield," Philip said.

"Everyone in town knows about her driving," Jesse added. "No matter how many tickets she's had, she doesn't get any better."

"It's a good thing she doesn't drive very often," Bill Draper said.

"Why don't they take her license?" I asked.

"It wouldn't matter. She'd drive anyway," Jesse explained.

"But—" I started.

Philip smiled at me and interrupted. "Elva is one of our town eccentrics. With the blessing of the chief, the police have decided to accept her the way she is. The rest of the town folk just stay out of her way when they see her coming."

"Besides, she seldom gets on the road," Jesse added.

"The rumor is that she's afraid to come out very often because someone will try to take her money," Bill Draper said.

"Another rumor is that she stays home and counts her money all the time." Jesse laughed. "Of course, there's a pile of it to count."

I didn't say anything further. I just watched as an older woman in a pink dress got out of the big black car with a basket of flowers.

She paused for a few moments and looked in our direction. She then walked to a grave, removed the old arrangement and replaced it with the basket. She didn't stay long, but I could tell she was intent on what she was doing and ignoring the activity in the churchyard. When she got back to her car, she paused and looked at us again. I expected her to walk in our direction, but she simply got into her car and roared off.

"I thought she was going to join us," I said.

Philip explained, "Elva never goes into a crowd. Doesn't

even come to church anymore. She's been a member here for most of her seventy-some years, but has become an almost recluse since her husband died fifteen years ago. She does show up every couple of months to replace the flowers on Leo's grave."

"I see she still drives that old Buick," Bill Draper said. "I remember Leo bought that thing new just a couple of years before he died. He was very proud of it."

"Yeah," Jesse said. "A young car salesman, knowing how rich the Kingfields were, tried to sell Elva a new one after Leo died. She told him she'd just drive the one he left for the rest of her life." He laughed. "Looks like she's going to do it."

"She must have some interesting stories to tell. Do you think I should visit her, Philip?" I asked.

"If you want to, I think it might do her good. I go to see her now and then and she's always glad to see me. She used to be very active in church, but things changed when Leo died."

"You might even be able to persuade her to come back to church," Jesse said.

Bill was opening his mouth to say something, but didn't get a chance.

A thunderous explosion in the graveyard made us all jump and several people screamed. The air in the southeast corner of the cemetery was immediately filled with dust, debris and chunks of a granite tombstone.

TWO

CHAOS DESCENDED ON the church parking lot. Some people ran toward the graveyard, others ran to their cars, and still others stood in place waiting for I have no idea what. I was in the group that ran to the graveyard. Philip was on my heels. Jesse and Bill followed. The newswoman and her camera-man beat us all to the gravesite. The camera whirred and she talked fast, trying to give her station the jump on the breaking news.

The explosion had made a mess of Leo Kingfield's grave. The stone was no longer in existence and there was a hole where it had stood. The opening exposed a section of the vault. I was relieved to see it had not cracked. That meant the coffin was still in place and the body had not been disturbed.

Philip must have been thinking the same thing because he said, "Thank God, only a corner of the vault is showing. I don't know how Elva would have taken it if that had been destroyed."

"Why would she care?" Jesse asked. "She's the one who planted the bomb, wasn't she? It had to be in that basket of flowers."

Philip shook his head. "We don't even know that it was a bomb. Besides, there's no way in the world Elva would do that to Leo's grave."

"She was the last one at the grave," Bill put in. He seemed to switch to his reporter demeanor when he asked, "Reverend Gallaway, as Mrs. Kingfield's minister, why do you think she blew up her husband's grave?"

"As I said," Philip explained, "I don't believe Mrs. Kingfield blew up the grave. I'm not sure what's going on, but I know she wouldn't do this to her beloved Leo."

Philip seemed to know Mrs. Kingfield pretty well and he seemed positive she wouldn't have done this. If she hadn't, I wondered who could have done such a thing. As Jesse had said, she was the one who put the flowers there. I didn't get a chance to voice my thoughts because Philip said, "Bill, do you have your cell phone?" When Bill nodded, Philip went on. "Will you please call the police? I'll have to go back into the church to get my phone."

Bill took a cell phone from his pocket and began to dial.

Philip took my arm and pulled me aside. "Willa," he almost whispered, "the TV reporter is heading this way. I'll keep her and Bill Draper busy if you'll please go tell Elva what has happened. She's going to be upset and I don't want her to hear it on the evening news."

"Of course. How do I get there?"

"Do you know where Blue Bell Road is?"

"I've seen the turnoff, and I've heard horror stories about a dangerous curve on it, but I've never driven down it."

He nodded and went on. "It's about half a mile after the curve. You can't miss the house. It's a big Victorian affair sitting on a hill on the left side of the road. At one time it was a beauty, but it has become somewhat run-down since Leo died." He paused, then added, "Just watch out for Blue Bell Curve. It's true that a lot of wrecks and even deaths have occurred there."

The TV reporter was almost upon us. I left Philip to talk with her and as casually as I could, I headed toward my apartment complex, which was across the street that ran behind the church and the graveyard.

I got into my car and headed toward Blue Bell Road, wondering what I would say to Mrs. Kingfield.

Philip's description of the curve was perfect. It was in the shape of a horseshoe and ended at a small bridge. I could see how one could lose control of a car there.

In exactly a half mile, I saw the huge Victorian structure on a hill. I knew this had to be the Kingfield home. I switched on my blinker and turned in the driveway which made a semi-circle in front of the house. I'm sure when it was new the house was a showplace. Now there were some loose shutters here and there and the two turrets were showing dilapidated areas. The trim on the rest of the house had faded from the once-bright yellow to a peeling beige. I couldn't understand why a woman with as much money as they said Mrs. Kingfield had would let such a beautiful home fall into disrepair.

As I crossed the cracked broken tile front porch, I couldn't help imagining the gatherings that had probably taken place on these premises. Testifying to the fact that people had been entertained here were four chairs and a large wicker table sitting at one end of the wraparound porch. It, too, had seen better days. There were missing sections in the chairs and the table was leaning to one side because of a broken leg. It made me sad to see all this decay.

There was no bell at the front door so I lifted the rusting ornate doorknocker and rapped three times. Hardly any time passed before a withered woman wearing a black maid's uniform opened the door.

"Hello," I said. "I'm Willa Hinshaw, the assistant minister at First United Methodist Church. I need to see Mrs. Kingfield, please."

"Follow me," she said.

I did.

She opened a door to the left of the entryway and I stepped into a room decorated in what were probably priceless antiques. A painting hung over the burgundy velvet sofa that was most likely done by one of the masters. I didn't see anything in the room that would be called a replica. From the Chippendale tables to the Duncan Fyffe pull-up chairs and sofa, I doubted there was a piece of furniture that wouldn't bring enough money to refurnish my whole apartment. Much of it reminded me of the furnishings in the Poole mansion where I'd spent a lot of time this summer.

I was admiring a Queen Anne table, which was almost a twin to one I'd admired the first time I was in the Pooles' home, when Elva Kingfield entered the room. "Hello, Reverend Hinshaw."

I turned to see a dignified little woman with a pile of white hair on top of her head and an infectious smile on her lightly painted lips. I couldn't help noticing the pink of her lipstick was a perfect match to the pink silk dress she wore.

"Mrs. Kingfield, I'm sorry to barge in on you like this, but I came to tell you about something that has happened." Now I was wondering why. There was no television in this room. There probably wasn't one in the house. Maybe Mrs. Kingfield wouldn't even hear about the explosion.

"Please sit down, Reverend Hinshaw. I'll have Bernice bring in some tea."

"That won't be necessary…"

Before I could finish my sentence she said, "Of course it's necessary. I can't have a guest and not serve tea."

She pulled the bell cord beside the door and then pointed to a grouping of chairs near the fireplace. "Let's sit down."

I obeyed and took a seat on the Chippendale chair she indicated. She sat opposite me in a matching chair.

Before I could speak the woman who had opened the front door reappeared. "Yes, ma'am?"

"Please serve tea, Bernice," my hostess commanded. "And get some of those little tea cakes we have."

"Yes, Ms. Elva," the maid said.

"Now, Reverend Hinshaw…" Elva Kingfield turned to me "…you seem to have something important on your mind. Would you like to explain?"

"Yes, Mrs. Kingfield. There was an incident at the church this afternoon and I was sure you and your family would want to know about it."

"My dear, I have very little family. My only child was

killed in Desert Storm and his wife moved to Oregon to be near her family. I hardly know my grandchildren. I have a few cousins and a couple of nieces in the area, but the only other family member who cares a whit about me is a nephew in Atlanta. I'm expecting him to visit sometime between now and Christmas. He usually comes up in the fall or early winter. The others only come around when they think I'm going to die. They want to know if they're mentioned in the will."

I didn't know what to say about her description of her family so I said, "I know you're aware that there was a festival at the church today."

"Yes. I saw the crowd when I took new flowers for Leo's grave."

"I noticed you when you brought the flowers." I paused as the maid brought in a silver tea service and sat it down on the table in front of Mrs. Kingfield. Not only did the big tray contain the teapot, creamer and sugar bowl, but it also sported two cups and a crystal plate of sugarcoated tea cakes. They looked delicious.

Mrs. Kingfield served the tea in fragile china cups, which were trimmed in pink roses. She insisted I take a cookie. She didn't have to work hard to persuade me. I bit into it and found it was as tasty as it looked.

Handing me a white linen napkin, she said, "Now. What was it you wanted to tell me?"

"As I said, I noticed you bring the flowers for your husband's grave." I was grappling for words to explain the situation.

She nodded and I went on. "Shortly after you left, there was a disturbance in the graveyard. Something exploded and I'm afraid Mr. Kingfield's tombstone was destroyed in the mayhem."

"Oh, my goodness." She put a dainty hand at her throat. "What caused the explosion?"

"We're not sure." I looked at her expecting more of an outburst. When it didn't come, I went on. "We felt sure you'd want to know about it."

"Of course I do, and it was kind of you to come tell me."

"Reverend Gallaway would have come himself, but the news reporters had him cornered. We didn't want you to hear about the explosion on the news."

"That was kind of you, Reverend Hinshaw."

"Why don't you call me Willa?"

She smiled at me. "Thank you, my dear. Then you must call me Elva." She took a deep breath. "I know you said the headstone was destroyed. What about Leo's grave?"

"The grave is fine. There will have to be some soil added and grass planted but other than that, it will be okay."

"That's good. I wouldn't want to think that Leo's body was disturbed." She picked up the teapot. "Would you like more, Willa?"

I shook my head and sipped the tea already in my cup. I was trying to understand what was going on in Elva Kingfield's mind. She was taking the news awfully well. Was she the one who blew up the grave or did she just not care that her husband's gravesite had been destroyed? Was she not the grieving widow everyone thought she was or was she just putting on a brave face for me? I tried to concentrate on these thoughts as I looked at the beautiful painting hanging over the sofa. Again I was drawn in by its exquisite colors and masterful strokes.

She sat the pot down and passed the cakes to me. I took one and said, "I'm sorry this happened. We're at a loss as to what actually went on. You didn't happen to see anyone or anything suspicious while you were in the graveyard, did you?"

"The only people I saw were the ones in the churchyard and parking lot. If there was anyone else in the graveyard they were out of my sight." Again she picked up the teapot. "Please let me refill your cup."

I knew she wouldn't give up until I had more tea so I held out my cup. "Thank you," was all I could think of to say.

She poured my tea and smiled at me. "Willa, I don't want you to think I'm insensitive, but when you're my age you learn to take things as they come. Of course I'd rather nothing had happened to Leo's grave, but since it has, there's really nothing I can do about it. I'm just grateful that he wasn't disturbed. Of course, I'll replace the headstone right away, but other than that, I'll just accept what has happened."

"That's a good attitude. I'm not sure I could be so philosophical about it."

"Again, my dear, that will come with age." She bit into a tea cake.

I shifted in the chair and sat my teacup down. "Can you think of any reason anyone would want to destroy your husband's grave, Elva?"

She frowned. "Of course not. Why would anyone want to do that?"

"That's what nobody seems to know."

"Then the explosion was not an accident?"

I saw the confusion in her eyes and knew I had not explained the situation well. "We think someone deliberately exploded your husband's tombstone, Elva. Probably with a bomb."

"Oh, my!" Again she clutched her throat. "I didn't know that."

I didn't want her to become more upset so I said, "I'm sure the police will be able to get to the bottom of it all soon."

"But why?"

"Eventually we'll know."

"Oh, I hope so. It hurts to think that someone would purposely try to—what were they trying to do?"

"Let's just leave it to the authorities. They'll let us know as soon as they can."

"Will you keep me informed, Willa?"

"Of course we will."

"No. Not we. You, Willa Hinshaw. I want you to be the one to keep me informed. Philip Gallaway is a nice man, but he has problems of his own and I don't want to cause him any more distress. I prefer that you be the one to get in touch with me."

"Then I'll be happy to let you know what's happening."

"Thank you, my dear. That means a lot to me."

After that, the conversation dwindled and I stayed only long enough to finish my tea and cakes. Elva Kingfield walked me to the door and I promised to call her soon.

THREE

WHEN I PULLED INTO the parking lot of my apartment complex my friend Trent Freeman, the pastor of Oak Street Baptist Church, was sitting in one of the wicker chairs on my front balcony. He and I had been dating fairly regularly since my ordeal back in the summer, but neither of us was ready to make a commitment, or in our case, concessions so we could make a commitment. There was no doubt that there was a deep attraction between us and we both felt the magic when we were together, but so far we'd managed to skirt the issues that would divide us. Though I was often referred to as "that Baptist preacher's girlfriend" and he was called "the Baptist preacher who is involved with that Methodist woman," at this point we were content to stay special friends.

He stood up and smiled as I got out of the car.

"Oh, Trent. I'm so glad to see you."

"I'm sorry I couldn't make your festival. I had to do a wedding in Asheville. I'd just arrived back at my office when I heard about the explosion. I went to the church and Philip told me where you'd gone. Are you okay?"

By the time he finished speaking I'd reached the top of the steps. I didn't care who was watching; I reached for him and he responded by putting his arms around me.

"For a day that started out so wonderful, it's turned into a nightmare," I said against his chest.

"I'm sure it's been awful for you." He released me and took the key from my hand to unlock the door.

We had barely stepped inside when the phone rang.

"Why don't you just let it ring?" Trent suggested.

I nodded. The answering machine picked up and it was a reporter asking to talk to me. She left a number.

"I just don't want to talk with anyone right now." I dropped into a chair.

"I understand." He started toward the door.

"I don't mean you, Trent. I'm glad you're here. I just don't want to talk to reporters and such. Maybe later."

He nodded and took a seat himself. "How was Mrs. Kingfield?"

"She took the news okay, I guess. I expected her to be more emotional, but she was kind of matter-of-fact." I looked at him. "It's strange, Trent. A bomb going off in the graveyard like that. I just don't understand it."

"Are they sure it was a bomb?"

I shook my head. "Everyone just assumes that it was. It made too big of a mess to be anything else."

"Do you think Mrs. Kingfield blew up the grave?"

"Philip was adamant that she wouldn't do such a thing and after meeting her, I'm not sure that she would do it either. I just can't imagine that delicate little woman messing with explosives of any kind."

"Then it's a good thing she'd left when it went off. She could have been killed."

This remark jolted me and I sat straight up. "You know, you could be right." I shook my head. "I don't want to think it, but someone may have intended to kill that sweet little lady."

"I'm sure it was just some kind of mishap. It could have been meant as a joke that got out of hand." His smile was wide and reassuring and his blue eyes twinkled as he looked at me.

I couldn't help smiling back as I shook my head again. My mind began conjuring up ideas of what might have happened. "Or as a warning of some kind."

"To Elva Kingfield?"

I shrugged. "I don't know, Trent. Like everyone else, at first I assumed Elva had blown up the grave for some reason but…

well…maybe she didn't know the basket would explode." I shuttered. "Maybe you were right in the first place. Someone may have been trying to blow her up or at least scare her."

"I hate to think that, Willa."

"So do I, but you have to admit, it's weird."

"Maybe the police will find the answers soon."

"I hope so." I was beginning to relax. He had that effect on me. "Do you know Elva, Trent?"

"I've never met her, but I've heard stories about her being a recluse since her husband died. As a matter of fact, some of her relatives attend my church."

"Oh." I was interested. "What relatives?"

"A niece, I think, and maybe a cousin. There could be others. You know how it is in a church. People are always related to each other and it's hard to keep kinfolk straight."

I nodded. "You're right about that. Sometimes I'll hear one person talking about another one—and not always in a flattering way—then I'll learn they're related and have been bickering for years."

"Same thing goes on at Oak Street."

A knock at the door interrupted our conversation. I started to get up, but Trent said, "I'll get it for you. Want me to get rid of them?"

"It doesn't matter. I can't hide forever."

Trent opened the door and then stepped aside, saying, "Come in, Blaire."

"I don't want to intrude."

"Don't be silly." I sat up straight to greet my neighbor and good friend, Blaire Peterson. "I'm glad you came over."

"I saw Trent here, but I wanted to see for myself that you're okay."

"I'm fine. Just baffled, like everyone else."

"I don't doubt that. Have you heard anything more?"

"No, but I did go see Elva Kingfield. It was her husband's grave that was destroyed."

"It's past dinnertime," Trent said, looking at his watch. "So if you ladies will excuse me, I'm going to raid Willa's kitchen and see what I can stir up for us to eat."

"Want me to help?" I asked.

"No. You keep Blaire company and I'll surprise you both."

"Don't fix anything for me. I'll—" Blaire started to say.

"Don't be silly," I said. "He makes a mean omelet and though I'm not a betting woman, I think that's what we'll be having."

"It does sound tempting." Blaire laughed. "After I left the festival, I spent the rest of the day shopping and my feet hurt. It would be good to have dinner prepared for me."

"Say no more." He went into the kitchen. "I'll call you when it's ready."

"Blaire, I know you haven't lived in Liverpool much longer than I have, but you do belong to Trent's church. He said he thought Elva Kingfield had some relatives there. Do you happen to know any of them?"

"I think Penny Saxon is a niece or something. I heard her talking about Mrs. Kingfield at one of our family-night dinners." Blaire dropped to the pull-up green chair. "She wasn't very complimentary in what she was saying though."

"Oh?"

"Yeah. She said the old woman was stingy and was planning on taking her money with her when she died. And those were her words, not mine. I don't know Mrs. Kingfield."

"Elva told me that most of her relatives are just waiting for her to die to see if they're mentioned in the will."

Blaire's aqua eyes with the golden flakes grew big. "You don't think somebody was trying to kill her, do you?"

"I'm not sure."

"On the news, the reporter kept calling the explosion a probable act of random vandalism."

"It could have been. Nobody knows yet. Maybe the police will sort it all out soon."

"I hope it wasn't an attempt to kill the poor lady. I

understand she's a recluse, but she has a right to live her life any way she wants to."

I shook my head. "Everyone keeps calling her a recluse, but I found her delightful. She seemed glad that I came to see her and even served tea and cakes. I think she's just a lonely little woman that most people have forgotten."

The phone rang and I heard Trent answer it in the kitchen. In a minute he appeared at the door. "It's your mom."

"Oh, dear," I said. "I hope this mess hasn't been on the news in their area."

I knew it had been when Mom said, "Willa, what in the world is going on there? Are you okay?"

I answered her last question first. "I'm fine, Mom, and the police are trying to decipher what has happened."

"And you're sure you're all right?"

"Absolutely. Trent and Blaire are here and we're going to have dinner together. I'm just like everyone else around here, baffled about what has happened."

"Do you want your dad and me to come up?"

"You know I'd love you to come see me anytime, but don't come because of what has happened. We're letting the police handle it. Everything is going on as usual."

"They said on the news that nobody was hurt, but they don't know who or why someone had planted a bomb in the graveyard," Mom said.

"That's true, Mom. I'm sure the police will get to the bottom of it as quickly as they can."

"You're certain you don't need us there?"

"As I said, I'd love to see you and Dad anytime, but not because of the bomb."

"We'd planned to go to Myrtle Beach this weekend, but if you need us…"

"Mom." I was kind, but firm. "Let me assure you that I'm fine. You and Dad go on to Myrtle Beach and have a good time. I'll call you there if I have any news about what happened here."

"If you're sure." There was still a little doubt in her voice.

"I am."

We said goodbye and I went back into the living room.

"Your parents are great to keep in touch with you, Willa," Blaire said as I sat down.

"I know. They hover sometimes though." I couldn't help chuckling.

"I think that would be nice." Blaire looked wishful.

"Do you have any green pepper?" Trent stuck his head in the door and asked.

"I think there's some in the drawer under the meat keeper," I said.

He disappeared back into the kitchen.

"I'm surprised the story was on the news at your mom's house," Blaire remarked. "Maybe they've found out more since I heard it on the radio this afternoon."

I picked up the remote and snapped on the TV. "Let's see," I said.

The explosion in the graveyard was the lead story. They interviewed Philip, then Jesse and then the police chief. "The police came after I left," I remarked.

The reporter was still at the church and reporting from the gravesite. I flipped the channel and found that the station in Greensboro was also reporting the incident.

"I wonder if I should go back over there," I said aloud.

"No, you shouldn't," Trent said with a smile as he came into the room. I looked at him and he added, "Dinner is ready and the kitchen table is where you need to come."

As I thought they would be, the omelets were delicious. The three of us devoured them in record time.

A short time later they both made excuses to leave. Trent said he had to go because he was still working on his sermon for Sunday. Blaire said the shopping had worn her out and she wanted to soak in a hot bath.

After closing the door behind them, I decided the hot bath

didn't sound bad, but first I'd check with Philip and see if I was needed back at church.

When he told me to stay home because all the reporters had packed up and left, I went into my tiny bathroom and filled the tub, adding a handful of lavender bubble beads. I placed the portable phone on the commode beside the tub and climbed into the water. I opened Dixie Land's newest romance novel that I'd been reading and leaned back on the neck pillow. I'd only read a couple of pages when the telephone rang. I started to let it ring, but changed my mind. Mom might call back and if I didn't answer she'd begin to worry.

I put the receiver to my ear. "Hello."

"Willa, are you all right? I heard on the news about a bomb at a Methodist church in Liverpool. It wasn't your church, was it? I sure hope it wasn't."

"Yes, I'm fine, Aunt Lila," I said and added, "and yes it was my church." I couldn't help smiling to myself. It was so like my aunt to begin asking one question after another without pausing for answers.

"Lord, child. I was afraid of that." Before I could say anything, she went on. "There's more mess going on in this world than I can keep up with. I don't see how you young people do it."

I ignored her remark and said, "I thought you told me last week that you were going on one of those bus trips to Las Vegas this week. I figured you were already out west having a ball."

"We're leaving in the morning at six. I was finishing my packing when I turned on the television and happened to catch the story about the bomb. Of course I had to stop and check on you."

"I appreciate that, Aunt Lila, and as I said, I'm fine." I changed the subject. "I hope you have a wonderful time on your trip."

"Oh, I think I will. I just hope it helps me get over breaking up with Sam."

"I hope it does also, Aunt Lila." I took a deep breath to keep from telling her that in my opinion breaking up with the overbearing Sam was the best thing that could have happened to her. Instead I said, "When you're in Las Vegas why don't you drop a quarter in one of those slot machines for me?"

"I'm surprised at you, Preacher Girl," she said with a laugh. "I didn't think people in your profession believed in gambling."

"We don't, but knowing you, you were going to play a slot for me anyway."

"That's right. I sure was."

We talked for another few minutes and when I hung up, I felt better because talking with my eccentric aunt Lila always put me in a good mood.

As soon as we hung up, the phone rang again.

"Willa, this is Elva Kingfield."

I sat straight up in the tub. "Is something wrong, Mrs. Kingfield?"

"I thought I asked you to call me Elva." Without giving me time to comment, she went on. "Nothing's wrong. Could you visit me after church tomorrow?"

"Of course. I don't have any obligations until four. There's an administrative board meeting then."

"Good. Will you come for lunch?"

"Of course," I said again and added, "Could I bring dessert or something?"

"No, dear. Just come straight after church."

I paused, then said, "Are you sure you're okay, Elva?"

"Yes, dear. I look forward to chatting with you to-morrow."

When we hung up, I had a hard time shaking the feeling that I should go see Elva Kingfield tonight.

FOUR

ABOUT TWELVE-THIRTY the following afternoon, I pulled into the long winding drive of the Kingfield home. I was surprised to see an almost new Lincoln parked here. *Maybe, Elva has invited someone besides me for lunch,* I thought as I climbed out of my car and headed across the porch.

The door opened before I reached it.

"Reverend Hinshaw," Bernice said flatly. "Mrs. Kingfield has had some sort of spell and we've sent for an ambulance."

"I'm so sorry. When did it happen?"

"Just a few minutes ago."

I heard the faint sounds of a siren and knew help was on its way. "May I come in and see her?"

Bernice looked doubtful, but stood aside and let me pass.

I wondered why she was reluctant to let me in, but didn't dwell on it as I went into the parlor. I found Elva Kingfield lying on the brocade sofa. A woman with salt-and-pepper hair was fanning her with a magazine.

"I'm Willa," I said as the woman lowered her magazine and turned to look at me.

"So you're the one she was expecting for lunch?" she said in a flat, unfriendly voice.

I guessed the salt-and-pepper lady to be in her forties. I ignored her remark about lunch and asked, "What happened?"

"I'm not sure. I heard the news about the explosion in the graveyard and came by to check on Aunt Elva. I'd only been here a few minutes when she crumpled to the floor. I think she just fainted but, as I said, I'm not sure."

I moved to the side of the sofa. "Hi, Elva. It's Willa Hinshaw."

Elva's shaky hand reached for mine. I caught it and held it tightly. I saw a smile form on her lips. They parted as if she was trying to speak.

"Don't talk," I said and followed it with a quick prayer for the tiny woman on the sofa.

She understood and tried to smile at me again.

In a soft voice, I said, "The ambulance is coming and they'll take care of you. Just know we're here and we'll keep praying for you."

The niece eyed me, but didn't say anything.

I heard a commotion on the front porch and in a matter of seconds two rescue workers came into the room. I stepped aside as one began taking her blood pressure while the other talked to her in a soothing voice. I knew I was in their way so I crossed the room and stood beside Bernice. They had to ask the niece to move.

"Bernice, what happened?" I asked.

"I'm not sure. She was in here with Miss Saxon. I was in the kitchen finishing up lunch."

"We've got to keep praying that everything will be all right."

"Oh, I hope it will," she said. "She got pretty upset last night. Maybe that had something to do with her having the spell."

Miss Saxon glared at us from across the room. "If people would just leave my aunt alone, maybe things like this wouldn't happen."

I wasn't sure who she was addressing, but I figured it was me. I bit my lip and didn't answer.

I wanted to ask Bernice what had upset Elva last night, but now wasn't the time.

"We have her stabilized," one of the emergency workers said. "We're going to transport her to the hospital now."

They began hoisting her to the gurney.

"Just a minute," Miss Saxon said. "Are you sure she needs to go to the hospital?"

The worker stared at her. "Of course she does."

"Well, I'm not sure…"

"What hospital are you taking her to?" Bernice interrupted.

"Forsyth Medical Center."

"But—" Miss Saxon started again.

Again Bernice interrupted. "As soon as I get the house locked up, I'll be right over."

"I'll follow you," Miss Saxon said to the attendant. Without speaking to either Bernice or me, she went out the door behind the stretcher.

"That was strange," I said. "It looks like she'd want her aunt to go to the hospital as a precautionary measure if for nothing else."

"High and mighty Miss Penny Saxon probably hoped that if Ms. Elva stayed home she'd die," Bernice said.

Without commenting on her assessment of the Saxon woman, I asked, "Do you need a ride to the hospital? I'm going to go over in case Elva needs me."

She smiled. "That's nice of you, Reverend Hinshaw, but I may want to stay longer than you do. I'll drive my car."

"Then I'll see you at the hospital."

She put her hand on my arm as I started for the door. "Wouldn't you like to eat a bite before you go? Ms. Elva had planned a lovely lunch."

"Thank you for offering, but I'll get something later. I think I should go to the hospital now."

She nodded and removed her hand.

I drove a little faster than I normally do down I-40. I knew I could take advantage of the privileged parking and probably get to the emergency-room waiting area almost as quickly as

Penny Saxon. For some reason I didn't quite understand, I had the feeling that I should be there when Miss Saxon talked with the doctors.

I had been right about the timing of my arrival. Penny Saxon was going through the door of the waiting room just as I got off the elevator. She was standing in front of the desk where a volunteer was talking on the telephone when I entered. I walked up beside her.

"Have you heard anything yet?" I asked, though I knew she hadn't been here long enough to talk with anyone; it was a way to open the conversation with her.

"I just got here," she snapped and glared at me. "You sure got here in a hurry."

I nodded and said, "I wanted to get here in case you needed me." I emphasized the word *you* in the statement.

She seemed to soften a little. "Thank you," she said.

The volunteer hung up the phone and asked, "How may I help you ladies?"

"They just brought my aunt in by ambulance. I wanted to find out what's going on," Penny said.

The volunteer looked at the minister badge I'd pinned on the collar of my dress and smiled. "Have a seat and I'll go see what I can find out."

Penny turned around and took a seat on one of the padded, but still hard, modern-style chairs near the desk. I sat in another one. An end table with a tall lamp separated us.

"Miss Saxon, do you mind if I ask you what happened?" I leaned around the lamp to look at her.

I felt that she wanted to tell me to mind my own business, but she bit her top lip and said, "I'm not sure. We talked about the graveyard incident, then she told me you were coming for lunch. In the middle of a sentence, she just keeled over."

"Does Elva have any problems that might cause her to suddenly pass out?"

"Not that I know of." She said no more because the volunteer came back and headed straight for us.

"Are you Mrs. Kingfield's next of kin?" She looked at Penny.

"I'm as close as she has in the area," Penny said.

"Then, the doctor asked that you come to the examining room." She glanced at me. "Your minister may come, too."

Before Penny Saxon could say that I wasn't her pastor, I stood and followed them.

We went into a huge room that was divided into cubicles, which surrounded a central nurses' station. A nurse, wearing a dark green top designed with leaves of all colors, came from behind the desk and the volunteer said, "This is Mrs. Kingfield's relative and their minister."

"I think the doctor wants to talk with you before you see Mrs. Kingfield. Wait here, please," the nurse said, and left us standing beside the central desk.

In a matter of minutes, a white-coated man came out of one of the cubicles. He had a crew cut and his glasses rested on the end of his nose. He had a definite New England accent when he spoke.

"Tell me what happened," he said after introducing himself as Dr. Strobel.

Penny Saxon told him basically the same story she told me.

"Mrs. Kingfield seems very agitated, but from the preliminary examination we haven't found a definite cause for her passing out. Her heart is strong, but it's beating a little too fast and her blood pressure is up slightly, though not yet to the danger level. There's some indication that she may have had a minor stroke, but we haven't found proof at this point. We have to do further tests. At this time, there doesn't seem to be any damage to her limbs."

"Oh, my," Penny said.

"Ministrokes are often common with older people," he continued. "To be thorough, we've taken blood and will do a complete workup on it. I'd also like to do a CAT scan or a body MRI. That should tell us what we need to know."

"Do whatever you think is necessary, Dr. Strobel," Penny said.

"Has she said what happened to her?" I asked.

"She's not very aware of what has happened. That's one reason I suspect a stroke. She seems confused." He smiled at me. "Maybe she will be able to tell us more if and when she's completely coherent."

"I hope so," I said.

He nodded and turned back to Penny. "One more thing. Do you know if she was overly stimulated before passing out?"

Penny looked at me, but said to the doctor, "She was somewhat keyed up about having lunch with her minister today. I don't think she was any more excited than she usually is when having company though."

When Penny didn't explain further, I said, "Mrs. Kingfield had a shock yesterday. Her husband's grave was bombed and the headstone was destroyed."

He nodded. "I heard about that on the news. That would be enough to upset someone."

"She took it pretty well," I said.

"When we discussed it this morning, she didn't seem overly concerned about it," Penny added. "She said she planned to replace the headstone and have the ground reseeded and that's about all she said."

"Well, we'll run the tests and go from there. I'm going to admit Mrs. Kingfield and we'll watch her closely tonight," Dr. Strobel explained. "The nurse will show you where to wait until we get her into a room."

"Is she going to make it, Doctor?" Penny asked.

His eyebrow shot up, but he said calmly, "I certainly hope so. There's no indication at this point that the episode is life-threatening, but let's do more tests and see what shows up."

I, too, was surprised by Penny's question. She continued, "Can I see her now?"

"I prefer you wait until she's in a room. We're still working with her at this time."

Before she could ask another question, he walked away and the nurse came to us. "If you'll wait outside, as soon as we have a room for Mrs. Kingfield, I'll come and let you know."

"Thank you," I said.

Penny simply nodded.

Bernice was sitting in the corner of the waiting room when we entered. A picnic basket sat at her feet. "How's Ms. Elva?" she asked before we could sit down.

Penny didn't respond so I said, "They're running more tests, but the doctor was encouraging. I think everything is going to be all right."

"Thank God," Bernice said.

"You didn't have to come to the hospital," Penny blurted to her.

"Of course I did," Bernice said. "Ms. Elva is not only my employer, she's my best friend."

"Yeah, I know," Penny said and looked away.

Bernice looked at me. "Since you didn't get a chance to eat lunch I took the liberty of packing one for you," she said.

"That was thoughtful," I said and smiled at her. Though I hadn't thought about food until now, I realized I was hungry.

"There's enough for you, too, Miss Saxon," Bernice said.

"No, thanks," she replied. "I'll go to the cafeteria later."

Noticing that others were eating in the room, Bernice opened her basket. She produced roast beef sandwiches, potato salad in individual cups, a big piece of German chocolate cake and a thermos of lemonade. It looked delicious.

"I hope you brought some for yourself so you can join me," I said.

"I did, Reverend Hinshaw. Thank you for inviting me to eat with you."

Penny stood. "It will probably be a while before Aunt Elva is in a room. I'm going to the cafeteria."

"You're welcome to a sandwich," Bernice said, but not very enthusiastically. "There's plenty."

Penny ignored her and said, "I trust that if they put Aunt Elva in a room before I return one of you will come and get me."

"Of course we will," I said.

Without another word, she left the room.

"What is her problem, Bernice?" I asked.

Bernice chuckled. "She probably didn't want to belittle herself by eating with the hired help."

"It's got to be more than that." I picked up my sandwich. "Shall we say a blessing?"

She nodded, then bowed her head.

I thanked God for Elva and asked Him to continue watching over her while she was here. I asked Him to help Penny with whatever her problems were and then I asked Him to bless our food. I closed with, "Amen."

I took a bite of my sandwich as Bernice poured lemonade for us.

"I'm glad you came today, Reverend Hinshaw. I'm sorry you had to miss lunch with Ms. Elva. She had this lovely meal planned and she was so looking forward to it."

"It's delicious. I'm sorry she can't be with us."

"I decided to slice the roast and make the sandwiches. I'm sorry I couldn't bring the rest of the vegetables."

"I couldn't ask for anything better." I took a spoonful of potato salad and asked, "Bernice, when I first got to the house you seemed uncertain whether or not to let me in. Did I cause a problem?"

"Oh, no, Reverend. Miss Penny was just up on her high horse. She was fussing because Ms. Elva had invited you. I didn't want you to come in and be insulted."

"Don't even worry about that. I've been insulted before and I'm still hanging in there." I chuckled.

"Well, it could be that Miss Saxon is still mad at me and she's decided to leave you alone."

"Why? You haven't done anything."

"I don't think she would have called the paramedics for Ms. Elva if I hadn't gone into the living room to ask a question about the lunch preparations."

"Oh?" I stared at her.

"She was standing there just looking at Ms. Elva on the floor. I kind of screamed and she whirled around. When I ran up to check Ms. Elva, Miss Penny told me to step back and she would handle things. I told her I'd call 911, but she said she didn't think it would be necessary. I called them anyway."

"I'm glad you did." I shook my head. "I don't see why Penny Saxon wouldn't want to call them for her aunt."

"As I said earlier, she probably wanted to see if Ms. Elva was going to die," Bernice said flatly.

"Surely not."

"Reverend Hinshaw, you just don't know Ms. Elva's family. They only care about her because she has money. Lord, forgive me for saying this, but they're just like vultures. They're only hovering around waiting for her to die and see what she's left them."

"She said something to me about that. She also mentioned a nephew in Atlanta, I think. She seemed to feel close to him."

"That would be Dennis. If you ask me, he's probably the worst of the lot."

"Why do you say that?"

"He comes around once or twice a year to butter her up, but I think it's mostly fake. He always goes home with a loan, if you can call it that."

"What do you mean?"

"He borrows money every time he visits and as far as I can tell, he's never paid her back a dime of it."

"How do you know about her finances?"

"I keep the bankbooks for her. Her eyes aren't what they used to be and I write her checks to pay the bills and I deposit all her incoming money. I've never seen anything come from Dennis Kingfield."

As Bernice had said, I didn't know Elva's family so there was no way I could disagree with her.

FIVE

AFTER LUNCH I DECIDED to call Philip and let him know what was happening.

When he answered I could hear talking in the background. "I don't mean to disturb you, Philip. I hear you have company," I said.

"No company, Willa. Mrs. Gallaway is talking to herself. She does that sometimes."

I didn't comment, but told him about Mrs. Kingfield. He was sympathetic and offered to come right over.

"There's no need," I informed him. "They still haven't put Elva in a room and I don't know when we'll get to see her."

"Then, please keep me posted. I'll have my cell phone with me. Call me at any time. I'm sure everyone will understand if we're interrupted."

"I will," I said, then added, "I'm not sure I'll make it back for the board meeting this afternoon."

"Don't worry about it. I'll cover for you. I'm just sorry you won't be here to report on the success of the festival. I'm sure the members will want to thank you."

"That's not necessary," I said. "I did make some notes on the participation and the expenses. They're on the corner of my desk. Feel free to get them."

"Thanks, Willa. I'll do that. Give Mrs. Kingfield my best. Tell her I'll pray for her and I'll visit tomorrow."

"I will, Philip. Thanks for covering for me."

"No problem. I'll talk with you later."

Mrs. Gallaway had continued talking through our conversation and was still going when I heard Philip hang up the phone. Though he didn't complain, I know it is hard for him to see his once vital and active wife succumb to the ravishing Alzheimer's disease and know there was little he could do but stand by and watch her deteriorate.

Shortly after I talked with Philip, Penny came back. She asked if we'd heard any news about Elva. When I said we hadn't, she moved to the other side of the waiting room and sat down. I had to admit that I was glad she did. She reeked of onions.

Bernice didn't say anything to her, but picked up a *Southern Living* magazine and mumbled to me, "I love to read the recipes in this book."

"They have some good ones." I took my trusty old straw bag from the arm of the chair, noting that it was time to switch to a more suitable one for fall and winter. I fished inside until I found the notes I'd been making for a Christmas pageant. If I wanted the children to do an original program, I had to get it written. It was, after all, the last week of October.

I was lost in my work when Bernice said, "Here comes a doctor."

He headed in my direction. Penny saw him and came over. "How's Aunt Elva?"

"As a precautionary measure, I've had her taken to ICU. Her heart is still beating a little unevenly and I want to keep a close watch on it." He went on to explain that he was giving her oxygen and some IVs and that we could only see her for a few minutes. He wouldn't speculate on the prognosis and when Penny insisted on an answer he said, "I can't tell you anything further. We're just going to watch her tonight."

Before she could ask him anything else, he walked out of the room.

A volunteer came and told us where the ICU waiting room was. We caught the elevator together.

"I sure hope Ms. Elva is going to be all right," Bernice said.

"So do I," I answered.

"I'll go see her first," Penny announced as the elevator doors opened. "You two can go in later if you must."

"If you like, I'd be happy to come with you," I said. For some reason I didn't think it was a good idea for Penny to visit her aunt alone.

"No, thanks."

There was nothing I could say, but I couldn't help wondering why she didn't want anyone with her. Of course, logically I knew that Elva would be okay in ICU. There were often nurses in the room and they monitored everything when they weren't there.

The volunteer paused in front of a door which stood open. "This is the waiting room. The hours to visit in Intensive Care are posted." She turned to Penny. "Of course they make an exception when someone is first brought in. If it's possible, they let family visit after the patient is settled. Please come with me and I'll see that you get in."

After visiting her aunt, Penny Saxon must have left without coming back into the waiting room because fifteen minutes later, Bernice and I were ushered in to see Elva, and Penny was nowhere in sight. I thought that was odd, but I didn't mention it to Bernice. I knew the two women didn't like each other and I didn't want to upset the housekeeper.

Elva looked even smaller than her tiny size as she lay still on the stark, white sheets. There were tubes and wires running to several different sections of her body. I recognized the heart monitor and the IV fluid bottle, but there were other attachments that I had no idea what their purposes were.

"Ms. Elva, it's Bernice. I just wanted to let you know that I'm here and that I want you to get well soon."

I could tell by her voice that she was emotional.

"I'm here, too, Elva." I took her hand. "I want to pray for you." I said a quick prayer and when I saw her trying to say something I added, "Now, don't you worry about a thing. Bernice is taking care of the house and you'll be back home soon."

A nurse came in and began checking the monitors. She didn't say anything, but she did smile at us.

"Elva, I'm going to go now," I said. "I'll be back to see you tomorrow."

I watched her mouth form the words, "Please do."

"I promise. You'll be stronger then and we'll talk."

She gave me a weak nod and closed her eyes.

"I think I'll sit with her a little longer, if it's okay." Bernice looked at the nurse, who nodded in the affirmative.

"I'll see you tomorrow, too, Bernice." I looked at her. "Take care of yourself and thanks again for the delicious lunch."

She walked me to the door of the cubicle. "I can tell you really care, Reverend Willa. Ms. Elva needs friends like you."

"I'll be happy to be her friend." I squeezed Bernice's hand and added, "And yours, too."

I saw tears form in her eyes and she whispered, "Thank you."

As I left the ICU I decided to visit the other parishioners who were in the hospital. Luke Underwood had been hurt during the Friday night football game at Liverpool High when half of the opposing team had landed on him. It twisted his leg and it was broken in two places. He'd undergone surgery and though he was expected to completely recover, he knew he was out of football for the rest of the year. And to Luke Underwood, there was nothing worse than not being able to play football.

The other member of First United Methodist in the hospital today was Sylvia Newsome. She'd given birth to twin boys on Saturday. Her husband, Adam, had been all aglow at church this morning. He'd even handed out bubble-gum cigars. I had one in my purse.

I got to the maternity ward first and I didn't even have to go by the desk and ask which room the Newsomes were in. I saw the two big blue bows on the door when I got off the elevator. I also heard lots of laughing and talking in the room.

I came through the door and Adam saw me immediately. "Reverend Willa." He got up from his sitting position on the side of Sylvia's bed. "Come in. It's great to see you."

"Hello," I said to him and smiled at the other people in the room. I didn't know any of them. "And how are you, Sylvia?"

"I'm fine. Let me introduce you to my mom and dad. They came up from Durham today."

"And these are my folks," Adam said. "They live in Archdale."

I greeted all the happy grandparents and before I could sit down, Adam said, "Let me take you down the hall to see my boys."

Of course his boys were precious. I couldn't help thinking that these were two lucky little babies to be born into a family where they were wanted and would be loved.

When we got back to the room, a couple from the young married class at church had come in to visit. I knew they wanted to spend time with their friends and family so I said I needed to get downstairs and see Luke. Sylvia asked me to say a prayer of thankfulness for her new family. I was pleased and we all held hands around her bed and I prayed.

In Luke's room, I found a different atmosphere. "Why, Reverend Willa? Why did God do this to me?" Luke demanded.

Before I could answer, his mother said, "Lukie, you shouldn't ask questions like that. Reverend Hinshaw might think you're mad at God."

"Well, I am mad."

"Lukie," she said again, "don't say that."

"It's okay," I said. "Sometimes we can't help wondering why something happens and sometimes there are no answers to our wonderings. Things just happen."

"But God could have kept my leg from breaking."

"Of course He could." I looked at Luke. In a soft voice, I

said, "He could have also let it have been your neck that was broken instead of your leg."

Luke stared at me and I went on. "Maybe you broke your leg because in the next game it would have been your neck. Or maybe it was because if you drove your car in the next few weeks you'd be in an accident and be killed. Or maybe you broke your leg because a bunch of big strong heavy guys fell on it and it had to break." I saw both Luke and his mother looking at me closely. "God gives us free will in this world. Sometimes we do things and make choices and then have to pay the consequences."

"But I didn't choose to break my leg."

"No, but you did choose to play football. Everyone knows that it's a dangerous game and there are times when people are going to get hurt. You just happened to hit one of those times."

"I guess you're right about that." He sighed.

"The thing to do is to use this time on the sidelines wisely. Instead of whining about not being able to play ball, think of what you can do," I suggested.

"Like what?"

"How are your grades? Maybe you should spend some time studying to pull up a low grade so you can get into a good college."

"My grades are okay."

"Then is there something that you've always wanted to do, but haven't had the time or the chance to do it?"

"Yeah. I've thought I might take up ballet dancing."

"Now, son," his mother put in, "you don't have to be rude to Reverend Willa."

"It's okay." I couldn't help mentally picturing this two-hundred-pound young man jumping around in tights. "I know you don't think there's anything you could do, but try giving it more thought."

He didn't answer and his mother said, "Lukie, you've said a million times that you were going to begin carving some of those little animals when you had the time. When you were younger you did a lot of them, but you quit when you got to high school."

"I did kind of like to do that." His voice was still a little huffy.

"That's wonderful." His mother broke into a big grin. "I'll get you some of the materials tomorrow and you can get started."

By the time I left, Luke had a list of things he was going to do while he was recuperating and his whole attitude had changed. His mother walked me to the elevator and thanked me profusely.

The sun was going down when I got to my car. I decided to call Blaire and see if she'd had dinner.

"I thought you might like to go get a bite to eat," I said after she answered.

"I just made a pot of spaghetti sauce. Why don't you come eat with me?" I heard her sniff and knew she'd been crying.

"Is something wrong?"

"Yeah. I think Nathan's getting ready to dump me."

"I'm sorry. I'm leaving the hospital parking lot," I said. I didn't want her to go into the reason for the breakup on the telephone. It would be easier to talk with her in person. "I'll be there shortly."

SIX

BEING SUNDAY EVENING, the traffic was fairly light. It took about twenty-five minutes to get to Liverpool. I pulled into my marked parking space and decided to go inside and change from my church clothes to jeans. Ten minutes later I was knocking on Blaire's door. She opened it immediately and I followed her to the kitchen.

Dropping to a chair at the table, I said, "Now, tell me what's going on."

Blaire took two individually filled salad bowls from the refrigerator and sat one in front of me. "This morning Nathan called and said he needed to go somewhere after church so we'd have to go in separate cars. You know we've been riding to church together for several weeks." She paused and looked at me.

"I didn't know, but I leave early on Sundays."

"Of course you do." She shook her head. "I wasn't thinking. Anyway, I didn't think anything about it until after the service. He walked me to the parking lot and said he probably wouldn't be home today, but we'd talk later this week."

I started to say something, but she shushed me and went on. "I could tell by his expression that he couldn't wait to get away from me. I hate to admit it, but I knew something was up, and I decided to find out what. Instead of driving out of the parking lot from the area where I was parked, I drove around the church. That was when I saw him holding his car door open for Mary Stillwell."

"Who's Mary Stillwell?"

"One of the many singles at Oak Street Baptist." She was

pouring iced tea for us. "Someone told me several weeks ago that she had the hots for Nathan."

"Blaire, that doesn't prove anything. He could have a very good reason to meet with Mary Stillwell. Don't jump to conclusions."

"I know I shouldn't, but I can't help it. Sometimes you just know these things." She began pouring spoonfuls of sauce over the plates of spaghetti. "How would you feel if it was Trent?"

Her remark caught me off guard. I hesitated a moment, then stammered, "I'm n-not sure."

"I think you'd be just as upset as I am right now." She brought the plates to the table and sat down facing me. "I think you care more for Trent than you want to admit, Willa."

"Trent and I are very good friends. That's how it has to be," I said.

"Why?"

"Oh, Blaire, I have so much in common with him in one respect. In another, we're complete opposites."

"But you could overcome those differences."

"I doubt that." I didn't want to discuss the many reasons I felt would keep anything serious from developing between Trent and me. "Anyway," I said. "Let's bless this food and eat before the sauce gets cold. We can discuss our love lives as we eat."

Blaire smiled for the first time. "You're right," she said. "No matter what, we have a lot to be thankful for." She bowed her head and began to pray.

During the meal we discussed the men in our lives. I even told her about Jacob's impending visit.

She seemed excited and said, "Maybe this fellow is the reason you won't let yourself get serious with Trent. After all, if you went to college together, it must be a special relationship."

I sighed. "Jacob Lowaski is a special person, Blaire, and I

think the world of him, but I have as many differences with him as I do with Trent."

"What do you mean?"

"Jacob is Jewish."

For a minute she just stared at me. Then she laughed out loud. "If I didn't know better," she said, "I'd think you keep picking out men that you don't feel you can ever get serious with."

I chuckled. "Maybe I do."

When we could think of nothing else to say on the subject without repeating ourselves, we then turned to other topics, including the graveyard incident and Elva Kingfield's hospitalization.

"Blaire, how well do you know Penny Saxon?"

She was pouring herself another glass of tea and indicated for me to hold mine forward so she could fill it, too. I did.

"I know who she is, but I don't know a lot about her. She's never been very friendly so I guess I haven't made an effort to get to know her. Why?"

"I can agree with the not-being-friendly part," I said and went on to explain the way she acted at the house and at the hospital.

Blaire shook her head. "It takes all kinds."

I left Blaire's apartment at nine. Though nothing had been settled about her relationship with Nathan, I think she was more optimistic than when I first arrived.

The first thing I did when I got in was my evening Bible study. After I finished, it was too early to go to bed, so I decided to take a hot bath. I ran the water almost up to my neck and then I picked up the Dixie Land book I'd been reading, *Return to Serenity*. I wasn't disappointed with the story. She was fast becoming one of my favorite romantic suspense authors.

At eleven I had finished the novel. I watched the news and then went to bed.

The next morning things were busy at the office. Philip

had gone to the hospital to visit and several people had come by to make donations to the festival fund or to retrieve things they'd left on Saturday. Some popped their heads in my office door to say hello or to thank me for suggesting the event. Almost everyone wanted to discuss the explosion. Of course we couldn't add much to what the news had reported.

It was close to noon when Philip came into my office. "I just got back from the hospital. Mrs. Kingfield wanted to make sure I told you she was doing better and that she is expecting you to come over."

"Thanks. I plan to go see her this afternoon."

He took a breath. "She was a little concerned because her housekeeper hadn't shown up today."

I frowned. "I don't understand that. Bernice said she'd be going over there early this morning."

"Well, she hadn't arrived when I left."

"I'll call the house and see what's going on."

"That's a good idea." He started out the door and then turned back toward me. "By the way, you did a good job consoling Luke Underwood. He was a different young man this morning. He was making animal sketches."

I smiled. "I'm glad I could help."

Philip headed for his office and I picked up the membership roster. I found Elva's phone number and dialed it. I let it ring several times, but there was no answer. This puzzled me. Maybe Bernice had left for the hospital and I'd missed her. I'd call again later just to be sure.

It was almost one o'clock and I was getting hungry. I decided to walk up the street to Helen's. The long, narrow restaurant was crowded, but I observed a couple of people seated on the stools at the counter eating dessert. I knew it wouldn't be long before I could get a seat.

Junior, the cook and owner, came up and said, "Hello, Preacher Willa."

"Hi." I smiled at him. "Still busy, I see."

"Come on," he said. "I think there's a seat in one of the booths."

I eased by the row of stools and headed toward the back of the café.

"Hey, guys," Junior said, leaning on the corner of one of the booths. "I brought a special lady to join you."

Before I could protest, Nevis Poole slipped over and said, "We'd be delighted to have you join us, Willa."

"I don't mind waiting for a stool. I don't want to interrupt your lunch."

"Don't be silly. Come on and sit down," Ed Walsh said with a twinkle in his eyes.

Though I considered Ed one of my dearest friends, I was still jarred sometimes when I looked at him. If there was a perfect Santa Claus look-alike, he was it.

"Thanks, gentlemen," I said and slipped into the booth beside Nevis.

Junior said, "The baked ham, stewed apples and cucumber salad are the special today, Willa. Or would you like to see the menu?"

"The special sounds good to me."

"Iced tea, right?"

I nodded and he scurried off to fill my order.

"Philip said at the meeting yesterday that Mrs. Kingfield had to go to the hospital. Have you heard from her today, Willa?" Nevis asked.

"Philip got back from the hospital visitation a little while ago. He said she was better physically, but was concerned because her housekeeper hasn't come to the hospital today. I tried to call the house to see what was holding Bernice up, but didn't get an answer. Maybe she has gone over by now."

"It's kind of strange that she'd be this late going over," Ed said. "From what I hear, those two women are very close."

"Yes, they are," I said. "I'm going to visit Elva later. If Bernice hasn't shown up by then, I'll go by and check on her."

"Good idea," Nevis said. "You just never know."

I knew he was referring to the ordeal he and his family went through last summer, but before I could say anything Junior walked up with an enormous plate of food for me. I stared at it and laughed. "I'm not sure I'll be able to eat all of this."

"Sure you can," Ed said with a grin. "I've seen you eat before."

Nevis stood with a chuckle. "Well, folks, I'd like to stay and enjoy the company but I have to get back to the plant." He paused a minute. "See you next Sunday, if not before, Willa."

"Have a good week," I said, still eyeing the food I was expected to eat.

"Is the talk about the excitement in the graveyard dying down yet?" Ed asked after Nevis walked away.

"I think it is a little."

"I'm glad nobody was hurt," he said.

"That was one thing to be thankful for."

"I just wonder…" Ed looked thoughtful.

"You wonder what, Ed?" I was interested in his perspective. As the retired police chief, he had an insight that was often right on the mark.

"You know Mrs. Kingfield is a wealthy lady." I nodded and he went on. "Could be somebody wanted to separate her from her money."

"I hope not. She's such a sweet little old lady."

He nodded and rubbed the side of his head.

"Are you okay, Ed?"

"I'm fine. Just a little twinge now and then."

"You need to find out what's causing it," I said. "It could stem from being hurt back in the summer."

"Yeah, I thought of that." He glanced at his watch. "Actually, I have an appointment this afternoon."

"Don't let me make you late."

"I don't want to leave you alone."

"Don't be silly. I'm a big girl, but you have to promise me one thing."

"What's that?"

"Let me hear from you when you get back," I said. "I want to know that you're going to be all right."

"I promise I'll call you," he said.

Though Junior had given me too much food, I managed to clean my plate. I was almost too full to walk back to work, but I managed. Anna stopped me as soon as I was inside the church.

"Willa, Mrs. Kingfield called. She was worried because her housekeeper hasn't shown up at the hospital today. She asked if you'd go by the house and see what's keeping her."

"I'll be glad to. Were there any other messages?"

"Nothing that can't wait."

"Okay. I'll go right now."

It began to get cloudy as I headed to Blue Bell Road. I wondered if it was going to rain, but didn't spend a lot of time thinking about it. It didn't take long to get to the Kingfield house. I don't know what I expected to see there when I arrived, but I felt a little surprised that there was no indication that anything was wrong. I parked on the circular driveway and went to the door. I lifted the knocker, rapped and waited. There was no answer.

I knocked again. Still no reply.

I knew it would be impossible to look in a window because the panes were covered with heavy drapes. *Bernice may be in the kitchen and can't hear me,* I thought as I knocked one more time.

I let a minute pass and decided to go around to the back door. Again, I knocked, but got no response. I tried the door and was surprised to find it wasn't locked. After only a slight hesitation, I pushed it open and went inside.

"Bernice," I called as I entered the kitchen.

Only silence answered me.

The house was large and rambling and the drapes were all

closed, making the lighting inside dim. It crossed my mind that some of the curtains were open the first time I came here. *But,* I thought to myself, *Bernice probably shut the house up before she went to the hospital. I probably just missed her.*

I decided since I was already in the house I would look around to be sure that Bernice was gone. I found my way to the dining room and then the front entry. My heart jumped and a short scream escaped my throat as I started toward the winding stairs. Bernice was in a crumpled heap at the bottom of the steps.

SEVEN

I RACED TO HER AND KNELT. Grabbing her wrist, I prayed aloud, "Oh, Heavenly Father. Please let her be alive!"

My prayer was answered. Though it was weak, I felt a pulse. I took my cell phone out of my purse and dialed 911.

Bernice was unconscious, and I wasn't sure what I should do while I waited for the paramedics. I was afraid to move her because if there were broken bones I could injure her further. I remembered hearing at some time that a person should be kept warm to avoid shock. I ran into the parlor and looked around. There was a handmade crocheted coverlet across one of the chairs. I grabbed it and hurried back to Bernice. As I spread it over her still body, I saw the pool of blood that had oozed out from under her. I couldn't tell where it came from, but I was afraid she'd hit hard enough for a wound to bleed.

I knew there was nothing more I could do for her. I went to the front door and turned the lock. I opened the door and let it stand ajar. When help arrived, I wanted them to get to her as soon as possible.

I opened the drapes covering the two windows on either side of the door. I then returned to sit beside Bernice. Though I knew she was past hearing me, I kept chatting about different things. I told her about Elva and I kept telling her that she was going to be all right.

Not much time passed until I heard the sound of sirens. In a matter of minutes an ambulance came up the driveway. It was followed closely by two police cars.

As the medics worked on Bernice, I talked with the officer, whose name I didn't catch.

"Tell me what happened?" he said.

"Mrs. Kingfield is in the hospital. She called and asked me to come and find out why her housekeeper hadn't made it over to see her."

One of the paramedics came up and said, "We are going to transport the patient to the hospital now. We have the stab wound bound and we've giving her blood, but she needs to be attended to as soon as possible."

"A stab wound?" I was surprised. "I thought she had fallen down the stairs."

"She did fall, ma'am. She's also been stabbed."

"Is she able to talk?" the officer asked.

"No, sir. She's unconscious." He put on his cap. "We'd better go now."

I turned back to the policeman. "I want to go to the hospital. Will you be here?"

"Probably. I'll call this in and I'm sure somebody from the force will come to the hospital to talk with her as soon as she is able to answer questions."

We talked a little more, and then I left. I realized as I drove down I-40 that I hadn't asked him to lock up Elva's house if he left. I decided I'd check back by on the way home. I put her house out of my mind because I knew I had to decide how to tell Elva about her friend.

When I got to the hospital a nurse informed me they had moved Elva from ICU to a private room. I found her in a half-sitting position in her bed. She still had some IVs, oxygen and a heart monitor, but the other machines were missing.

"Willa," she said as I came in. "I was about to give up on you coming." Before I could answer she added, "And Bernice hasn't shown up either. I was counting on you two."

"I'm sorry, Elva," I said. "I would have been here earlier, but I was delayed." I took a deep breath. "I went by your house and found that Bernice had fallen." When I saw the stricken look on her face, I added quickly, "I'm sure she's going to be all right, but they brought her to the hospital to check her out."

Elva put her hand to her throat. "Oh, dear. I was afraid something bad had happened to her, but I wouldn't let myself believe it."

I put my hand on her shoulder. "I'll go find out about her in a little while. I just wanted to check on you and to let you know what was going on."

"I'm going to be fine." She moved her hand from her throat and took hold of mine. "They did some tests today and said they'd know the results by tomorrow or next day." She took a breath. "I love having you here, dear, but I do wish you'd go check on Bernice for me."

I smiled at her. "Of course. I'll be back as soon as I know something."

As I started down the hall I met Penny Saxon headed to her aunt's room. I simply said hello, though I did wonder why she had those bad scratches on her face. She simply nodded to me without speaking.

I was surprised to see Dr. Strobel when I got on the elevator to go down to the emergency room. He had a glint of recognition in his eye and I knew he remembered me when he said, "Good afternoon, Reverend."

"Hello," I said with a smile and added, "I was glad to find Mrs. Kingfield moved from ICU today."

He returned the smile. "Yes. She is improving quickly. I'm anxious to see the results of her tests."

"I had to bring her some bad news and I hope it doesn't set her back."

"Oh?" He looked concerned.

"I found her housekeeper unconscious today. She'd been attacked and stabbed. She's in the emergency room. She and Mrs. Kingfield are very close."

He frowned. "I hate that." He glanced at his watch. "I was getting ready to go home, but I have a few minutes. I think

I'll go down to the E.R. and see what's going on. It might help Mrs. Kingfield to know I've checked on her friend."

"That would be nice of you, Dr. Strobel."

"No problem." He smiled again. "My wife's parents are coming to dinner and like a lot of men, I'm putting off going home."

I didn't know how to answer him so I just smiled.

The elevator opened and he pointed me to the waiting room. "Someone will let you know what's going on."

"Thank you."

About twenty minutes later a nurse came out and ushered me back. A woman about my age and size came forward and held out her hand. "Hello. I'm Dr. Suzanne Bryant."

"Willa Hinshaw," I said, taking her hand.

"Dr. Strobel told me you were the patient's minister. Is any of her family here?"

"No. I really don't know any of Bernice's family. The woman she works for is a patient of Dr. Strobel's."

"Yes. He told me." She added, "Mrs. Wallace has a broken collar bone, a fractured tibia in her left leg, a fractured left wrist and three broken ribs."

"Oh, my," I said.

"She has also lost a lot of blood from the stab wound under her right shoulder blade. It punctured a lung, but missed other vital organs."

"When I found her, I thought she had just fallen down the stairs. Then the medic told me she had been stabbed."

"It looks as if Mrs. Wallace had help falling down those stairs."

"I didn't see a knife anywhere."

"The puncture didn't look like a knife wound. It was more cylinder shaped."

I couldn't understand why anyone would want to harm Bernice. I didn't dwell on the thought. "Dr. Bryant, is she going to be all right?"

The doctor was noncommittal. "Let's take it one day at a

time. Right now, we're giving her transfusions to build up the blood. Her heart is strong, but because of the lung, we have her on a respirator."

"Has she regained consciousness?"

"Not yet, but with these injuries that is not uncommon." She took a breath. "I do think you should get in touch with her family. We need permission for surgery."

"I'll see what I can find out."

Dr. Bryant told me that they would let me know when Bernice was sent to ICU. I gave her Elva's room number and headed back upstairs.

I told Elva about the broken bones, but I didn't tell her that someone had stabbed Bernice. I thought that news could come later. I did ask her about Bernice's family.

"She really doesn't have a lot of family here. There's a nephew that goes to Winston-Salem State. He calls her occasionally. The rest of her family is in the eastern part of the state. Benson, I think."

"Do you know the nephew's name?"

"Tyrone, I believe." She scrunched her face as if she was thinking hard. "Yes, I'm sure that's it. Tyrone Wallace. He's her brother's child."

I glanced at my watch. It was almost five o'clock, and I thought I might catch someone in the administrative offices at Winston-Salem State. I was right. A Mrs. Barnes was most helpful. She not only gave me Tyrone Wallace's class schedule, she rang his room and when she didn't get an answer, she promised to track him down. I gave her the phone numbers to my cell phone, my home, the church and Elva's room.

"I'll make sure he calls you as soon as I locate him, Reverend Hinshaw," she promised.

"Thank you, Mrs. Barnes," I said and hung up the phone. "Well, that's all we can do right now," I said, sitting back and looking at the tiny woman before me. "Now I have some questions for you."

"And just what might they be?"

"I want to know what happened before your spell, as Bernice called it."

"I'm really not sure, Willa. I know I was looking forward to our lunch and then that nosy niece of mine dropped in. She only came to see if the incident in the graveyard was enough to do me in."

I couldn't help smiling. Elva certainly was not fond of Penny Saxon, and after meeting her, I understood why. I didn't voice this to Elva. Instead, I prodded, "Go on."

"I asked her to leave because I was expecting company whom I would enjoy. She didn't say anything, but her face turned white and in a strange voice she said there was a man looking in the window at us. She said he looked awful."

Elva closed her eyes and her voice came out in an almost whisper. "I swear to you, Willa, when I turned around and looked, Leo Kingfield was standing there staring back at me."

I noticed how the heart monitor had gone crazy as she spoke and it frightened me. "Elva, relax." I took her hand and tried to calm her. "We can talk about this later."

She took some deep breaths. "I'll be okay. I want to tell you."

"Only if you try to stay calm."

"I will," she assured me.

The monitor, though it showed her heart beating a little faster, had gone back to a more normal rhythm.

Elva went on. "He looked almost like a mummy. He was all gray-looking and his clothes were tattered, but it was Leo. I know it was, Willa."

"Elva, somebody is trying…"

"No, Willa, it was him. He got out of his grave and came back. He stood outside the window and he was singing."

"Singing?"

"Yes, singing. I could tell by the way he threw back his head and opened his mouth. Leo always liked to belt out a song. He sang in the church choir for years and he belonged to a group that did barbershop singing."

I shook my head. "Your husband is dead, Elva. He can't come back. He can't sing or talk or anything. The only time you will see him again is when you get to heaven, too."

"I know that. I'm not saying that Leo is alive. I'm just telling you that I saw Leo outside that window. He wasn't alive, but he was there."

I knew that nothing I could say would change her mind. "I wonder why Miss Saxon didn't tell us about the face in the window."

"All she said to me was, 'I guess the bomb opened the grave enough for him to get out to visit you, Aunt Elva.' Then she gave me a snide smile that would make a cow give buttermilk. I don't remember anything after that. The next thing I knew, I woke up here."

She lay back and closed her eyes. I waited until her heart seemed to be beating normally again and said, "I'm sure they're going to take good care of you here." I wanted to get her mind off thinking she'd seen her husband.

"They are very nice. I really like Dr. Strobel." Her words were slurred a little.

"Yes, he is very nice. He went down to check on Bernice."

"That's good. She'll…like…him…too."

"Yes, she will," I whispered.

There was no more talking and in a matter of minutes her breathing told me that she had gone to sleep. I left her a note and eased out of the room. I decided to forgo visiting with the other hospitalized church members because I knew Philip had been there today. I did check on Bernice's condition, which hadn't changed, and then I headed to Liverpool.

I wanted to go by Elva's house before it got dark. I knew the police were probably gone by now and I wanted to do a little snooping on my own. On the drive I tried to figure out some of the things that had happened in just three days.

Whoever attacked Bernice may have been trying to get to

Elva through her, I thought. *After the strange story she told me, I don't know if she dreamed about her husband when she had the seizure or if there are some underhanded dealings going on in that house. Maybe someone is trying to frighten Elva to death or simply trying to make people think she was crazy. I definitely don't want someone shipping the sweet old lady off to a rest home because they think they can prove she is delusional. I know without Bernice there to help her, there is nobody she can count on. Certainly Penny Saxon wouldn't be any help.*

I took a deep breath. I instinctively knew that I had inherited the job as her protector. I also knew that I really didn't mind.

EIGHT

I PULLED INTO THE Kingfield driveway and saw the house
was still being invaded by the police. As I turned off the
motor, my phone rang. Mrs. Barnes at Winston-Salem State
had been true to her word. The caller was Tyrone Wallace. I
told him about his aunt and he said he was going directly to
the hospital. I asked him to call me if there was any change
or if they had to do surgery right away. He said he would.

I hung up and debated with myself about going inside Elva's
house. I finally decided I would. I got out of my car and
headed toward the long wraparound porch. I was glad to see
that the officer standing near the door was Gary Bumgarner.
He greeted me with a smile on his face. "Hello, Reverend
Hinshaw. I might have known if there was trouble afoot, you'd
show up."

I returned his smile. Officer Bumgarner had come to my
apartment when I'd had some break-ins last summer so I said,
"At least they're not breaking into my place this time."

"That's true, but I hear you're the one who found the Wallace lady."

"I did. Mrs. Kingfield is a member of our church and she
asked me to come here to check on her housekeeper. That's
when I found Mrs. Wallace."

He nodded, and said, "The detectives are probably gonna
want to talk to you."

"Of course," I said and started toward the door.

"Maybe you'd better wait out here. They're gathering evidence inside."

"I'm sorry. I wasn't thinking." Before I could say anything further, my phone rang again.

"Willa, it's Anna Casey at church. Philip wondered if you could come back to the office right away."

"What going on, Anna?"

"There's a meeting of the Liverpool Ministerial Association here at seven and he's having a problem with Myra."

"I'm at Elva Kingfield's house. I can be there in fifteen minutes."

I hung up and told Gary that if the police needed to talk to me, to contact me at church. He said that would be fine.

By breaking the speed limit only slightly, in twelve minutes I pulled into the church parking lot. Betty Nichols was waiting on the steps. "Oh, Willa, I'm glad you're here."

"What's going on, Betty?" I knew the secretaries usually left at five and felt there was a real problem to keep them this late.

"It's Myra. Philip and Anna are looking for her." She took a deep breath. "Philip was in the conference room getting ready for the Ministerial Association meeting when he happened to glance out the window. He saw Myra running across the yard butt-naked. By the time he got outside, she was nowhere in sight."

"Oh, dear. What can I do?"

"Philip wanted you to take care of the meeting if you would."

"Of course. Do you know what they had planned?"

"Not really. Maybe the Thanksgiving services." She held the door open for me. "Most of them are already here. I put them in the conference room."

"Let me put my bag in my office and I'll be right there."

"I'll bring in tea and coffee and the sugar cookies that Myrtle Johnson brought."

I nodded as I unlocked my office. I threw my purse on the small flowered sofa in the corner and picked up a legal pad. I wanted to look as if I knew what I was doing.

As I entered the conference room I said, "Hello, gentlemen."

John Shaffer, the Presbyterian minister, was the first one to his feet. The others followed him.

I said, "Unfortunately Philip has had an emergency. I hope you don't mind my filling in for him."

David Staples, the Moravian cleric, said with a chuckle, "I'm sure nobody minds. You are, after all, much prettier than Philip."

I took no offense at his remark. Reverend Staples was pushing seventy and had always treated me with kindness and respect. I smiled and said, "I must admit, I didn't get a chance to talk with Philip, so you're going to have to bring me up to speed with the plans."

"No problem," Jeffrey Pierce from St. Stephen's Episcopal said. "For one thing, we've been discussing a pancake breakfast for the holiday season."

"Another project is the charity float for the needy we're planning for the Christmas parade," said Pastor Jerry Nifong from Mt. Carmel AME.

"That's probably what we need to decide on first," suggested Trent Freeman.

The others agreed and I said, "Okay. Jeffrey, if you'll lead us in prayer, we'll begin making plans."

"I'd be happy to," he said and we bowed as he started to pray.

When he finished we began discussing the float and Betty appeared with the food. Because I hadn't had dinner, the cookies looked wonderful. One bite told me that I hadn't been wrong because every time I had an opportunity to taste her cooking I was more convinced that Myrtle Johnson was one of the best cooks in our church.

Forty-five minutes later we had the plans laid out for a float in the parade. There would be a crèche on the float with a joint choir singing carols behind it. The words *God gave His Son to save you* would be over their heads and under that would be the words *What will you give to help those in need?* Members of the clergy and laypersons would walk beside the float with buckets taking offerings and donations. Everyone seemed pleased with the plan and Jerry Nifong and John Shaffer were elected co-chairmen of the project. We decided to table the pancake breakfast and adjourned the meeting.

As everyone took their leave, Trent lingered. "How are things going, Willa?"

I looked at him. "What do you mean?"

He looked at me suspiciously. "I was referring to Mrs. Kingfield's situation, but is there another problem?"

I nodded, but before I could say anything, Anna came running down the hall. "Oh, Willa, I'm glad you're through with the meeting. I think Philip could use your help."

"Of course. Where is he?"

"On the stairs to the belfry platform. That's where we found Myra. But Philip can't get her to come down. She doesn't seem to know him and when he starts to go into the steeple, she goes wild. She doesn't respond to me either. He thought that maybe you could reason with her."

"I'll certainly try."

"Do you think I could help?" Trent asked.

"You might," Anna said. "Just follow Willa. I'm going to find something to put around her in case we can get her to come down."

The access to the belfry was through a small closet behind the balcony. It was narrow and there was barely enough room for the pull-down stairs that led to the area where the chimes had been installed.

"Philip, I'm here to see if I can help," I said.

"Okay, Willa. I'll come down so you can get in."

I saw he was visibly shaken as he eased down the stairs and went through the door to the balcony. I climbed the stairs as Trent greeted him. I heard the two men sit down on a bench. I felt glad that Trent was there to comfort him. My heart swelled as I remembered what a gentle person Trent is.

I didn't have time to dwell on Trent long because I'd climbed the stairs and was peering into the dimness of the area leading to the steeple. At first I couldn't see anyone, then the small figure crouched in the corner began to become distinguishable.

Oh, God. Please help me say the right thing, I prayed silently. Aloud, but in a soft voice, I said, "Myra. It's Willa. Is something wrong?"

She didn't answer.

I tried again. "Myra, may I help you? I really want to help you."

She turned her head and looked at me, but said nothing.

"Is something scaring you, Myra?"

She nodded.

Good, I thought. *I'm making a little progress.*

"Do you want to tell me about it?"

She mumbled something, but I couldn't understand what it was.

"Would you say that again?"

"The dead man's here. He's trying to get me. I'm afraid of the dead man. Get him away. Get him away." She crouched closer to the corner and covered her head with both hands.

"Try to relax and I'll do what I can to get him away, Myra."

She peeped out from under her arm. "Please, please. I'm afraid of him. He sees me. I don't want him to see me."

"I won't let him see you, Myra." I took a deep breath. "Why don't you come over here and take my hand? I'll lead you away from him." She hesitated and I added, "Please come. I want to help you."

"You won't let him get me, will you?"

"I promise. I won't let him get you."

Myra moved a little closer to me and I reached out my hand toward her. She grabbed on to me with a hand that was so cold it didn't feel real. Her grip made me flinch and I wondered how someone so frail could have that much strength.

"Myra, you seem cold. Would you like something to put on?"

She nodded.

I glanced down and asked, "Did you get something to cover her with?"

Anna handed me a choir robe.

With my free hand, I spread the dark blue robe across Myra's shoulder. She shivered.

"Let me help you down the steps," I said. "There's nobody here except the two of us."

The ones waiting took the hint and left the area so I could bring Myra down into an empty room. Still shaking, she put her foot on the first step. She stopped and tried to pull away. "I can't come down. He'll be there."

I held on to her hand. "No, Myra. There's no one here except you and me. Bend over and look."

She did as I asked her to. "There's nobody here," she mumbled.

"Just like I said, nobody except you and me."

When I finally got her down the steps, I straightened the robe on her and zipped it up. It seemed to swallow the frail woman. I was amazed at how much weight she had lost in the months I'd worked here.

I was getting ready to ask her if she wanted to go home when she blurted, "Where's Philip, Willa? Why isn't he here? I came over to find him."

Startled by her quick change of mood, I stuttered, "H-he's here…he's in the next room. I'll take you to him, Myra."

I pushed the door open that led to the balcony and let Myra go out in front of me. She saw Philip and rushed to him. "Where have you been?"

"I've been here, dear."

"Why am I here, Philip?"

He didn't hesitate when he said, "You were looking for something. I think you must have found it."

"Good." She looked at him with almost blank eyes. "Can we go home now?"

"Yes, dear. We'll go right now." He took her arm and led her toward the balcony steps. Looking over his shoulder at us, he mouthed, "Thank you."

As Anna, Trent and I left the balcony, I said, "I wonder what triggered that incident?"

"Philip said that before he came over for the meeting, she was having a good time looking at a catalog of Halloween costumes. She wouldn't even put it down when he tried to get her to eat her snack," Anna said.

"That would explain the obsession with the dead man." I shook my head. "Poor Philip. I wonder how much longer..." I didn't finish my sentence because I didn't know exactly what I wanted to say.

"It is frustrating," Trent said. "I have a member with Alzheimer's and he's to the point of not recognizing any of his family or friends."

"It's such a terrible disease. It's just as hard on the family as it is on the person who has it," I said.

"Maybe even harder on them," Anna said.

We reached the office area and Anna thanked Trent for coming to our aid. She then went into the front office to tell Betty it was over and they could go home.

Betty had stuck the messages she had written on sticky notes on my office door. I pulled them off and went inside. Trent followed me. He closed the door behind him.

"You look tired, Willa. Are you okay?"

"I'm fine, but I am tired. A lot has been going on today. I think I need to sit back and kick my shoes off for a while."

"Why don't you do that?"

"I'm going to see if there are any calls I need to return and then do that very thing." I glanced through the notes. There was nothing urgent, but there was one from Blaire. This surprised me. She seldom called me at work. I laid the rest of them on my desk and picked up the phone. "There's just one I want to make. Blaire Peterson."

He nodded.

Blaire answered on the second ring. I could tell she'd been crying. "What's going on, my friend?" I asked.

"Nathan and I have called it quits. I feel awful and I need to talk to someone. I even called Trent, but he was at some kind of meeting."

"Trent is here. Would you like to speak to him?"

"It doesn't matter. I'd just as soon talk to you."

"I'm getting ready to come home. Why don't I meet you at my place? I'll be there in ten or fifteen minutes."

"I'll watch for you."

We hung up and I turned to Trent. "Blaire and Nathan have split up. She needs a shoulder to cry on."

"I guess that blows my idea. I wanted to go to your place, order a pizza, sit on the couch with you in my arms and get lost in some silly movie."

I shook my head. "That sounds great, but it will have to be later."

There was a knock on my door.

"Come in," I said.

Anna opened the door and said, "Willa, this is Detective Clay Fisher. He needs to talk with you."

"Of course," I said. "Please come in."

He glanced at Trent. "If you're busy, I can wait, Reverend."

Trent stood. "We're through," he said to the detective. To me he said, "Why don't I go see Blaire and let her know you've been detained?"

"Thank you, Trent."

I pointed to the sofa Trent had vacated. "Have a seat, Detective."

"Thank you." He took a small notebook from his pocket and sat down. "I'm sorry if you had other plans, Reverend Hinshaw, but I really need to ask you a few questions."

"It's no problem. Reverend Freeman is going to keep the appointment for me."

There was not a lot I could tell Detective Fisher. No, I didn't know anyone who would want to hurt Bernice Wallace. No, I didn't see anything suspicious around her house. Yes, I'd be glad to call him if I thought of anything that might be of help to him.

Thirty minutes later, I headed home. Trent's car was parked in front of Blaire's building across the parking lot from mine. I didn't want to interrupt the counseling session so I went up the steps to my own apartment.

The light was flashing on my answering machine. I tossed my straw purse to the sofa, noting again that I needed to change for the season, and flipped the on switch.

"Hi, Preacher Girl," the distinct New York accent greeted me. "I'm sorry I didn't get to speak to you in person, but I'm on the run as usual. I'm headed to China to film the pandas, so I'll have to postpone my visit with you. Hope you hadn't made lavish plans. I really do hate it worked out this way, but we'll do it later, okay? Love you as ever."

I don't know if it was because Jacob wasn't coming or if I'd just gone through so much in the past couple of days that I'd reached my breaking point. But whatever the reason, I dropped into the big green chair and began to sob.

NINE

IT WAS WELL INTO the evening when I felt settled down enough to call and check on Blaire. She thanked me for sending Trent to see her and proceeded to tell me that she was beginning to feel much better about the situation. I offered to come over, but she said not to bother. She was going to cuddle up with a new Helen Goodman mystery novel and maybe read the whole thing before she went to bed.

I felt a little guilty that I was secretly glad she didn't need me. I chose to push it out of my mind and called Ed. I wanted to find out how it went at the doctor's.

"Would you believe it was an inner ear infection?" he said as soon as he recognized my voice. "And believe it or not, I planned to call you tonight."

I took a deep breath. "I do believe you and I'm glad it was the inner ear. That relieves my mind," I said. "I was so afraid it was from the incident last summer."

"Me, too, but the doctor said it was something that could easily be treated."

I hung up, and said a prayer of thanksgiving. I was hungry so I settled on a scrambled egg, a sliced tomato and some toast for supper. After eating, I did my studying and decided to make an early night of it.

By nine, I was propped up in bed, waiting for a movie I'd seen advertised on one of the cable networks. I had my diet Coke sitting on the nightstand and had a big bowl of popcorn on my lap. The introduction to the movie came on just as my telephone rang.

"I'm sorry to bother you, Willa, but I need you to do me a

favor." Elva Kingfield's voice came over the wire as soon as I said hello.

"Of course I will," I said, putting the popcorn beside me, feeling a little apprehensive. I knew she must be okay or she wouldn't be able to call, but illogically, I was afraid something was wrong. "What do you need me to do?"

"Please call my nephew in Atlanta for me. I'd do it myself, but I can't make a long-distance call from this phone."

"What do you want me to tell him?" I wondered if she wanted me to relate to him the unbelievable story that she'd told me about Leo coming back from the dead.

"I want you to ask him to come up here."

When she said nothing further, I asked, "Is there some reason besides your illness that I should tell him why you need him?"

"Just tell him that I think Penny is trying to get me put away."

I sat up straight. This was something that I had feared. "Why would Ms. Saxon do that?"

"She wants me to give her my power of attorney. When I told her there was no way in h— I mean there was no way that I would do that, she got mad and flew out of here like a deranged antelope."

I couldn't help smiling at Elva's assessment of Penny's reaction, but I didn't mention it to her. "I met her in the hall as she was leaving the hospital today. I didn't know she had asked you to do that."

"Oh, she didn't ask me today. She came back tonight with that smart-mouthed niece of hers and they both jumped on me."

"I'm sorry that happened, Elva."

"I think it scared them. I got so mad that my heart monitor went off. The nurse was just coming in the door to check on me and she ran them off. She wouldn't even let them apologize." Elva chuckled.

I was too concerned about her to let her humorous remarks sink in. "Are you okay now?"

"Of course I am." She changed the subject. "Will you make the call for me?"

"I will. Do you have your nephew's number?"

"No. You'll have to get it from information." She gave me his full name and the street he lived on.

I told her I'd let her know when he could come.

"I don't think they'll allow calls to the rooms after nine. You can just let me know tomorrow. You are coming to see me, aren't you?"

"I'll come, but I'm not sure what time."

We hung up and I dialed information. When I reached Dennis Kingfield's number, his answering machine picked up. It said, "I'll be in California on business until Sunday. Please leave a message or, if you have an emergency, please call Ray Allen, my partner."

I thought about trying to track down Ray Allen, but I had no idea of his address and there were probably a slew of Ray Allens in Atlanta. I knew it was smarter to leave a message. Into the receiver, I said, "Mr. Kingfield, this is Willa Hinshaw, one of your aunt's ministers. She asked me to call you for her. Don't let this frighten you, but she's in the hospital. She is much better and should be home in a few days. This is my home number and my cell number in case you call home for your messages." I left the two numbers and added, "Please call me when you get this. Thank you."

There was nothing more I could do tonight. I turned back to the movie, which had started, but I soon caught on to the plot line.

It was raining when I got up the next morning and the temperature had dropped several degrees. I decided to wear my gray flannel pantsuit and red silk blouse to work. I had a habit of wearing something red on a cloudy wet day. I started this when I was in college and continued it when I got my first job. For some reason it seemed to make the gloomy days seem brighter.

By the time I got dressed, made a hot breakfast of oatmeal, and headed for the church, I was in high spirits. I had a feeling it was going to be a good day.

There was nothing pressing at the office when I arrived, so I decided to close my door and work on the children's Christmas play then go to the hospital to visit Elva and Bernice. By noon, I had the first draft of the play completed. I pushed the chair back from the computer desk and stretched my arms over my head. I felt good, but there wasn't a lot of time to relish in my accomplishment because the phone buzzed and Betty informed me I had a call.

"Yes, Elva," I said into the phone after I greeted her. "I called your nephew, but he was out of town. I left a message."

"Then I guess I'll just have to wait until he gets back." I could almost hear the disappointment in her voice.

"I presume he'll call," I said. "I asked him to do so as soon as he returned home."

She changed the subject. "Are you coming to the hospital today?"

"Yes. I'm getting ready to leave now."

"You'll be sure to check on Bernice, won't you?"

"Of course."

"I keep asking the nurses, but they won't tell me a thing."

"I'll see about her as soon as I get there. Is there anything you need me to bring to you?"

"Not a thing, dear. I'm just looking forward to seeing you."

We hung up and I headed for the hospital.

When I arrived, I found there had been little change in Bernice's condition. She was still in ICU. I left my card on her nightstand and caught the elevator to Elva's floor. As I approached the room, I heard loud voices. I hurried my steps.

As I neared the room, Elva was saying, "I don't give a whit what you think, Penny. I'm not going to do it."

"You're being stupid, Aunt Elva. And I bet Dennis would agree with me."

"We'll just see when he gets here."

"What do you mean by that?" Penny yelled.

"Willa called him for me and…"

"You crazy old woman, why did you get her involved in a private family matter?"

"She's my…friend. She cares. She…" Elva collapsed backward to her pillows as I entered the room.

Before I could say anything a nurse pushed past me and demanded, "What's going on in here?"

Penny whirled around and saw both of us. "It's her fault," she said, pointing at me. "She won't stay out of our family business."

The nurse moved to the bed and took Elva's wrist in her hand. I heard the older woman mumble something that I couldn't make out.

The nurse nodded and turned to us. "Which one of you is the niece?"

Penny grinned and said, "That's me."

The nurse replied in a flat voice, "Please step into the hall with me."

When the door closed behind them, Elva reached out toward me. "Willa, I'm so glad you're here."

I took her hand. "What is going on, Elva?"

"Penny is having a conniption because I won't consent to give her my power of attorney. She wants to put me away. I know she does, Willa."

I patted the aged hand. "We're going to make sure that doesn't happen."

She smiled and closed her eyes. "Please be on my side in this issue. She says I'm losing my mind."

"I don't believe that."

She squeezed my hand. "Thank you, dear."

The nurse came back through the door and said, "Mrs. Kingfield, you don't have to worry about being bothered by your niece again. I asked her to leave and told her that she would no longer be allowed to visit you unless you request that she come."

"Oh, thank you."

"Now, let me check out those vitals. We don't need to be getting upset like that."

"I know I shouldn't let her upset me, but that woman would upset a rabid dog."

I had to hide a smile. I couldn't help trying to picture a rabid dog that was not already upset. I bit my lip and said, "Maybe I should leave and let you rest."

"I think she's fine. Her heart is strong and her pulse is settling down." The nurse turned to me. "And I think she wants you to stay."

Elva spoke. She had a thermometer in her mouth, but I understood she was saying yes.

When the nurse was satisfied and left the room, I pulled a chair close to Elva's bed. "I'm sorry Penny upset you."

"It's okay now and that's not what is important. How's Bernice?"

I explained that her condition was the same, and that I had been in touch with her nephew. "He's seeing that she is getting the best of care."

"Thank you, Willa. Bernice is my best friend. I can't stand the thought of something happening to her. I planned for the two of us to stay together until we each reach the ripe age of at least one hundred."

"I think that's a lovely plan."

"Maybe it will still happen."

I nodded and changed the subject. "Elva, are you sure things are okay with you?"

"I think so, Willa. I don't understand why all of a sudden Penny Saxon has decided to take over my life. I wonder if she knows that I didn't mention her in my will."

"Do you have a recent will, Elva?"

She looked at me strangely. "I had one drawn up after my husband died. Why would you ask?"

"I know it's none of my business, but they say some of the older wills aren't holding up. I think there are simpler ways to write them now."

"Oh, I see. Maybe I should call Jesse Snow and have him check on it."

"Let's hope it will be many years before it becomes an issue." I changed the subject again. "Has the doctor given you any idea of how long he plans to keep you in the hospital?"

"A few more days is all he'll tell me."

"I'll be glad to see you come home." I wondered if I really meant what I was saying. I didn't want this sweet old lady going back to a house where someone had attacked her friend. Especially now that she might be alone. Maybe, I decided, I could talk her into having someone stay there when she did get out of the hospital. There were several people in the church that sat with the elderly. One of them might be the answer. I made a mental note to talk to her about it later.

At that moment a young doctor—probably an intern—entered the room. "Hello, Mrs. Kingfield. How are we feeling today?"

"I feel fine. I'm not sure how you may be feeling," Elva said with a smile.

The doctor didn't seem to catch the irony of her reply. He continued, "Let's have a look and see what that tells me."

I stood. "I'll come back tomorrow, Elva. Let me know if you need anything."

"Thank you, Willa."

The doctor ignored me as I left the room.

The Newsomes had gone home with their twins. Luke Underwood was scheduled to be released today. I made a quick stop by his room to speak to him. He was sitting on the side of the bed, dressed and ready to leave.

"I'm just waiting until Dad settles up the bill." He grinned.

"Mom decided to stay home so she could have a good hot meal ready when I get there."

"I know you'll be glad to get home and to taste your mom's cooking again." I returned his smile. "I'll be over to see how you're doing in a few days."

"Thanks, Reverend."

We talked a little more. I then said goodbye and headed for the parking lot. On impulse, I decided to go by Elva's house before returning to the office.

When I rounded the curve in the driveway, I was surprised to see a Lincoln parked in the drive leading to the back of the house. Penny Saxon was coming toward her car with two huge silver candlesticks in her hands. I remembered they had adorned the parlor fireplace. She looked as startled as I was, but she stood motionless as she watched me come to a stop.

I jumped out of my car and ran toward her. "What are you doing?" I demanded. When she didn't answer, I went on. "How dare you come to pilfer Elva's things while she's in the hospital."

"It's none of your business," she said.

"Oh, I disagree. Someone who cares for Elva needs to look out for her interests."

"Are you saying I don't care about my aunt?" The familiar haughtiness was coming back into her voice.

"That's exactly what I'm saying."

"Well, I do care."

"And I see just how much," I snapped.

She glanced down at the candlesticks. "How do you know these aren't mine?"

"Because I've seen them in the house."

Penny acted as if she didn't know what to say. There was a few seconds pause as I glared at her. Finally she mumbled, "I was just going to clean them up for her."

"Right! Is there anything else that you were going to clean?"

Penny glanced at her car. "It's none of your business what I'm doing," she yelled.

I bit my lip to stay calm. "As I said, someone has to look out for Elva. Maybe I should ask the police to come out and check things over."

For a moment I thought Penny was going to hit me with one of the candlesticks, but instead she thrust them into my arms and ran to her car. Before I could say anything else, she jumped inside and started the motor. I headed toward the car and she wheeled through the yard, barely missing my car as she backed out of the driveway. She was gone before I could get a good look inside of her car. I thought I might have seen a table leg sticking up beside the window, but I wasn't positive.

For a minute I didn't know what to do. If I left now, she might be watching and then she could come back to continue taking Elva's things. On the other hand, I couldn't stay here all day and night to protect them. There was one person I could call who would know exactly the right thing to do. I entered the house through the back door, went directly to the parlor, put the candlesticks back on the mantel, opened the drapes so I could see if anyone came up the drive and then took my cell phone from my pocket. I dialed Ed Walsh's number from memory.

TEN

ED ANSWERED THE PHONE on the second ring. "What's the matter, Willa?" he asked as soon as he heard my voice.

"I'm not sure, Ed, but I think Elva Kingfield's niece, Penny Saxon, is trying to steal some of the valuable antiques in the house while Elva is in the hospital." I went on to explain the confrontation with the candlesticks.

"It certainly sounds like Ms. Saxon is up to no good."

"I'm concerned about what is going to happen when Elva comes home."

"Doesn't she have a housekeeper?"

I told him about Bernice.

"Let me check around a bit, Willa. I'll see if I can figure out something."

"I'm sorry to bother you with this, Ed. Especially when you're not feeling well. I just didn't know who else to turn to."

"I'm already feeling better. The medicine is kicking in. Don't you worry about me. I'm going to be fine."

"I'm glad about that."

We talked a little longer then said our goodbyes.

After hanging up, I took the opportunity to look around in the rooms of the house that I had been in. The entryway looked as it had on my first visit. Of course, I realized, I didn't take inventory the times I'd been there because I didn't expect to have to remember what I'd seen. Back in the parlor I looked around. The mantel looked a little more empty than the first visit, but I couldn't recall what else had been there.

I moved to the chairs where Elva and I sat the first day

we met. I sat down in the one I had occupied. I methodically looked around the room. The Queen Anne table I had admired was in its spot, and as far as I could tell, everything that had been on it was still there. I kept looking. Nothing stood out and I was about to give up when the picture over the sofa caught my eye.

Didn't it have a lake in it? This one was a mountain scene, but there was no lake.

Something was wrong. I got up and walked to the sofa. I looked at the picture closely. It was an original painting, but it didn't have the beautiful brush strokes or color mixes one expects to see in an expensive work of art. This one was definitely not the one that had been over the sofa the first time I had sat here and admired it.

That settled it for me. I knew I couldn't prove it, but Penny was replacing some things in Elva's house with items that she didn't think Elva would notice. I hoped Ed could come up with a plan to stop this. I was certainly at a loss.

I locked up Elva's house and headed to the church. I was pulling into the parking lot when my cell phone rang.

"This is Willa," I said. "How may I help you?"

"Hi, Willa. It's Trent."

"Hi, my friend."

"I know it's short notice, but a parishioner gave me tickets to the Barn Dinner Theater in Greensboro tonight. Wondered if you'd be interested in going?"

"Oh, that sounds wonderful. Do you know what's playing?"

"*Smoke on the Mountain,* I think."

"Oh, I love that play. What time should we go?"

"Is six-thirty too early?"

"No. I'll be ready."

"Good. See you then."

There was nothing pressing at work. Philip's office door was closed and I knew he was out, so I told Betty and Anna that I was going to call it a day. I went home, took a hot bubble bath, and dressed in my almost new teal pantsuit. I took the time to put my shoulder-length hair up in a French twist and clipped it with the pearl clasp that my aunt Lila had given me for my birthday. I slipped on the bracelet and matching earrings that had been designed by Lanie of Lanie's Fine Things—a gift from Mom and Dad. I hoped that Trent would approve of the way I looked.

When he knocked on my door a few minutes later, his eyes told me he did. And I approved of his appearance, too. He was wearing light gray slacks and a bulky knit burgundy sweater. His blue eyes sparkled as he smiled at me.

"I appreciate a woman who is ready when she says she'll be," he kidded.

I laughed. "I guess it's my training." I locked my door and we went down the stairs to his SUV.

We were headed to I-40 when I said, "I'm looking forward to this. I've had a rough day."

He answered correctly. "Tell me about it."

It took a while, but I told him the events of my entire day. I ended with "I'm not sure what to do about Penny. I've called Ed Walsh and I hope he'll have some idea."

Trent shook his head. "Boy, you have had a busy day and I'm sure Ed will think of something because the situation definitely needs to be taken care of."

"I agree."

We spent the rest of the drive discussing possibilities of what could be done about Penny. In what seemed like no time at all, we'd reached Greensboro and were pulling into the parking lot at the Barn Dinner Theater.

The lot was almost full. We had to park in the back. "I should have let you out at the door," Trent said.

"I don't mind walking with you."

We got out of the car and started toward the door. Trent took my hand in his and squeezed it. A little chill ran down my spine as it always did when he made a romantic move toward me. He said, "Don't worry, honey. Things are going to work out with Mrs. Kingfield."

"I know." I moved closer to him. "Tonight I just want to get it all out of my mind and have a good time with you."

"Then that's exactly what we're going to do."

And we did. We had excellent seats, the food was great, and the play was hilarious.

When we got back to my apartment, it was close to midnight. Trent walked me to my door. "It's getting pretty late, but you're welcome to come in," I said.

"I think I'd better get on."

I unlocked my door and turned to him. "Then, let me thank you for a wonderful night. I'm really glad your church member couldn't use the tickets."

"I had a good time, too, Willa. Of course, I always do with you."

I felt my heart quicken, but I didn't say anything.

Neither did Trent. He simply took me in his arms and kissed me passionately.

I felt myself returning his kiss. "Oh, Trent." I pulled away and whispered, "We'd better slow down."

"I agree," he said. "I know we have to watch it, but you're beginning to become more and more important to me."

"You mean a lot to me, too, Trent."

"We've got to face our feelings for each other one of these days."

"I know."

"But not tonight, right?" He chuckled.

"Not tonight." I kissed his cheek. "We'll talk soon."

"Yes. Let me know if I can help with the Kingfield situation."

"I will."

He kissed me again, this time quickly. He then turned and went down the steps and got into his car, but he didn't pull away until I went through the door and closed it behind me.

Inside my apartment, I leaned against the door and listened

to his car leaving the parking lot. My heart was pounding and thoughts were whirling in my head. I had known for a long time that I cared for Reverend Trent Freeman, but now I knew I was beginning to fall in love with him. And from his actions tonight, I realized he was feeling the same way. Unless we wanted to take our relationship to another level, we needed to call it off now. But to face breaking it off with him was almost more than I could bear to think about. He was an important part of my life.

I shook my head. I'd make those decisions later.

As I went through the living room I noticed the flashing light on my answering machine. It told me I had a message, but I decided to wait until morning to listen to it. Right now I was going to bed and letting the memory of Trent's kiss lull me to sleep.

ELEVEN

I WOKE UP FEELING GOOD. I took a quick shower, got dressed and headed to the kitchen. I was hungry. I cut up a big bowl of fruit and fixed myself some oatmeal. The fruit would be tasty and the oatmeal was something that filled me up and would keep me feeling full until lunchtime.

After putting it in the microwave, I returned to the living room and flipped on the answering machine. I expected to hear Ed's voice giving me an idea of what could be done about Elva's problem. I was totally surprised when Penny Saxon spoke. She gave me her name and number, then she said, "Reverend Hinshaw, I need to talk to you. If you get in early enough tonight, please call me. If not, please call tomorrow morning."

Stunned, I wrote down the number she left and stuck it into my purse. I decided I'd call her as soon as I got to the office. The microwave buzzed and I went back into the kitchen. I took my oatmeal and flipped on the TV. I was going to watch a little of the morning show while I ate. I'd get into other matters soon enough.

I got to work at eight-thirty. After greeting everyone, I went to my office and sat at my desk. I knew the first thing I had to do was call Penny. Though I dreaded a confrontation with her, I picked up the phone and dialed her number.

On the fourth ring, her answering machine picked up. After her greeting and the beep, I said, "Miss Saxon, this is Willa Hinshaw. I didn't get in early enough to return your call last night. You can get me at the church until noon today. Afterward, you can call my cell." I left both numbers and then hung up.

There was a knock on my open door.

"Come in," I said.

Myrtle Johnson came through the door. "Hello, Reverend Willa."

"Hi, Myrtle."

"May I talk to you for a few minutes?"

"Of course."

She set a grocery bag beside my desk. "I brought you some fall apples. They make great pies or they can be fried or stewed. They're good that way, too."

"Thank you. I love apples. Have a seat." I indicated my small couch. "Would you like to close the door?"

"I think I will," she said as she pushed the door together. "I don't want to hurt anyone's feelings by talking about a private matter."

I wondered what this gentle woman had on her mind. She was one of the members of the church who loved everyone. And from what I could tell, the feeling was returned.

She took a seat on the sofa. She must have seen the concern on my face because she said, "I'm not going to say anything against anyone, Reverend Willa. I just don't want Philip to think I'm trying to stick my nose in his business." She smiled, took a deep breath and continued. "There was a meeting of the Tuesday Night Ladies' Circle and we were discussing Myra's condition. She seems to be getting much worse."

I now understood why she wanted to be discreet. Everyone knew Philip was sensitive about Myra's illness. "She has deteriorated some. It has been hard on Philip."

"That's what we thought. We decided to talk to you and see what you thought we could do to help him out."

I smiled at her. "I think that's a lovely idea. I'm sure he'd enjoy a few home-cooked meals."

"We discussed that. Do you think three a week are okay, or should we do more?"

"I think that's just perfect. You don't want to bring so much that he has to throw some out."

"We also thought that he might need someone to stay with Myra occasionally. We weren't sure how to approach him about that."

"Oh, Myrtle, what a wonderful idea. If you could set up a schedule of two or three mornings a week, that would give him some relief."

"That's just what I needed to know. We'll get right on it." She stood. "I'm expecting you to come out to the house for Sunday dinner again soon, Willa."

"I'll look forward to it."

"Well, thanks for the information. I won't keep you any longer."

"You're not keeping me. I enjoy having folks drop in for a chat."

She smiled. "I would stay and talk today, but I'd better get to work on this. I'll see you Sunday."

"Thanks again for what you're doing, Myrtle."

She nodded and closed the door behind her.

I turned to my paperwork with a smile. *Those ladies are one of the reasons this church is such a wonderful place to worship and to work,* I thought.

I turned back to my paperwork.

An hour later, my phone buzzed. "Willa, there's a Penny Saxon on the phone for you."

"Thanks, Betty." I picked up the phone. "This is Willa Hinshaw."

"Reverend Hinshaw, this is Penny. I just wanted to apologize for the way I acted yesterday. I was just so upset about what has been happening to Aunt Elva."

I was surprised by her comment and just mumbled, "I don't think I'm the one you should be apologizing to."

"Of course I should apologize to you. I know you thought I was stealing things from my aunt." When I didn't answer she said, "You just don't know what she's been doing."

"Oh?"

"Well, she's been giving away some of her valuables and I was just putting some in storage for her so she wouldn't give them all away."

I didn't believe a word Penny was saying, but I asked, "Who is she giving them to?"

This must have encouraged her because she said, "I'm not sure, but I suspect that Bernice has been selling some of Aunt Elva's things."

"That's hard to believe."

"Oh, you just don't know her like I do. She has a big family and I'm sure she sends them money. I think she's been doing it for years. You know how maids are when they work for rich people."

I ignored her last statement and asked, "If Bernice has been selling off items for years, why hasn't Elva noticed some of her possessions were missing?"

"Aunt Elva isn't as sharp as she used to be. Besides, I think she might be senile. Somebody has to look out for her and I think that somebody should be me."

"Penny, I've found your aunt to be an articulate and wise person. I think at her age, she is a remarkable lady."

"Oh, yes. She can fool some people, but she really is getting senile." Penny took a deep breath and went on. "I called in hopes that you would understand and help me convince her to give me her power of attorney. It's vital that she do so."

I couldn't believe this request. "You must be kidding."

"Not at all. I know she likes you and if you asked her to turn her affairs over to me, I'm sure she'd do it."

It was all I could do to keep from yelling at Penny. I know my voice must have shook a little when I said, "You have the wrong person. I have no intention of asking Elva to do such a thing. In fact, if she were to appoint you to have her power of attorney, I think it would be a big mistake."

"Well, you sure disappoint me. I thought a preacher would be more understanding."

"Oh, I think I understand completely."

Her whole attitude changed. Her voice became whiney and it rose an octave or two. "Aunt Elva needs to be put in a home. If you can't see that, then you're stupid."

I bit my lip to keep from telling her what I really thought of her. Instead, I said, "I think it's time we ended this conversation."

"You're right about that and as far as I'm concerned you can go to hell!" She slammed the phone down so hard it hurt my ear.

I was shaking when I replaced the receiver. I closed my eyes and prayed silently that I wouldn't have bad thoughts about Penny all day. I also asked the Lord to help her see what she was doing to a sweet gentle lady.

After taking a thirty-minute quiet break, I decided I needed to get out a while and go to lunch early. I told Betty to take messages.

To help clear my head I walked to the Knife and Fork Café. I was halfway there when I had to pull my sweater close around me. "Should have worn a jacket this morning," I said and picked up my pace.

Since it wasn't yet twelve, the restaurant wasn't crowded. Fran Stevens, the new owner, greeted me. "How are you today, Reverend Hinshaw?"

"Fine, Fran. How are you?"

She smiled. "I couldn't be better." She led me to a table next to the window. "Is this okay?"

"It's perfect."

She handed me a menu and asked, "Iced tea?"

I nodded and she scurried away.

I had my tea and was studying the menu when Jesse Snow came in. "Hi, Willa," he said. "Are you alone?"

I nodded, and he walked over. "Mind if I join you?"

"I'd love to have your company, Mayor."

"I appreciate that." He took a chair in front of me. "How's everything going today?"

"So far, it has been interesting."

"Oh?" He cocked an eye at me.

Fran appeared with a glass of tea for Jesse. "Hello, Mayor."

"Hello, Fran." He took the menu she handed to him. "I hope you don't mind me finding a seat on my own."

"Of course not." She smiled at us. "The waitress will be right with you."

"I think I'll have the chicken salad," I said, putting my menu aside. "When you've decided, may I ask you something?"

He put his menu down and looked at her. "You can ask me anything, Willa."

"You're Elva Kingfield's lawyer, aren't you?" He nodded and I went on. "I thought she said you were. I think you should visit her, Jesse."

"If you think I should."

The waitress came to our table and I ordered the chicken salad on a croissant and a five-bean salad. Jesse asked for the roast beef on rye with a tossed salad.

When we were alone again, I said, "I think Elva's family is trying to get rid of her."

"What do you mean?"

I told him how Penny had acted on the day Elva had her spell and about catching her carrying Elva's belongings out of the house. I ended with the telephone conversation I had with Penny this morning.

"You're right. I need to go see Elva. I don't think I have any appointments this afternoon. I'll go see her right after lunch."

When our food arrived, we dropped the subject of Elva and turned to Philip. Like me, he was concerned about the strain Myra's illness was putting on her husband.

"It doesn't look like it will be much longer until he will have to make the decision to have her institutionalized. I know it's hard for him to think like that though," Jesse said.

"Very hard. I think he knows it's close, but he doesn't want to accept it."

"I'm glad you're here to help him, Willa. I don't know what the church ever did without you."

"You're going to make me feel prideful, Jesse. But thanks for the compliment."

Fran walked up. "I've come up with a new dessert that I want to add to the menu and I wondered if you two would be willing to test it for me."

"Of course," Jesse said. "I'm not one to turn down a good dessert."

"I'd love to try it, Fran," I said.

She brought out a chocolate concoction that, as the kids say, was to die for. She beamed when I told her so.

"Great," Jesse said. "You've got to add it."

"I'm going to print up a note on it and put them on the tables now. Maybe I can sell some of it today." She moved away.

"I'm sure glad she bought this place," I said.

"Me, too. I was afraid when the former owner had that stroke it would close. But her taking it over has been a plus to the town and to her, too."

"I agree. When her husband walked off, I was afraid she was going to give up. Instead she's showing that she can make it in this world on her own." I put my napkin on the table and said, "Boy, I'm full. I'm glad I walked up here. I need to exercise some of this off."

"I walked from the other direction, or I'd offer to take you back to the church."

We said our goodbyes and both headed to our respective offices.

Back at church, I thought I'd do a little more work before going to see Elva. That would give Jesse time to visit her and I definitely thought his visit was more important than mine. I looked at the two calls that Betty had taken while I was at lunch. One was from Blaire. I dialed her number at work.

As soon as we said hello, she asked, "If you're not busy tonight, could we have dinner?"

"Sure. How does Mexican sound?"

"Sounds great. Let's go to Don Juan's in Kernersville. I hear it's good."

"I'll be going to the hospital this afternoon. I'll give you a call as soon as I leave there."

"See you then."

It was a fast conversation, but I knew she was busy. I heard a lot of talking in the background. I looked at the next number. It was Tyrone Wallace. I dialed it, with dread in my heart.

"Reverend Hinshaw," he said when I told him who I was. "They're going to operate on Aunt Bernice at seven o'clock in the morning."

"I'm so glad you let me know. I'll be there."

"You don't have to come, but I knew you'd want to know."

"Of course I'll come. I've been checking on your aunt every day."

"Thank you. I know she would appreciate it."

"I'll see you in the morning, Tyrone."

"Thanks."

I said a prayer for Bernice and all her family. I had a good feeling after the prayer. I knew I had done all I could. She was in God's hands now.

There was a tap on my open door. "Willa," Anna said. "There's a man on line two for you. Betty said he called while you were at lunch, but wouldn't leave a number."

"Thanks, Anna." I punched up line two. "This is Willa Hinshaw."

"I'm glad I caught you this time, Reverend Hinshaw. This is Dennis Kingfield. I called my home phone to get my calls and got your message. I'm very concerned about Aunt Elva. What has happened?"

"I'm glad you called, Mr. Kingfield. Elva had some kind

of attack and was taken to the hospital, but she's doing fine. She should be going home in the next day or two."

"That's a relief. She's such a dear person. I don't want to think of anything happening to her."

"She is a special lady and I know she cares about you. She asked me to call you and let you know she wants you to come visit as soon as you can."

"I'm in California and I haven't finished my business here. It might be a couple of weeks before I can get there. Of course, if there's an emergency, I'll come right away."

"I don't think that will be necessary. If you'll give me a number where I can reach you, I'll call if necessary."

"I can give you the hotel where I am now, but I'm leaving for San Diego in the morning. I don't know what that number will be."

"Do you have a cell?"

"Yes. Let me give you that number."

He did and I said, "I won't call unless it is absolutely necessary."

"Is there any way I can talk with Aunt Elva? Maybe you could have her call me."

"You can call her at the hospital if you like. She has a phone in her room."

"Oh, that would be great. Do you have the number?"

I gave it to him and he thanked me profusely. He also told me to be sure and call him any time I felt it was necessary.

I hung up and thought about our conversation. I then re-membered what Bernice had told me about Dennis Kingfield borrowing money from his aunt. It was hard to reconcile the two. He had shown a lot of concern during the call. I didn't doubt that he really cared for Elva.

I packed up my work and got ready to go to the hospital. At least Dennis would have talked with her before I arrived. Maybe that would soften the blow when I told her that Bernice was scheduled for surgery.

When I got to the hospital, the visit with Elva went well.

She was thrilled that Dennis had called and she said she assured him that two weeks would be great if he could get here then. She was also excited that Jesse had come by. She said he was coming back to finalize her new will. The only thing that bothered her was the fact that Bernice was facing surgery. I told her I had promised to come sit with Tyrone and this made her feel better.

I left Elva and went by to see Bernice. She was still motionless on the stark white sheets. I held her hand and said a prayer for her and for success of the surgery the following day. I then told her that Elva was doing fine and that she was praying for her, too.

When I turned to leave, a young man was standing in the doorway, staring at me. I smiled at him. "You must be Tyrone."

"Yes, ma'am."

I held out my hand. "I'm Willa."

"It's nice to meet you, Reverend." He took my hand and shook it.

"I've been visiting Mrs. Kingfield and I always come by to see your aunt."

"That's nice of you. I'm sure she would appreciate it."

"Bernice and I like each other. I'm sure she would do the same for me."

He just nodded.

"I'll see you in the morning," I said.

"Don't feel you have to come."

"I don't feel that way. I want to be here. As I said, Bernice is my friend."

I left him and headed for the parking lot. The sun was going down and it was getting a little chilly. I pulled my sweater together and hurried to my car. I paused as I put the key in the lock. There was a paper stuck under the windshield wiper.

"I hate those ads," I mumbled as I reached for it. "I bet they don't drum up much business either."

I glanced at it and saw it wasn't an ad, after all. It was a message to me. I read it and my heart began to beat faster. The note said, *You need to get out of Elva Kingfield's life. I don't care if you are a minister, if you keep putting your nose in her business, it may get chopped off—or worse!*

TWELVE

I HURRIED INTO MY CAR and locked the door. I looked about the parking lot, but saw only a few people coming and going. I didn't see anyone that looked as if they were lying in wait to jump me. Regardless, I drove a little faster than usual as I headed back to Liverpool.

By the time I reached the town limits I had calmed down enough to call Blaire. When I pulled into our parking lot, she came out on her porch. I pulled in front of her apartment and put my window down.

"Come on and get in," I said. "I'll drive."

"I had planned on driving."

"It doesn't matter. My car is already warm."

She got in the passenger side. "I'm glad you were able to go tonight. I needed a night out."

"I've been looking forward to it. I haven't had Mexican since the last time we ate it together."

The note I'd gotten at the hospital floated from the dash, where I'd thrown it. It landed in Blaire's lap. "What's this?" she asked.

"Nothing. Probably just a prank."

Blaire read the note. "Prank, my foot. Have you told the police?"

"Of course not. I just found it when I got in my car."

"Well, I think you should."

"As I said, it's probably a prank."

Blaire shook her head. "You know better than that. This is no prank. Somebody is threatening you."

"If it will make you feel better, I'll show it to Ed."

"That does make me feel better." She folded the note and stuck it in my open purse. "Now don't you forget."

"Yes, Mama," I said and she laughed. I went on. "How are you doing?"

"Okay, but I didn't want to go to the church supper tonight because I was afraid they would be there."

I didn't have to ask who they were. I knew she referred to my downstairs neighbor Nathan and his new girlfriend. I said, "I can understand that."

"It's hard enough living across the parking lot from him, and seeing her go in and out of his apartment. I can't meet him on a social level." She shifted her position. "Anyway, not yet. I'm not going to let him run me away from church though."

"I don't blame you for that."

There was a moment of silence, then in a quivering voice, she said, "Her car was in the parking lot all night last night."

"Oh, Blaire, I'm sorry."

"I thought maybe you'd notice."

"No. Trent and I went to the Barn Dinner Theater last night. I wasn't paying attention."

"Did you have a good time?"

"It was great." I smiled to myself as I thought about it.

"I'm glad," she mumbled.

I could tell by her voice she was near tears. "I know it's tough, my friend," I said.

"If I didn't have to see them together when I'm home, I think I'd feel better about it."

"Maybe he'll move."

Blaire chuckled. "Maybe he will, or maybe I will."

"Oh, I don't want you to move." As soon as it was out of my mouth a fleeting thought drifted across my mind. I didn't voice it because I wanted to bring it up again when I was alone and could really think it through.

"Don't worry. I was just talking. I can't afford any of the other apartments in town." She shifted her position again.

"That's enough about my lost romance. Tell me about the date with Trent."

"As I said, we had a wonderful time. Have you ever seen *Smoke on the Mountain?*"

"No, but I've heard it's a good comedy."

"It is," I said, and then launched into a description of the play and some of the funniest scenes. When I finished we were pulling into the parking lot of Don Juan's in the small town of Kernersville.

When we went through the door we were immediately ushered to one of the booths. Almost as quickly, a basket of chips and a serving of salsa were put on the table. The waiter took our drink order—we both had iced tea—and I tried the salsa and chips. "Good," I said between bites.

Our drinks arrived and we said we'd like a little more time to look over the extensive menu. I chose chicken fajitas and Blaire had beef.

The food arrived quickly. We said a prayer of thanksgiving and dived into our meal. It was good and we were chatting and enjoying it more than either of us thought we would. We were getting close to the end of our dinner when a familiar voice said, "Well, well, well. If it isn't the esteemed Reverend Hinshaw."

I looked up and saw Penny Saxon glaring at me. I simply nodded.

Penny looked at Blaire. "Let me give you a little piece of good advice. If you need help with something, you've gone to the wrong person. This reverend is a fraud. She doesn't believe in helping people that really need it."

"Come on, Aunt Penny," a dark-headed teenager said. "Don't bother these people."

"I'm not bothering them. I just want to give this young lady some good advice. Somebody has to warn people about this gal that calls herself a preacher."

Penny's voice was loud enough that several people around

at nearby booths and tables put down their forks and looked at us.

"Miss Saxon—" I started, but she broke in.

"Don't you dare speak to me," she shouted.

Before anyone could say anything else, two waiters came up and asked if they could help. Penny must have realized that she was making a scene, because she walked off without another word.

"I'm sorry, ma'am," a waiter said.

I smiled at him. "No problem. She was just upset."

When we were alone again, Blaire asked, "What in the world was that all about?"

"She called me today and asked me to talk Elva Kingfield into giving her power of attorney."

"No!"

"Sure did." I took a bite of my food and then told her the whole story.

When I finished, Blaire said, "Maybe Penny Saxon was the person who left the note on your car."

"I thought of that and now that this has happened, I'm beginning to think that's right on the money."

After we finished eating, we paid our bill and went into the clear cool night. As we were going through Kernersville we saw a shop with a big cone of ice cream out front.

"Hey, look," Blaire said. "An ice cream shop. Do you feel like splurging?"

I laughed. "Why not? We've blown our diets already by eating all that sour cream."

"I want chocolate," Blaire said.

"Is there any other kind?" I asked.

Giggling like teenagers, we went into the small restaurant and spent thirty minutes eating our double-deck cones. Stuffed and shivering, we went to the car and decided it was time to call it a night.

I headed toward Liverpool.

"You know, this was more fun that I thought it would be. Even Miss Saxon didn't spoil it," Blaire said.

"I'm glad you enjoyed it. I did, too."

I flipped on the radio and we sang with the popular songs all the way to our parking lot. I pulled into my spot and we both got out.

Blaire sighed. "Well, she's here again."

"Who?"

"Mary Stillwell. That little red car there is hers."

"Blaire, I know it sounds trite, but if this is the way he wants to live, you're better off without him."

"Logically, I know that. Eventually my emotions will catch up."

"Sure they will." I put my arm around my friend. "If you need me, call. I don't care what time it is. You know I'm here for you, no matter what Penny Saxon said."

She laughed. "That's right. I do know it. Thanks, friend."

She started toward her apartment on the other side of the parking lot. I went up the steps to my balcony and watched her. Her apartment was on the ground level. There were several cars parked in the spaces in the center of the lot and she walked around two that were parked too close together. I was about to turn and go inside when I saw her come to an abrupt stop. Before I could call and ask her what was wrong, she let out with a blood-curdling scream.

I raced down the steps, two at a time, and crossed the distance to Blaire in seconds. I stopped short and almost screamed myself when I saw what had frightened her. Slumped over the steering wheel of the tan Lincoln was Penny Saxon.

THIRTEEN

PORCH LIGHTS CLICKED ON and people began coming out onto their porches or balconies. When I saw Nathan come out, I yelled, "Call 911. There's someone hurt here."

Blaire reached for the car door. As soon as she got it open, I felt the vein in Penny's neck. I didn't feel a pulse. "I think she's dead," I whispered.

"Oh, Lord, Willa. We just saw her a couple of hours ago."

"I know."

Nathan walked up. "What's going on?"

"I think this woman is dead. Did you call 911?" I asked.

"Mary's calling. I thought I'd come and see if I could help."

I saw Blaire flinch at the mention of Mary's name. "Why don't you see if you can keep the people back until the ambulance gets here." I pointed to the rear of the car. "Blaire and I will keep them back on this end."

"Sure," he said. He walked to the back of the car and I saw him talking with a neighbor who was approaching.

I nudged Blaire toward the front of the car and had her run interference to an approaching neighbor on that side. I hoped this would take her mind off Nathan's presence.

The sound of a siren ripped through the silence in the parking lot. Only seconds passed before a police car pulled in and stopped beside the gathering crowd. An ambulance and a fire truck were following close behind.

An officer got out of the car. It was Gary Bumgarner. He

said something to the crowd, and the man he spoke to, pointed toward me. The police officer headed in my direction.

"Well, Reverend, I might have known that every time something happens in our fair town, you're right in the middle of it." He smiled when he said it.

I returned the smile. "It does seem I always end up at the wrong place at the wrong time, doesn't it?"

"What's happened here?"

"There's a woman in this car. I think she's dead."

The paramedics headed toward the car with their stretcher. Gary took my arm and moved me out of the way.

It wasn't long until we learned that Penny was indeed dead. The detective, Clay Fisher, began to rope off the car so it could be inspected before evidence was destroyed. He also looked at the body after the medics put it on the stretcher. I heard him say, "Looks like she was strangled."

How horrible, I thought. I said a silent prayer that Penny didn't suffer long.

People began to drift back toward their apartments and I wondered if the detective was going to talk with Blaire and me.

I got my answer when he walked over to Officer Bumgarner and me. "I understand you found the body, Reverend Hinshaw."

"Not really. It was my friend, Blaire Peterson. I came down after I heard her scream." I motioned for Blaire to come closer to where we were.

"Willa and I had been out to eat and I was just walking across the lot to my apartment," she said, in answer to his question. "I just happened to look over in that car and I saw Penny. It frightened me and I screamed. Willa came running."

"Then you know the deceased?" He eyed her.

"Yes. She goes to my church. Oak Street Baptist."

"I see." He wrote in his little notebook and then asked, "Did you touch anything?"

"I opened the door."

"And I felt for a pulse, but I didn't touch anything else," I said.

"Somebody had to call it in, did either of you?"

"No," I said. "Neighbors were coming out of their apartments. I yelled at one of them to call."

"I see." He closed his little book, then changed his mind and opened it again. "Did you know the lady, Reverend?"

"Her name is Penny Saxon. She is the niece to one of my members at First United Methodist. I've met her on a few occasions when I was visiting her aunt, Elva Kingfield, at the hospital."

"So, she was related to Mrs. Kingfield?"

I nodded.

"When was the last time either of you saw Penny Saxon?" he asked.

I glanced at Blaire, but she said nothing. "We saw her with her niece tonight at Don Juan's Mexican Restaurant in Kernersville," I said.

"What's the niece's name?"

I started to say I didn't know, when Blaire said, "It's Jackie Meyer. She's Penny's brother's daughter."

"Did you talk with Miss Saxon?"

"She told me that I was interfering in her family business. She was mad at me because I refused to help her get the power of attorney for her aunt's affairs."

"Maybe you'd better tell me what that was all about."

I took a deep breath and told him everything, beginning with the way Penny acted at the hospital.

When I finished, he said, "So it would be safe to say that you didn't like Penny Saxon very much, Reverend?"

"I try not to judge people, Detective, but you're right. Miss Saxon was not one of my favorite people. I didn't like what she was doing to her aunt."

"And you, Miss Peterson. Did you dislike Miss Saxon, too?"

"I didn't know Miss Saxon very well. I just saw her at church."

"I see." This time he did close his book. "Thank you for the information and I'll be back in touch if I have more questions."

He went over and said something to Lieutenant Bumgarner. They were out of earshot so I turned to Blaire. "Are you okay?"

"I think so. I just wonder who did this to Penny."

"I don't know, but I bet it has something to do with what happened to Bernice Wallace."

"You're probably right."

I saw her looking at Nathan's apartment. He and Mary were standing on the porch. "Don't let it get you down, my friend," I said. "Things will work out."

"I know." She took a deep breath. "If they're through with us, I think I'll go in and go to bed."

"Me, too. I need to be at the hospital early in the morning. They're operating on Bernice."

"Let me know how she is tomorrow night."

"I'll do that," I said, then I told the police that I was going in and to call later if they needed anything else.

Inside my apartment, I ran a full tub of water, filled it with bath beads and eased down in it. I needed to think and sitting in a bubble bath always helped me think. I pulled up the thought I'd had earlier and found it just as attractive as it was the first time it had crossed my mind. I decided I would discuss it with Elva tomorrow.

I turned my thoughts to Penny. I couldn't imagine why anyone would kill her and choose my parking lot to do it. And what had happened to the niece? Had she killed her aunt? Was there someone else with them when they got back from Kernersville? Had they harmed the niece? Was this connected to Bernice's attack or was it just a coincidence?

After thirty minutes of racking my brain, I got out of the water and put on my fuzzy robe. I curled my feet up under

me on the sofa and picked up my Bible. I was going to do my
night studies and go to bed early. I didn't want to be late for
the operation in the morning.

FOURTEEN

TYRONE WALLACE WAS IN the waiting room when I arrived at the hospital. "Good morning," I said.

"Good morning, Reverend."

"Have you seen your aunt?"

"I went in to see her for a few minutes."

"I think I'll see if they'll let me go in and have a prayer with her, if they haven't taken her to the operating room."

"That would be nice."

I handed him the sack I had in my hand. "Here are some muffins. I didn't know if you had time for breakfast or not. I thought we could munch on these."

"Thanks, I really didn't take time to eat anything."

I did go in and have a prayer with Bernice. Then, I rejoined Tyrone in the waiting room. He was standing at the coffeepot that was provided for families who were waiting. "Would you like a cup?" he asked.

"Yes, thank you. Just cream please." I took a seat in front of the table where he had put the muffins.

He came back with the coffee and handed me a cup. He dropped to a chair in front of me. "Thanks for bringing the muffins."

"I didn't have breakfast and I thought they'd be filling." I took out a blueberry one. "What are they going to do to your aunt or have they told you?"

"The doctor said there was some internal bleeding and they're going to try to stop it. I'm not sure what else."

"I see," I said. "We will keep saying prayers for her complete recovery."

He nodded and changed the subject. "She's a wonderful person. I've always thought of her as my second mom and she says I'm the closest thing to a son she's ever had. She and Uncle John never had any children."

"Is she a widow?"

"Yes. Her husband died in a farming accident when she was still a young woman. She never remarried."

"Are you from Benson, too?"

"Yes. Aunt Bernice couldn't stay on the farm after her husband died. She moved to Winston-Salem and worked in a sock factory. She cooked pastries for a caterer on the side. Mr. Kingfield was at some kind of party where they were serving some of her food and he really liked it. Mrs. Kingfield was sick at the time and he was looking for a housekeeper and cook to help her out. He asked for my aunt's name and number." He took a breath. "As they say, I guess the rest is history. Mr. Kingfield offered Aunt Bernice more money than she was making on both jobs. Of course she accepted and she's worked there ever since. I think it's been more than thirty years. She and Mrs. Kingfield are best friends."

"I knew they were very close, but I didn't know their whole story. Thanks for telling me."

"Mrs. Kingfield is a fine lady. I went up to see her last night."

"That was nice of you and I know she appreciated it."

"Yes, I think she did. She was real concerned about Aunt Bernice. I'm glad I went because it seemed to make her feel better." He tossed the paper from his muffin in the trash and reached for another one. "Do you mind if I have two?"

"Not at all." I stood. "I'm going to refill my coffee. Would you like me to get you some more?"

"Thank you. I drink it with cream and sugar."

I returned with the coffee. "Now, Tyrone. Tell me about school. What are you studying?"

"I'm not positive yet, but I think I'm going into computers. That seems to be a good occupation nowadays."

"It really is, but I don't think I could ever learn enough about them to make a living at it. They seem to know that I'm helpless when they go on the blink."

"What made you choose to be a preacher?"

"I'm not sure I did choose it. I think it chose me." I smiled. "I really feel that I was called to the ministry."

"I guess that's what all ministers should feel."

"I agree. I also think people are called into other occupations. Writers, artists, doctors and so on. I know a lady that says she knows God meant her to be a housewife and mother and she is thrilled with this role."

He smiled. "How do you know God wants you to be in a certain occupation?"

"I guess it's up to the individual, but I think God gives us clues. He gives us talents and he gives us likes and dislikes. Sometimes a person might know what he wants to do from the time he is a child, but on the other hand, you might see something for the first time and down in your heart of hearts you know that is what you want to do for the rest of your life."

"I've always wanted to be an architect."

I looked at him and asked, "Then why are you thinking about computers?"

"Well…the money's good."

"Don't just settle for money, Tyrone. You're too young to give up your dream. If you want to be an architect then be one."

"Do you think I could?"

"If you want it badly enough and you work hard enough, I don't see why not."

He got quiet and seemed to be thinking over what I had said. I drank my coffee and didn't say anything else. I wanted him to digest what I had said.

Before either of us spoke again, a doctor came into the room. "Mr. Wallace?"

"Yes." Tyrone stood and I stood beside him.

"Your aunt came through the surgery fine. We're going to send her back to ICU after she gets out of recovery. You can see her there in a little while."

"Is she going to be all right, Doctor?"

"She seems to be doing well at the moment. We'll know more in a day or two."

"Thank you, Doctor," he said.

The doctor left and he turned to me. "Thank you for coming, Reverend Hinshaw. I've enjoyed talking with you. I'm going to think about what you said."

"I hope you will, Tyrone. And I'd appreciate it if you'd call me Willa." I picked up my purse. "I'm going to see Elva. I'll tell her the good news about your aunt."

"Thank you, Reverend Willa."

I went down the hall and caught the elevator to Elva's floor. When I reached her room, I found her sitting in the lounge chair. "Well, look at you," I said. "You look like you can go home at any minute."

"Hello, dear." She held out her hand to me. "The doctor told me that I might go home tomorrow."

"That's great, Elva."

"Enough about me. You know what I want to know, don't you?"

"I do and our prayers were answered. Bernice came through the surgery fine and is in recovery. I'll drop by and see her as I leave."

"Oh, thank God. He has answered our prayers."

"Shall we say a prayer of thanksgiving right now?" I asked.

"I think that would be lovely."

I held her hand and said a short prayer, thanking God for bringing Bernice through the surgery and for helping Elva improve each day. After saying amen, I pulled up a chair beside her. "Now," I said with a sigh, "there is something I have to tell you."

"You sound serious, Willa."

"It is serious, Elva." When she said nothing, I went on. "Someone murdered Penny Saxon last night."

"Oh, my goodness. Are you sure?"

"I'm sure."

"Do they know who did it?"

"Not yet. I'm sure they'll find out though."

"How did it happen?"

I told her about coming home and finding Penny dead in her car in my parking lot. I did not tell her about the confrontation at the restaurant. I didn't want to upset her by pointing out that I thought Penny was trying to get her committed.

When I finished my story, Elva said, "Poor Penny. She wanted so much and was never able to acquire all the material possessions she desired. She probably died an unhappy woman. That's sad."

"Yes, it is very sad. I only hope she is at peace now."

Elva nodded. "So do I."

I sat back, glad that Elva had taken the news of Penny's death so well. "There is one other thing that I want to talk with you about, Elva."

"Oh, dear. This sounds serious, too. Nobody else has died, have they?"

I smiled. "No, it has nothing to do with death."

"Good. I don't want anyone else I know to bite it."

I smiled again. I wasn't sure how this little senior lady came up with these expressions. I went on. "You know that when you and Bernice get home, you're going to need someone in the house with you."

"Why?"

"Well, for one thing, Bernice is probably going to be in bed for a while. I know you'll have a nurse for her, but it isn't safe for you two to be in that big house alone."

"You're probably right. I can find a temporary house-keeper."

"I think you should do that, but I want someone to be there at night with you, too."

"Willa, I can tell you have something on your mind. Just come out with it."

"Okay. I will. A friend of mine has just had her heart broken by the man who lives across the parking lot from her. She wants to move, but she can't afford a more expensive apartment. I thought it would be nice if she could stay with you for a while." There, I had said it. Now it was up to Elva.

"Well, Willa, why didn't you say so in the first place? Of course your friend can stay at my house." She shook her head. "I don't know why you thought I'd say no."

I reached over and patted her arm. "You are a wonderful woman, Elva Kingfield."

"Thank you, my dear."

"Now, I haven't yet approached my friend with the idea of moving into your house. She might nix the whole thing. I wanted to talk with you before I said anything to her."

"Well, you can tell her that I love the idea of having someone young and lively in my house again. It will make me feel younger."

"I'll tell her. I know you two will get along famously. I'm sure Bernice will like her, too. By the way, her name is Blaire Peterson."

Elva nodded. "Have her come to meet me as soon as she can."

"I'll do that." I stood. "I'll check on Bernice on my way home. I'll call you back this afternoon and let you know how she is doing and if Blaire is receptive to moving into your house right away."

"That sounds wonderful, dear."

Bernice was in ICU when I went down. The nurse said she was doing nicely. I thanked her and headed for my car. I had just gotten inside when my cell phone rang.

"Hello, Preacher," a deep voice said.

I recognized it immediately and said, "Ed, my friend, how are you?"

"Great. Where are you?"

"Just leaving the hospital."

"I called the church and they said they thought you'd still be there. Could you swing by Elva Kingfield's house on the way back to town?"

"Sure. Has something happened there?"

"Not that I know of. I'm changing the locks on her doors."

"Oh, Ed, that's a great idea. I should have thought of it." I started my car. "I'll see you in a few minutes."

I was on I-40 when my cell rang again. "Willa Hinshaw," I said.

"Reverend, it's Dennis Kingfield. I called the church and they said you'd gone to the hospital. I thought I'd take a chance on catching you before I go out to a breakfast meeting."

For an instant I wondered what he meant by breakfast meeting since it was approaching eleven o'clock. Then I remembered the three-hour difference between Eastern and Pacific time.

"What can I do for you, Mr. Kingfield?"

"I just wanted to check on Mrs. Wallace. Aunt Elva told me they were going to operate on her this morning."

"She came through the surgery fine. We're hoping for the best."

"That's good. I know how close Aunt Elva is to Bernice. I know it would really upset her if something happened to her friend."

"Yes, it would be bad." I changed the subject. "I do have some bad news for you, Mr. Kingfield."

"Nothing has happened to my aunt, has it?" He sounded concerned.

"No. No. She's fine. In fact, she may get to come home tomorrow."

"That's a relief. You scared me."

"I'm sorry. The bad news I have is about Penny Saxon. Someone murdered her last night."

"My heavens! What's going on in Liverpool?"

"It does seem that for a small town, we have our problems."

"Do they know who killed Penny?"

"I don't think they have a clue, but I wanted you to hear the news from me."

"I appreciate that, Reverend, but I've never been very close to Penny. Oh, don't get me wrong. I'm sorry this has happened, but according to my aunt, Penny wasn't a very nice person."

"She was trying to get Elva's power of attorney assigned to her."

"She didn't get it, did she?"

"No. Elva never signed it over."

Dennis Kingfield seemed to take a breath then went on. "Good for her. There's no reason why she should sign it over to anyone. Aunt Elva is still as sharp as she always was."

I knew Bernice didn't trust Dennis, but I was beginning to like this man. He really cared about his aunt and he seemed only to want what was best for her.

We chatted a little further and then said goodbye. By the time I clicked off the phone, I was at the turnoff to Elva's house.

In minutes I pulled into the driveway. Ed's red Ford truck was parked there. I pulled in behind it. I hopped out and headed for the porch. The front door was closed and Ed wasn't there. I decided he was probably working on the back door. I walked around the house. He wasn't at the back door either. For a minute, I didn't know what to do. Then it hit me. I went back to my car and grabbed my cell phone. I dialed Ed's cell number. It rang and rang again. He didn't answer.

"Where are you, Ed?" I asked out loud.

I turned off the phone. *Maybe I dialed it wrong,* I thought. I punched in his number again.

There was no answer.

I was stunned. I didn't know what to do. I looked around, but there was nobody in sight. I walked up to Ed's truck. I was almost afraid to look inside. The truck was empty except for a tool box sitting on the front seat. This looked strange, because there was a big silver professional-size box fitted across the bed of the truck. I thought men used these to house their tools or any other items they wanted to carry.

My heart almost stopped when another thought crossed my mind. The big silver box could easily hold a man.

FIFTEEN

I DIDN'T HESITATE FURTHER. I climbed on the side of the truck and reached for the lid of the box. Thankfully, it wasn't locked. My heart pounded as I tried to prepare myself for anything. Holding my breath, I lifted the lid and peered inside. There were some tools, a dog collar, a rope and some rags. Otherwise, it was empty.

I relaxed and caught my breath. "Thank You," I said, looking toward heaven.

I didn't know what my next move should be. I stepped down and looked around again. As loud as I could, I yelled, "Ed! Where are you?" I waited and when I didn't get an answer, I called again.

I decided to walk around the house again. I didn't see any signs of Ed on the side of the house next to the gazebo. I walked on around to the backyard. There was a sunroom that jutted into the garden section of the yard. I looked toward the pond that was several yards beyond the lawn. I was about to move on when I saw a figure walking back toward the house. My heart again began to pound, but I stayed put and watched as he approached.

In a few minutes I recognized the man. I called out, "Ed Walsh, where have you been? I was scared something had happened to you."

He didn't answer until he got back to the yard. "Hello, Willa," he said. "Been here long?"

"Long enough to imagine you lying somewhere hurt or maybe even dead. Where have you been?"

"Chasing a shadow."

"What?"

"I was finishing up the locks when I saw a strange figure coming up behind the house. When he saw me, he took off toward the pond. I ran after him, but he must have been younger and faster. I lost him in the woods beyond the pond."

"I wonder who it could be."

"Probably someone who knows the women are both in the hospital. It would be the perfect time to rob this place."

"Elva may come home tomorrow."

"I hope she's not going to be here alone."

"I'm going to ask a friend of mine to come stay with her."

"That's good." He took my arm and propelled me toward the front yard.

"By the way, did you have a special reason for asking me to come by here?"

"I wanted to give you the keys to the new locks and I wanted to ask you about that note you found on your windshield."

"How did you know about that?"

"I ran into your friend Blaire this morning. She asked me if you had told me about it."

"I was going to," I said.

"Why don't we go get lunch and you can tell me."

"That sounds good. I'm beginning to get hungry."

"Wanna go to Pizza Hut? I like their buffet at lunch."

"I'll follow you."

After Ed and I ate a big lunch at Pizza Hut, and I let him fuss at me for not telling him about the threatening note sooner, I headed back to the office. I wanted to get in touch with Blaire before she made plans for the evening. I hoped it wouldn't take much convincing to get her to move into Elva's house—at least temporarily.

There was a call from Trent in my messages. I decided to call him first.

After the greeting, he said, "I wanted to invite you to lunch, but I assume you've already eaten by now."

"Another man beat you to me," I teased. "I had lunch with Ed Walsh."

"I couldn't have lost out to a better man."

I laughed. "I don't yet have plans for tonight. Want to come over and grill a steak?"

"I'd love to, but unfortunately, I do have plans. I have to meet with Penny Saxon's family to make the funeral arrangements."

"I understand. Maybe another time."

"Of course, but if it's not too late, how about I come by for dessert?"

"Sounds good. Myrtle Johnson brought me some apples. I'll make a pie."

"Then I'll definitely be there."

We said goodbye and I dialed Blaire's number at work. I heard the usual background noise that I always hear when I called her office. "Could you possibly get off early today?" I asked.

"I guess. What's up?"

"I'll tell you then. Meet me in the parking lot at home about four."

"I'll be there."

I hung up. That would give me plenty of time to show her around Elva's house and to get back in time to bake the pie.

I turned to my other calls and it was then that I saw the pretty little package sitting on the sofa. I smiled. Somebody had brought me a gift. I loved this type of surprise. I put the phone down and went to the sofa and picked it up. It was wrapped in pretty pink paper with a multicolored ribbon. It was almost too pretty to open, but that didn't stop me.

I opened the package and took the tissue-wrapped item from the box. Unwrapping it, I saw a beautiful carved cardinal painted in the authentic red of his natural colors. The carved feathers on the bird looked almost real. I looked in the box and found a small card. It read, "Thanks for everything, Preacher Willa! Luke Underwood."

"That young man is really talented," I said aloud.

Anna Casey was going by my door. She paused. "Did you say something, Willa?"

"Look what Luke Underwood gave me. Isn't it lovely?"

She stepped in the door. "Oh, it is. His mom came by and dropped it off. She insisted we put it in your office."

"I think he could do well selling these carvings."

"There's probably lots of places that would let him show them. Angie Jarman runs Southwinds Gallery in Kernersville. She shows lots of artists' works besides her dad's. I bet Ellie's Gift Shop here in town would carry them, too."

"I'm going to visit him soon. I'll mention it and see if he's interested." I put the cardinal on my desk. "In the meantime, I'm going to put this here where everyone can see it."

"I would, too," Anna said as she went out the door.

I finished up what I needed to do at the office and decided to go home early. When I got to my apartment, I changed from my work dress to a pair of jeans and a turtle-necked shirt. I made a glass of tea. Dropping to the sofa, I flipped on the television and found an old black-and-white movie starring Kathryn Hepburn, Cary Grant and a lion named Baby.

A few minutes later, the phone rang. It was Blaire. "I'm pulling into the parking lot. Do I have time to run inside a moment?"

"Yes. I've changed into jeans. You might want to change clothes, too."

"I will. I won't be long."

I turned off the television and put my empty glass in the sink. I went outside, locked my door, and went downstairs to my car. I decided to pull across the lot and pick Blaire up. I had just pulled in front of her apartment when I saw Nathan pulling into the lot. The car that Blaire had told me belonged to his new girlfriend pulled in behind him.

Yes, I thought. *If Blaire will go for it, it will be good to get her away from here.*

It wasn't long until her door opened. She locked up and then opened the passenger side and slid in. "You really have piqued my curiosity."

"I hope you're going to like what I suggest."

"Lay it on me."

"Actually, I want to show you something first."

She looked at me. "What?"

"You'll soon see." I changed the subject. "How was your day?"

"I guess you're going to make me wait." She laughed and said, "My day was fine. How was yours?"

We chatted about work and the weather and other neutral subjects until I turned into the Kingfield driveway off Blue Bell Road. "I want you to see this house," I said, pulling to a stop.

"It's lovely, but why are we stopping?"

"We're not just stopping. We're going inside."

"Why?" She looked at me as if I'd lost my mind.

"This is Elva Kingfield's house. I'm checking something out." I cut off the motor and opened my door.

Blaire followed suit.

We were standing on the front porch and I was fishing in my pocket for the keys that Ed had given me when she asked, "Can you imagine living in a place like this?"

I found the key and inserted it. "Wait until you see the inside," I said.

We went into the entry and I found the light switch. After giving her a few minutes to look around, I went into the parlor. Blaire followed. I didn't say anything because I wanted her to take in the grandeur of the place.

She walked around the room, looking first at one thing and then another. Finally she said, "This is very nice."

I took a deep breath, and asked, "How would you like to live here?"

"I'd love to live here. Wouldn't you?"

"Okay, Blaire. It's time to level with you. I want you to move in here for a while."

She whirled around and looked at me. "Are you nuts, Willa? Mrs. Kingfield would have a fit. You can't just move into someone's home while they're in the hospital."

"Elva will probably be coming home tomorrow and she said it was a good idea if you had already moved in." I took her arm. "Let me show you the rooms she told me would be yours."

Blaire was too stunned to argue with me. We went up the winding stairway. I followed the directions that Elva had given me to the rooms she said she thought Blaire would like.

"I think this is the correct room," I said, opening a door.

We went inside. It was gorgeous. The ornate bed was cherry and its cover was an off-white satin with an elaborate design. The rest of the matching furniture was placed against the front and the left walls. There was a collection of fluffy pillows on the bed and in the love seat in the alcove connected to the bedroom. There was a small table and chairs near the sofa. The room looked like it could have been set up for a photograph to be used in *House Beautiful*. There was an adjoining room that was furnished as a den with a television, comfortable chairs and a computer desk in the corner.

"If you decide you don't want to move in here, Blaire, I may just move in myself," I said.

"I can't believe this." She shook her head. "You think I should do it, don't you?"

I was walking across the room to a closed door. "I can't make you do it, but yes, I think this is a wonderful opportunity to live in a beautiful setting." I opened the door. It led to a beautifully appointed bathroom. I motioned for her to come look.

"It's gorgeous," she whispered.

"Blaire, you wouldn't just be doing yourself a favor. Elva

Kingfield needs someone here when she comes home. You know her housekeeper is in the hospital, too."

"I wouldn't have any idea of how to take care of Mrs. Kingfield."

"That's not what you'd be doing. She will have nurses for that. She'll also have someone to come in and do the cleaning. You might have to do a little cooking, but that's it."

"When you think about it, I guess this could be the answer to my prayer to get away from Nathan and Mary."

"Then may I tell Elva that you're going to do it?"

Before she could answer a door banged downstairs. We both jumped.

"Who could that be?" I whispered.

"I don't know," she whispered back. "What should we do?"

"I don't intend to stand here and let someone sneak up on me. Come on." I walked out into the hall and headed to the stairs. "Who is down there?" I called.

There was no answer. "Is someone in this house?" I called again—a little sharper this time.

There was a short silence, then I heard running footsteps in the area of the kitchen. In a few seconds the back door banged.

I raced down the steps and to the kitchen. Blaire was on my heels. I ran to the open back door and looked out. I got a glimpse of a figure running around the edge of the lake in the backyard. "I wonder if that's the person Ed saw?"

Blaire didn't answer that question. Instead she said, "I thought you said Ed put new locks on all the doors."

"He did." I looked at the lock on the back door. It had been opened with a key and the key was still in the lock on the outside of the door. I frowned.

"You don't think Ed would have come in, do you?"

"Of course not," I said. "Besides, the man at the lake wasn't as big as Ed." Still I wondered how the stranger had gotten a key. "I'll call Ed and tell him what has happened." I took the key out of the lock and closed the door and relocked it from the inside. I also attached the chain that fastened only on the inside.

"I don't think I want to stay here until Mrs. Kingfield gets home," Blaire said.

I didn't say so, but I agreed.

I called Ed's cell phone on the way back to the apartment. He couldn't understand how anyone could get a key to the lock he'd just installed, but he said he'd go to the Kingfield place and check it out. When I hung up, I asked Blaire what she wanted for dinner.

"Why don't we stop and get a sandwich?" she suggested. "I need to start packing some things if I'm going to be moving right away."

"I need to go home and bake an apple pie. If Trent gets through with the Saxon family, he's coming for dessert."

We went by Subway and both got a twelve-inch sandwich. The place wasn't crowded and we ate rather quickly. In thirty minutes, Blaire was at home deciding what to pack and I was in my kitchen peeling apples.

SIXTEEN

THE NEXT MORNING I sat at my small table waiting for the coffee to finish making. I eyed the apple pie sitting in its container on my counter. Abruptly I got up, opened the plastic container and took out the whole pie. I cut a large slice and put it on a plate. I was just about to pick up a fork and taste it when the phone rang.

"I'm sorry I couldn't make it last night, Willa," Trent said after my hello. "It was almost midnight when I left the Saxons'. I figured you were asleep and I didn't want to call and wake you."

"That was thoughtful," I said. I knew my voice was sharp, but I couldn't help it. I didn't want to tell him that I had waited until after midnight to hear from him.

"I hoped I could take you to breakfast to make up for it," he said.

"I'm just getting ready to eat breakfast," I said. I tried to keep the sarcasm out of my voice, but it was hard.

"I'll bring biscuits."

I couldn't help laughing. "Forget the biscuits and come on over. I'll put on the bacon."

"I'll be there in ten minutes."

I slid the slice of pie back into the pie plate, opened the drawer on the bottom of the stove and took out a frying pan. I turned to the refrigerator and took out the carton of eggs and a pack of bacon. Shoving the door closed, I put in as many slices of bacon as the frying pan would hold and laid four eggs on the counter. I put two slices of wheat bread in the toaster and turned back to the refrigerator. I returned the remaining eggs and bacon and took out the milk and filled the cream pitcher. I sat the carton back on the shelf and removed the butter dish. Closing the refrigerator again, I retrieved the salt and pepper from the back of the stove and got the sugar bowl from the cabinet. The bacon began to sizzle and I turned it. From the freezer, I took a carton of frozen orange juice, mixed it and filled two glasses. I broke the four eggs in a bowl, added a little milk, salt and pepper, then whipped them until they were well mixed. All the time I was humming one of my favorite hymns—"Go Tell It on the Mountain."

The doorbell rang. I turned down the burner under the bacon and answered it.

As always, my heart melted when I looked into Trent's blue eyes. "Come in," I said.

"Good morning," he said, stepping inside.

I closed the door and headed back to the kitchen. Trent followed and took a seat at the table. I felt him watching me.

The bacon was ready. I drained it on a paper towel and put the eggs in the pan. As they cooked, I pushed the arm down on the toaster and took two plates from the cabinet.

"I could get used to watching you cook breakfast," Trent said.

"I don't do this often," I said with a laugh. "You'd have to settle for a muffin or just a piece of toast most of the time."

"Would you have a vase?"

"What?" I whirled around.

He was holding a bouquet of flowers toward me. "I'm tired of trying to hide these things. Could you put them somewhere?"

"Oh, Trent. How nice." I took out a vase, filled it with water, put the flowers in it and set them in the center of the table.

When the toaster popped up, and the eggs were done, I put some on each plate and added the bacon. I set one before Trent and put the other on the table for me. I then poured two cups of coffee and sat down.

He took my hand and said a blessing and we began to eat. "Am I forgiven?" he asked.

"For what?"

"Don't be coy. The minute I heard your voice this morning, I knew you were peeved at me for not calling last night."

I chuckled. "I guess I was. I waited until after midnight for you to come or call."

"With a fresh baked pie, I bet."

"Yes, I made the pie."

"I'll have a piece this morning if I may."

"I was going to eat a piece for breakfast until you called." I changed the subject. "Tell me about the Saxon funeral."

"Visitation tomorrow night at Brooks Funeral Home. The service will be Sunday at two at Oak Street." He stood. "I'm going to refill my coffee. Would you like some?"

"Please." I held out my cup. "I assume you'll be conducting the service."

He refilled our cups and sat back down. Nodding, he said, "Though I've known who Penny Saxon is for several years, I didn't really know her very well. She attended on Sunday and she'd come to a function now and then, but she didn't take part in much else."

"What about the niece. I forget her name?"

"Jackie Meyer," he said. "Penny did bring her to church and she has become active in our youth group."

"What about Jackie's parents? Do they come to your church?"

"No. There was a divorce a year or so ago. The father is Penny's brother, but he lives out of state. Jackie's mother lives in Winston-Salem and from what I gather, she doesn't always get along very well with Penny. But when she developed breast cancer, she asked Penny to take care of Jackie until she got back on her feet."

"Is Penny married?"

"She's been divorced for years. She has a son who lives in Ohio and a son in Florida. While I was talking with the family last night, I picked up that there was some strain between Penny and her sons. Neither of them had any idea what their mother might want at her service. I think I heard one of them say that he hadn't seen his mother in five years."

"That's sad, but it was nice of Penny to take the niece."

"Yes. Jackie had given her mother problems. She was caught shoplifting and I was told that she took her mom's car without permission and was caught driving under the influence."

"I'll have to admit, in the few dealings that I had with Penny, I would never have guessed her to care this much for someone else."

"They were close, from what I gather. Jackie was pretty broken up last night."

"Did I tell you that I saw Penny and Jackie when Blaire and I went out to eat on the night that she died?"

"No. What happened?"

I didn't want to talk about Penny, now that she was dead, so I simply said, "Not much. We only saw them as they left the restaurant."

"Well, I'm glad Penny took Jackie in. I think the teenager needed to get away from her mom for a while. There was a lot of bitterness over the breakup of her parents' marriage. The kid fits right in with the youth at church. She's been coming about six weeks now."

He pushed back his plate. "I think I'm going to have to wait for the pie. I'm full."

"So am I."

He looked at his watch. "I'd love to stay here and chat with you all day, sweetheart, but I've got to get to work."

"So have I. Elva Kingfield is probably coming home today and I want to make sure she has people to look after her."

He stood and began clearing the table. "I thought Friday was your day off."

"Sometimes it is, but I work when things have to be done." I began putting the things in the refrigerator. In a matter of minutes we had the kitchen clean and I walked him to the door.

"You know we still need to talk about us," he said. He reached to open the door, but instead he turned and put his hands on my shoulders. "Got plans tonight?" I shook my head and he went on. "Let's get a pizza and hide out for a while."

"Sounds good. We still have apple pie, too."

He pulled me to him and kissed me firmly. Of course, I returned it.

"See you about seven," he whispered, and before I could answer, he was out the door.

I watched him go down the steps and get into his SUV. I smiled to myself as I turned to get my purse. I really did care for this man—maybe I loved him. But did I dare give my heart away to someone who had beliefs that conflicted with mine? Could I really handle a romance with a Baptist preacher? Most Baptists were against a woman being a minister, and I had no intention of giving up my ministry. Could he handle my remaining active in the Methodist church if we took our relationship to another level?

I shook my head. I didn't want to deal with these questions right now. I grabbed my purse and headed toward the door. The telephone rang.

"Willa, this is Ed. I got your message and I'm going back out to the Kingfield place. I don't have a clue as to how someone got a key."

"I appreciate that, Ed. I think Elva is coming home this morning and I don't want somebody breaking in on her."

"I'll call you later. Will you be at your church office?"

"I'll be running around. Call my cell and keep yours with you. I may want to get in touch."

He didn't ask why, and I didn't explain. I didn't want him to know that I wanted to check later to be sure he was okay. We said our goodbyes and again I picked up my purse, the black leather one that I'd finally changed to for cold weather.

I went out and locked the door behind me. I was half-way down the steps when I saw Blaire open the blinds on her living-room window. I walked across the parking lot and knocked on her door. I was surprised to see her in pajamas when she opened it.

"Are you not going to work today?"

"Nope. I called in and said I was going to take a personal day. I decided that if I'm going to move in with Mrs. Kingfield, I had to start packing in earnest."

I smiled. "I have a couple of places to go, but if you like, I'll come back and help you later."

"Thanks. But I think I can handle it." She held the door open. "Want to come in? I'll make us some breakfast."

"I just cooked a big breakfast for Trent and me."

"I understand," she said. "Are you going out to the Kingfield place?"

"Probably later. I'm going to the hospital first to check on Bernice and I'll stop to make sure Elva has everything arranged to come home."

"I'd like to go today and meet Mrs. Kingfield. She may not like me."

"I doubt that. Why don't I call and let you know when she'll be home. We'll go this afternoon so you can meet her. I truly think you two are going to really enjoy each other."

"That sounds great. I'll be here whenever you're ready."

"See you then." I turned to go to my car. As I started to open my door, I noticed a note on the windshield and I reached for it. I got inside before I read it. It said, *Look, Preacher. I've warned you one time to get out of Elva Kingfield's business. This is twice. You're smart enough to know that three strikes means you're out.*

SEVENTEEN

I TRIED NOT TO APPEAR UPSET. In case someone was nearby and watching, I didn't want them to think it was getting to me. I folded the paper, slipped it into my purse and started my car.

In minutes I was on I-40 headed to the hospital. I didn't think about the note, or at least tried not to think about it. I was thinking of Trent. I decided I'd surprise him and get home in time to cook a good dinner. I know he gets home-cooked meals from his church members, but I hadn't cooked for him very often. He seemed to enjoy it when I did.

That settled, I thought about Elva. If she hadn't made arrangements for a nurse, that was something I'd have to push her to do. I also wanted to see if she'd get someone in to do the housework because it would be a long time before either she or Bernice would be able.

When I arrived at the hospital, I went directly to Bernice's room. A nurse met me at the door with a smile. "Good morning, Reverend," she said. "You're in for a nice surprise."

"Oh?"

"Mrs. Wallace is beginning to wake up. She spoke to the night nurse when she was taking vitals at three this morning."

"That's wonderful."

"I just checked her and I swear she smiled at me."

"Thank God."

The nurse headed down the hall and I went into Bernice's room. Someone had brushed her hair and her bed was rolled up in a slight incline. I stood beside her. "Bernice," I said in a soft voice, "I hear you're getting much better." Her eyelids fluttered. "I'm so thankful," I went on. "I'm going to say a prayer. Dear Holy Father," I began to pray. "I thank You for this wonderful news about our friend Bernice. I ask You to continue to hold her in Your hands and to bless her as she continues to recover. Thank You in the name of Your Son and our Savior, Jesus Christ. Amen."

"Thank you," Bernice whispered.

"Oh, Bernice. Thank God, not me."

"Mrs....Elva...?"

"She's doing fine, Bernice. She'll probably go home today. Now you must concentrate on getting better so you can come home soon."

She didn't answer and I knew she'd gone back to sleep. I said a few more words of thanksgiving to God and slipped out of the room.

When I got to Elva's room and gave her the good news, I thought she was going to shout. It took a while to settle her down so I could ask her some questions. I was delighted to find out that, with the help of a social worker, she had made arrangements for around-the-clock nurses. In fact, she was waiting for one of them to accompany her home this morning. I decided that with everything here handled, I'd go to her house and open it up and straighten a little. Besides, I wanted to check on Ed. I know I could call, but I wanted to see for myself that he was okay.

I went directly to the house. Ed's truck was in the driveway. I shuddered when I parked, because I didn't want to be worried about him again. I didn't have to be. He came around the house and met me.

"Hi," I said.

"Hello, Reverend. How are you today?"

"I'm fine. Have you found anything suspicious?"

"Not really. There's some footprints around the back steps, but I can't tell how old they are. I found some rags under one of the windows, but they could have been used for cleaning.

The lock on the back door hadn't been forced, but I changed them all again."

"I don't understand how someone could have gotten a key to the new lock, but I'm glad you changed them again."

"Well, it could have been my fault. I threw the wrappings from the locks I put on the other day in the trash can in the garage. I noticed most of the wrappings were gone today. I think the person got enough information off them to get keys made or replaced. If not, I have no idea how they did it."

"I didn't know you could do that."

"I'm not sure you can, but just in case, I'm taking all the wrappings with me today."

I changed the subject. "Elva's coming home today. I thought I'd go in and see if there was anything I could do to cheer things up in the house. Maybe let some sunshine in and dust a bit."

"I'm sure she'd appreciate that." He looked around. "The yard could use a little cleaning, too. I'll putter about and see what I can get done."

"Thanks, Ed. I'll take you to lunch when we finish."

I went inside. The first thing I did was open all the drapes and blinds so it wouldn't be so dark inside. I then went upstairs and found Elva's room. I changed the sheets on her bed and dusted the furniture. I was just going downstairs when there was a knock on the door. I wondered what Ed wanted, and hurried to the door.

I was surprised to see Myrtle Johnson standing there with a dish in her hand.

"Philip said Mrs. Kingfield was coming home today. I decided to come out and see if I could do anything to help. Some of the other women of the church are coming, too." She stepped inside. "I brought a casserole. I knew there wasn't anyone here to do the cooking."

"That's wonderful, Myrtle. Why don't you put it in the kitchen?"

In the next thirty minutes, three more women showed up.

Kathy Gordon brought a jug of tea; Connie Underwood, a garden salad; and Helen Chambers, a chocolate cake. The five of us made quick work of cleaning the big house. Of course, Bernice had it in good shape to begin with or we wouldn't have finished so soon.

"Ladies," I said as we all gathered in the kitchen, "you are a great advertisement for Christianity. Thank you so much."

"A couple of others would have come, but it was short notice. Rose Poole had a dentist appointment, Kate Aster was out of town and Lou Stone was babysitting her grandchildren," Connie said.

"Rose said she'd bring the entire meal for Sunday," Myrtle said.

"I'll be back on Tuesday. Junior said he'd cook a ham and make potato salad and another vegetable. I'll make a couple of pies," said Helen, whose son owns and runs Helen's Restaurant.

"This is wonderful. I appreciate it and I know Elva will, too," I said.

"Elva used to be really active in the church. She just lost interest when Leo died," Myrtle said. "Maybe this will bring her back into the fold."

"Who knows?" I said. "Stranger things have happened."

"I didn't know the lady, but I've heard good things about her," Connie Underwood added.

I changed the subject. "Connie, I love the carving that Luke sent me. Tell him that I'll be out to see him next week."

"I will and I appreciate the help you have been to him. Now he's like a new person. He's even talking about starting a business with his carvings."

We chatted a little longer then they left. I went out in the yard to find Ed. "Hey, fellow," I said when I found him dragging loose tree limbs from the side yard.

"What's up?" He paused and looked at me.

"Do you want some water or something?"

"No, thanks. I have my thermos. I always travel with water and coffee."

I laughed. "In the same thermos?" I teased.

"No, Miss Smarty Preacher. I have two." He laughed, too.

"You've sure made the yard look better," I said.

"Thanks."

"You should quit and rest now."

"How about you? You've been working just as long as I have." He cocked an eye at me.

"I thought I'd wait around until Elva gets here."

"You don't think I'm going to leave you out here by yourself, do you?"

"No. I didn't think you would." I took a deep breath. "I'm going back in. If you need me, give a yell."

I went back in and looked around the entry. It smelled of lemon polish. I moved to the kitchen and got a drink of water from the tap. I decided to call Blaire and see how she was progressing with the packing. If she needed a break, I thought she might like to come out here now.

She agreed it would be a good idea to come.

After our conversation, I went into the parlor. I sat in the Chippendale chair and looked at the lovely room. I hadn't cleaned in here and I hadn't looked around since the day I noticed the strange painting. Now something else was different. I racked my brain. I kept looking until I noticed that the candlesticks I had taken away from Penny were gone. I knew I put them back on the mantel myself. They were not there. I surveyed the room to see if one of the ladies had put them in another place, but they were nowhere in sight.

I frowned. Somebody had to have taken those candlesticks and changed the painting. I was beginning to think that Penny's death wasn't going to change anything that had been going on. Certainly someone was upset that I was trying to befriend Elva. Maybe I should take the notes more seriously.

I got up and went back outside. "Ed," I called. "Could you come here? I want to show you something."

He came toward the porch. "What's up?"

"Come in a minute, please."

He followed me inside. "My feet might be dirty," he said. "Can you show me here in the entryway?"

"I can." I picked up the purse I'd put on the table in the corner. I took out the note and handed it to him. "This was on my car this morning."

Ed read the note and then looked at me. "Of course you didn't see who put it there?"

I shook my head.

"Willa, you're going to have to be careful. Remember the mess you got in last summer by trusting everyone."

"I know, but I can't just avoid people, Ed. I have a duty to help the people in my church. And I intend to do that duty. Elva Kingfield needs a friend and I'm going to be there for her."

"I know you will. That's the way you are." He took a deep breath. "I'll tell you what I heard from the grapevine." I looked at him and he went on. "They think the same person that attacked Mrs. Wallace is the same person that killed Penny Saxon."

"Really?"

He nodded.

"But Bernice was stabbed and Penny was strangled."

"There were still some similarities."

"What?"

"Just take my word for it. Okay?"

"Okay."

"I'm going to give these notes to the police, Willa. Some-body will probably call you."

"I figured you would turn them in. I'll expect their call."

"I just want to keep you safe."

"Thank you, Ed."

There was the sound of crunching gravel in the driveway.

I looked outside and saw an ambulance pulling closely to the front steps. A Ford Taurus stopped behind it and a nurse got out.

I smiled and said, "Well, Ed. It looks like Elva is home. Let's hope there are no more problems."

The attendants brought Elva in and put her in bed. They left and the nurse began puttering around her, setting up oxygen and arranging the night table to hold supplies. I waited at the door until she had everything settled like she wanted it.

My cue was when she said, "Now, Mrs. Kingfield, I think you're ready for company."

I came into the room. "Hello, Elva," I said with a big grin.

"Oh, Willa, I'm so glad you're here. Everything looks so nice."

"You can thank your friends from church for that. Three of them came by and worked all morning."

She looked surprised. "I didn't know anyone at church remembered me."

"Of course they do." I took the chair the nurse had placed beside the bed.

"Willa, this is Ms. Eaton. She's going to help take care of me for a while." To Ms. Eaton she said, "Willa Hinshaw, one of my ministers."

The nurse nodded and I did likewise. "The ladies also brought lunch for both of you. I bet you're ready for some home-cooked meals?"

"I definitely am," Elva said. "Of course, you'll join us, Willa."

"I'd love to, but I promised to have lunch with Ed. He changed your locks and he's been working in the yard."

"He came to the hospital and asked me if I minded if he changed them. I insisted he give me a bill after he did it. Would you see that he does that?" She looked at me.

There was a knock at the door before I could answer.

"That's probably Blaire Peterson. I called and asked her to come out."

It was Blaire. I ushered her upstairs to meet Elva. As I knew they would, they liked each other instantly. In a matter of minutes, they were chatting away. I told them I had to see if Ed was ready to go eat and that I would see them later.

Ed and I went to Helen's for lunch. As usually happened when I ate there, a mound of food was on my plate. I had a baked chicken breast with roasted potatoes, green beans and sliced tomatoes. Ed ate country-fried steak, mashed potatoes, green beans and slaw. Junior also set down a plate of biscuits, rolls and cornbread. *At least,* I thought, *I won't nibble while I'm cooking supper. I'll be too full.*

After we ate, we said goodbye and I headed to the grocery store. I'd decided I'd make lasagna and salad. I knew how much Trent liked it. I needed just about everything to make it—noodles, cheese, sour cream, ground meat and the right spices. I did have the onion and green pepper that I liked to chop and add to the meat sauce.

I was about to get in line to check out when someone said, "Willa, hello."

I looked around to see a young woman rounding the end of the line and starting to go down another one. "LeeAnn Poole, I mean Swanson. How are you?"

"Great. And you?"

"I thought you and Justin were still in Europe on your honeymoon."

"We got home about a week ago. We've been staying with our parents, but we decided we wanted to move into a place of our own right away. We found an apartment Wednesday and we got everything moved in yesterday. Of course, our cupboard was bare and I had to come get groceries."

"It's going to be great to be out on your own, I'm sure." I smiled at her. "You look wonderful, LeeAnn."

"Thank you. It is wonderful being in our own place. The honeymoon was a start in getting over the horror we went through this summer and now having our own place makes it real that we are really together again."

"I'm so glad."

"And of course, since Mom and Dad have opened their arms to Justin, I couldn't be happier."

"You deserve to be happy."

"We certainly haven't forgotten what you did for us either. As soon as we get settled, we'd like to have you for dinner."

"I'd love to come. Just let me know."

"We'll do that."

I paid for my groceries and headed home. It was almost three. I still had plenty of time. I decided I'd take a long bubble bath and think about the part of the service I was responsible for on Sunday morning. Then I'd have it in my mind before I started writing it out in the morning.

Instead, as I relaxed in the soft soapy water, I found myself praying that God would guide me in my relationship with Trent Freeman.

EIGHTEEN

BY SIX-THIRTY, the lasagna was almost done, the salad was in the refrigerator, the tea made, and the table set with my best china and candles. The flowers Trent had given me this morning were in the middle of the table and I had done a fancy fold with the linen napkins.

I was dressed in tan slacks and an off-white silk blouse. I accessorized with several gold necklace chains, gold hoop earrings and gold bangle bracelets. I had done my makeup with care and I let my shoulder-length blond hair hang loose. I felt good and I knew I looked well put together. I just hoped Trent thought so. I seldom spent this much time on my appearance.

Since it wasn't time for Trent to arrive, I decided to call my mom. There were times when a girl just needed to hear her mother's voice. I dialed their Myrtle Beach number.

"Hello," Mom answered.

"Hi, Mom."

"Willa. It's good to hear from you. Is everything okay?"

My mother, the worrier. She always thought something was wrong when she got an unexpected call from one of her kids. "Everything is fine. I just need some motherly advice."

"Oh?"

I thought the best thing to do was to come to the point immediately. "Mom, I'm scared that I'm falling in love with Trent Freeman."

There was only the slightest pause then she said, "Trent seems like a nice man, Willa. What's the problem?"

"He's a Baptist preacher, Mom. Baptists don't allow women to be ministers."

This time the pause was longer. Finally she said, "This is something that you're going to have to face on your own, Willa. I suggest you do a lot of praying and then see what your heart has to say to you." She took a deep breath, and went on. "This could be a test for you…or for him or—and this is what you're going to have to decide—this could be the man for you."

"Oh, Mom, I was hoping you'd tell me what to do."

She laughed. "I haven't done that since you were in high school. I have a smart daughter. She'll reach the right conclusion."

"Sometimes I wish you and Dad didn't have so much faith in your kids."

"Of course we have faith in all of you. We raised you to make your own decisions with the help of the Good Lord."

"It's good to talk to you anyway, Mom. Are you and Dad having fun?"

"It's been a nice trip so far. We're going out deep-sea fishing tomorrow. I just hope we don't get seasick."

"You have fun, but take some seasick pills before you go."

"We will, honey. By the way, have they caught the person who put the bomb in your church graveyard?"

"Not yet, but they're working on it. There hasn't been any more trouble."

"That's good."

"I guess I'd better hang up. It's almost time for Trent."

"Okay. It was good to talk with you." She chuckled. "Call and let me know what happens. If I have to plan a wedding, I need plenty of time."

I couldn't help laughing, too. "Goodbye, Mom. I love you."

I was hanging up the phone when the doorbell rang. I patted my hair, adjusted my blouse and then answered it.

Trent let out a low whistle as he stepped inside. "You look beautiful," he said.

"I wanted you to see that I clean up pretty good sometimes," I said. "You don't look so bad yourself."

He was wearing dark slacks and a blue sweater that made his eyes dance. He wrinkled his nose. "I smell real food," he said. "I thought we were going to order a pizza."

"I decided to cook. I hope you're not disappointed."

"I'm not disappointed at all. In fact, I'm thrilled. You know how much I like your cooking."

I smiled. "Come on in the kitchen. I think it's ready to come out of the oven."

"It looks lovely," he said. "You'd think this was a special occasion."

"I thought it would be nice to go a little fancy tonight. We don't pamper ourselves very often."

"I agree." He turned and looked at me. "What can I do to help?"

"You can get the salads out of the refrigerator and maybe put some ice in the glasses for tea."

In a matter of minutes we were seated, Trent said a beautiful blessing and I served each of us a large slice of lasagna.

"It's very good, Willa."

"Thank you."

"Well, tell me about your day. Did Mrs. Kingfield get home?"

I told him about her return home and about the women of the church and what they had done. I concluded with Blaire's arrival and how quickly she and Elva took to each other.

"Living out there will be good for Blaire," he said. "I know breaking up with Nathan has been hard for her."

"Especially since his new girlfriend is spending so much time at his place."

"That would be hard." He smiled at me and reached for my hand. "I wouldn't like seeing you with another man all the time."

My heart melted. "Oh, Trent, it goes without saying, I wouldn't like some pretty young thing with you either."

He squeezed my hand. "You don't have to worry about that." He let my hand go and added, "While you're still letting me hang around here, could I have another slice of that lasagna?"

I laughed and served him another piece. "Are you going to the visitation for Penny Saxon tomorrow night?"

"I plan to. Are you?"

"Probably not. Penny Saxon didn't like me very much. She thought I was interfering in family business."

We fell into conversation about Penny and, though we'd touched on it earlier, I told him the details about my encounters with her.

We had apple pie with ice cream for dessert and then cleaned the kitchen together. When we headed to the living room, Trent sat on the sofa and patted the seat beside him. I picked up the remote and sat down. "I think there's a special on that is supposed to be good, is that okay?"

"Sounds fine."

I handed him the remote, kicked off my shoes and tucked my feet up under me. Trent snapped on the TV, found the right channel and put his arm across my shoulder. The telephone rang.

We both chuckled.

"Would you consider letting the answering machine get it?" he asked.

I took a breath. "I think I will. At least I'll see who is calling."

The message machine clicked on and the female voice said, "Don't give me that good preacher message. You messed up Penny Saxon's life. Now you're trying to corrupt Preacher Freeman. Whey don't you mind your own business?"

I grabbed the phone. "I'm here," I said. "Who is this?" The phone clicked and I dropped it back in its cradle. "Don't think very much of me, do they?"

Trent was frowning. "Did you recognize the voice?"

"No. It wasn't familiar at all."

"This may sound crazy, but it was kind of familiar to me."

I looked at him. "Maybe it's one of your many female admirers just trying to eliminate the competition."

"Don't make light of this, Willa."

"Trent, I did nothing to Penny Saxon except refuse to help her get Elva Kingfield's power of attorney. As far as you're concerned…"

He nodded. "I know. There has been no corruption on your part there."

"I'll keep the tape of this call, just in case I need it later. In the meantime, I'm going to forget about it and enjoy the rest of this program."

"I'm not sure…"

Before he could say anything further, I reached for his arm and pulled it around me as I snuggled against his side. "There. Isn't that pleasant?"

"It's more than pleasant. It's wonderful." He kissed the top of my head. "I could get used to this as a daily thing."

I bit my lip to keep from jumping up and throwing my arms around him and telling him how much I loved him. I took a deep breath and whispered, "I like it, too, but I think we need to take it a little slow."

"I know, I know…it's just hard. When you care for someone…"

"We have a lot of things to discuss to see if we can come to some agreement before we take our relationship any further, Trent."

He chuckled. "Wouldn't it be simple if we were both Baptist?"

"Or Methodist?" I added.

He chuckled and pulled me tighter. "We'll discuss it all at another time. Right now I'm happy to watch this program with you in my arms."

I relaxed. "So am I, Trent. So am I."

We watched the rest of the program, had another piece of apple pie, and then it was time to say good night.

It felt good when Trent took me in his arms and kissed me gently, then passionately. Finally he let me go. "I had a wonderful time," he said.

"Me, too."

"We'll do it again soon. Next time, I'll cook."

"That's fair. I think a man should do the cooking sometimes."

He kissed me again and went out the door. I closed it behind him and smiled to myself. It had been a good night. Even the phone call hadn't messed it up. I knew I wasn't going to have a hard time sleeping tonight because I was going to bed with pleasant thoughts on my mind.

NINETEEN

A BANGING ON MY FRONT DOOR woke me. It continued as I jumped out of bed. I glanced at the bedside clock. Four a.m.

"Who in the world?" I muttered as I wrapped my robe around me and went to the door. I peeped outside and was shocked to see a small woman huddling against the wall.

I opened the door. "Myra," I said. "Is something wrong?"

She bolted into the door. "The dead man came to get me," she cried.

"Sit down," I said, leading her to a chair. "Let me get you a robe."

"No!" She almost screamed. "Don't leave me."

"Okay." I sat down beside her.

"Where am I?"

"You're safe, Myra. You're with Willa."

"Willa is nice. She keeps the dead man away."

"Yes." I patted her hand. "Would you like some tea, Myra?"

"Yes, but don't leave me."

"I won't leave you. You can come with me." I took her hand and she stood.

We went into the kitchen and I sat her at the table. I poured her a glass of tea and moved to the phone.

"Who are you calling?"

"I've got a call to make. You don't mind, do you?"

"No." She looked at her glass and said, "This is good tea."

I nodded and dialed the parsonage number. Philip answered

on the second ring. I didn't want to alarm anyone, so I said into the phone. "I'm calling because I have a guest named Myra who just dropped in and I thought you might want to come over here."

"Oh, Willa. Thank God. I woke up a few minutes ago and missed her. I'll be right over."

"You might want to bring a bathrobe."

I hung up the phone and said, "I think I'll have a glass of tea with you, Myra."

"Okay. This is good tea."

I sat down beside her. "Are you cold?" I looked at the thin nightgown she was wearing.

"I'm fine."

I chose my words carefully when I asked, "Myra, do you know where you are now?"

She laughed. "I'm at Willa's house, of course." She looked around. "Why am I here, anyway?"

"You just dropped in to say hi."

"Oh."

I wondered if she had forgotten all about the dead man, but I didn't dare bring him up. She was calm and seemed satisfied to sit there and sip her tea. I knew it wouldn't be long until Philip got there.

There was a knock on the door.

"I'll be right back," I said and headed for the door before she could protest. I opened the door and Philip came in.

"I'm sorry, Willa."

"Don't be. I'm just glad she came to my door instead of some stranger's." I motioned for him to come into the kitchen. "Myra, Philip is here."

"I'm glad you came, Philip. This is good tea."

He put the robe he had over his arm around her. "Put this on, Myra. It's a little cool out there."

"Okay." She slipped her arms into the sleeves.

"Are you ready to go home, dear?" he asked.

"No. I want to finish my tea." She took a small sip. "It's good tea."

Philip looked at me with sorrowful eyes. "I'll have to watch her more carefully."

"Philip, you can't watch her twenty-four hours a day." I took a deep breath and went on. "I know the decision you're going to have to make isn't an easy one, but you've got to take care of yourself, too."

"I know, Willa. I know." He looked at her. She was turning the glass of tea around and around in her hand, lost in her own world. "We've been together forty-two years. It's the hardest decision I've ever had to make."

"I'm sure it is." I smiled at him. "I just want you to know I care."

"Thank you, Willa. I've counseled husbands and wives who have been in my position many times. I now know why they put off the inevitable as long as they can."

"This is good tea," Myra said.

"Repetition is one of the symptoms of the disease. I'm sorry she keeps saying that over and over."

"I know she can't help it, Philip." I changed the subject. "When she first arrived, she talked about the dead man again."

"It's that blasted costume book. She is possessed with it. She looks at it for hours every day. I've tried to get it from her, but she cries every time she can't find it, and I end up giving it back to her. It's the one thing she never seems to forget."

"If she enjoys it, why not let her keep it? It doesn't really matter that she talks about the dead man."

"That's what I finally decided."

"This is good tea," she said.

Philip put his hands on her shoulders. "Myra, honey, it's time to go. Willa needs us to go now."

"Okay." She stood and pushed her glass away. "This is good tea."

"I'll talk with you later, Willa. Thanks again," Philip said as they went out the door.

I watched them go down the steps and get into his Buick. My heart was touched. I was glad they had had so many wonderful years together and I was sorry their marriage wasn't going to remain a happy one until the end of their lives.

I started to close the door when I saw a movement at the corner of the building across the parking lot. It moved into the shadows and I caught my breath. It looked like a person in a ragged coat. I shook my head and looked again, but it was gone.

I locked my door and convinced myself that the movement at the end of the building could have been anything from a dog to some odd item caught and moved by the wind. I clicked off the light and went back to my bedroom. It was four-forty-five. There was still time to sleep some more. I climbed back in bed and pushed thoughts of Myra out of my mind by thinking of the lovely time Trent and I had earlier. In a short time I was falling asleep, oblivious of anything going on inside or outside my apartment.

TWENTY

I HAD DONE MY LAUNDRY, and written my children's sermon for Sunday and was just getting ready to reheat some lasagna for lunch when Blaire knocked on my door.

"Willa, I love Elva. She and I had a wonderful talk last night, and this morning, we laughed and talked some more. I want to thank you for introducing us. I'm going to love living there."

"I'm so glad. I thought it would be a good match."

"I'm going to get a few things together to take out there. Did you know she offered to have a couple of rooms cleaned out so I could bring all my furniture to her house?"

"Are you going to do it?"

"No. I told her I'd put some things in the attic, but most of what I have isn't worth storing. I'm giving it to a charity."

"That's very generous of you, Blaire."

"It's no big deal. As I said, most of it was old and some secondhand anyway."

I smiled at my friend. "I was just getting ready to have lunch. Would you like to eat with me?"

"Sure. May I help?"

"You can make a salad, if you want. We're having the leftover lasagna I cooked for Trent last night."

"Oh?" She cocked an eye at me.

"Yes, we had a good time. No, nothing happened. We're tabling it for a while."

Blaire took the vegetables out of the refrigerator and got the cutting board from behind the sink. I put water on to heat so I could brew fresh tea. I cut two hefty chunks of lasagna and put them on a microwavable plate. I then set the table and put out napkins.

In a few minutes our lunch was ready and we sat down. After the blessing, she put her napkin in her lap and said, "Okay. Tell me all about the date."

"I know you wish there was a torrid romance between Trent and me, but there isn't. We ate, we watched TV and he went home. And, before you ask, yes, he did kiss me goodnight before he left."

She laughed. "So, that was that."

"Yes," I said. "When you get back to Elva's, tell her that I'm going to see Bernice this afternoon. I'll come by and tell her about the visit."

"She'd like that. She's really concerned about her friend."

"They're very close."

"Bernice's nephew called to check on Elva last night. He said he'd come out to see her in a few days so he could report back to his aunt."

"Tyrone is a nice young man. I'm glad he's going to school in Winston-Salem. He's a big help to Bernice."

Blaire got up and refilled her tea. I held out my glass and she filled it, too.

"One odd thing did happen last night," I said. "I got a strange phone call." I told her about the call telling me not to corrupt Trent.

"Probably some jealous woman who wants him herself," Blaire said.

"That's what I thought. He is a good catch in this town."

Blaire laughed. "You don't know the half of it. Every mom in town with a single daughter from twenty to fifty had him to dinner when he came to Liverpool. Many of them are still pushing their girls at him. Then there are the ones who are just now getting to the age that they think they could make him the perfect girlfriend. This includes most of the female teenagers at church because most of them have a crush on him."

"Most men would love to have this problem."

"Not Trent. He's taken a few women out, but nothing ever came of it. Most of the ones I know he dated said he was the perfect gentleman and that he didn't even try to kiss them. Then you hit town and stole his heart. I don't think he's looked at another woman since."

"Right," I said sarcastically.

"I'm serious, Willa. There's been talk about it at church."

"What do you mean?"

"Comments like, 'With all the nice Baptist girls in town I don't see why he has to go after that Methodist preacher' or 'This Methodist woman can't be the right person for him.'"

"Well, I'm sorry the people of his church feel that way. I would never do anything to make Trent compromise his beliefs or his church."

"I know that, but you know some people." She pushed back her plate. "I bet there are people at your church that don't like you seeing him."

"If so, they've never told me," I said, but I couldn't help wondering how my parishioners felt about my friendship with Trent. I didn't want to think about it. I stood and said, "There's a bit of apple pie left. Want a piece?"

"Sure."

After we finished eating, Blaire left to gather some things to take back to Elva's house with her. I took my shower and dressed in navy slacks, a white blouse and a navy jacket. I put on silver jewelry and pulled my hair back with a navy scarf and headed to the hospital.

Bernice was able to talk a little. I told her how well Elva was doing and that Blaire had moved in with her. I assured her that Elva wouldn't be happy until she was home again. I held her hand and said a prayer. I could see she was getting sleepy so I told her I would see her later.

As I was leaving, I met Tyrone in the hall. "Hi," I said.

"Hi, Reverend Willa. How nice of you to stop in and see Aunt Bernice."

"I'm looking forward to when I can visit her at home."

"I'm sure she can't wait to get out of here and back to Ms. Elva's house."

"She seems to be doing better every day. I hope it won't be long until she can get out of here."

He smiled. "I hope not, too. I think it will be good for the two of them to be together again."

"So do I. Elva is excited about having her home again," I said.

"I'll try to help them as much as I can. I know they're going to need it with them both still in bed."

"I'm sure they'll love to have you there as much as you can be, Tyrone. The doctors have lined up nurses and a friend of mine has moved into the house. Elva has even hired a temporary housekeeper until Bernice is back on her feet. I think they're going to do fine."

"That sounds good." He smiled at me again. "I guess I'd better visit a little while. I have a class later this afternoon so I can't stay too long."

"I'm sure I'll see you again soon, Tyrone."

He nodded and disappeared into his aunt's room.

When I got to Elva's house I parked in the driveway behind a silver Lincoln. I was careful not to block it in. I didn't have time to wonder who it belonged to because Rose Poole stepped out on the porch as I started up the steps.

"Willa, hello," she said warmly.

"Hello, Rose. How are you?"

"I'm fine. I just brought some food to Elva and I'm delighted to see you."

"I'm always glad to see you, too, Rose. I saw LeeAnn at the grocery yesterday. She looks happy and healthy."

"She is so happy, Willa. And that is thanks to you."

"The thanks needs to go to God, not me."

"I thank you both." Rose started down the steps. "I'd love to stay and talk but LeeAnn and Justin are having his folks and Nevis and me for dinner tonight. It's the first time we've been invited to their new apartment and I'm looking forward to it."

"That will be fun. Please give Gaylord and Portia my regards. It's been a while since I've seen them."

"I'll do that and I'll probably see you at church tomorrow."

"Goodbye, Rose."

"Bye-bye."

I went to the door, but Blaire opened it before I could knock. "We meet again," she said, laughing.

"That we do."

"Go on up to see Elva. Mrs. Poole brought enough food to feed us for a week. I've got to see what I can do with it all."

"I'll help you."

We went into the kitchen. There were several dishes sitting on the counter. "See what I mean?" Blaire said, waving her hand to indicate all the food.

"I sure do. What all did she bring?"

"Well, there's a big roast, wild rice, a vegetable casserole, makings for a salad, mashed potatoes, green beans and a jar of gravy. Then there's two pans of pecan pie squares, a carrot cake and some snack foods. Just in case we want something to munch on while watching TV, Mrs. Poole said."

"Boy, she did bring a lot."

"She said she felt bad because she wasn't able to help yesterday."

"Rose is a special lady. I really got to know her this past summer."

"I can tell. I liked her immediately. She doesn't flaunt her money, does she?"

"No, she doesn't."

We got all the food in the refrigerator. "Thanks for the help."

I didn't have time to answer. Ms. Eaton came through the door.

"Mrs. Kingfield asked for hot tea. Do you know where the tea bags are?" She looked at both of us.

"They're in the pantry at the end of the kitchen. I found them last night when she wanted a cup," Blaire said.

The nurse headed toward the pantry and I turned to say something to Blaire. I forgot all about it when an ear-piercing scream came from Elva's room.

Blaire and I took the stairs two at a time. The nurse was on our heels.

TWENTY-ONE

ELVA WAS SITTING UP in bed, flinging her arms in all directions and babbling incoherently. Her body jerked as if she was having a spasm, and she had a horrified look on her face.

The nurse ran around us and took Elva's wrist. "Relax, Mrs. Kingfield. We're here. Try to calm down enough to tell us what happened."

"Willa? Where's Willa?" Elva was trying to look around the nurse.

I went to the other side of the bed. "I'm here, Elva. Please listen to the nurse and then we'll talk."

"Leo. It was Leo," Elva said in a shaky voice. Her eyes pierced mine.

I nodded and shuddered. I didn't like seeing her in this agitated condition, but knew there was little I could do to help her.

"Mrs. Kingfield, please. Sit back. Your heart is beating too fast." The nurse looked at me as if she were asking for help.

I took the hint. "Elva, are you telling me Leo was here?"

She nodded and pointed toward the door. "He stood at the foot of my bed and sang to me."

"Okay, Elva," I said. "If you'll listen to the nurse and try to calm yourself, I'll see if I can find anyone in the hall."

She leaned back on her pillow. "Come back and tell me."

"I will." I moved toward the door and motioned for Blaire to follow me.

In the hallway, Blaire asked, "Is she going to be all right?"

"I think so. Before, when she thought she saw Leo, she had

the episode that put her in the hospital. That time she passed out. Today she's still awake, thank the Lord."

"Who is Leo?"

"Her dead husband."

Blaire shivered. "Well, she certainly saw something, or she thought she did."

"I agree." I looked around the hallway. Nothing seemed different to me. "I don't see how anyone could get in here."

"And they definitely couldn't get out without us meeting them on the way up the stairs," Blaire added.

"Maybe she was dreaming. That's about the only thing that makes sense to me. Yet..." I shook my head. "I don't know how to explain it, but when I looked into her eyes I knew she believed what she was saying."

"So you think she saw Leo?"

"No. I know she couldn't really see him, but Elva is a smart lady. It would be hard to fool her."

"Okay," Blaire said. "Let's look at this logically. There is only one window in this hall. It's in that alcove over there. We're on the second floor and unless someone uses a ladder and climbs in, they have to come up the stairs."

I walked to the alcove and looked out the window. "No ladder here." I tried the window. It was stuck tight. "And it doesn't look like this window has been opened in years."

"That leaves out the window as an entryway, so it has to be the stairs."

"But when? Or how? And how would someone get out or..." I looked about. "Or is someone still here?"

Blaire's eyebrows shot up. "But where? Elva's room and bath are here. Down the hall are Bernice's rooms. The two rooms and bath she gave me are on the other side of the stairs. The little room beside the alcove is used as a storage room... maybe there."

I went to it and reached for the door. I turned the knob, but the door wouldn't open. "Nobody went in here because the door is locked the old-fashioned way. You can't just push a button on the inside to lock it. It requires a key to get in and out and there's no key here."

"Maybe you were right the first time. She could have dozed off and dreamed about her husband," Blaire said. "She went to sleep a couple of times when she was talking with me."

"That has to be it," I said. "There's no other explanation."

We went back to Elva's room. The nurse had her calmed down. Just to be sure there was no one in here, I glanced about her room as we entered. Of course, there was nowhere for anyone to hide. I wanted to check out the bathroom, but decided I'd do that later. I didn't want to upset Elva further.

"You didn't see him, did you, dear?" Elva asked as I came closer to her.

"No, we didn't, Elva. We looked everywhere we knew to look."

She sighed. "I didn't think you'd see anything." She stared past me toward the door as if she expected her apparition to come back in. "It may be that I'm the only one he will let see or hear him."

Before I could answer, the telephone rang. The nurse answered it and then held her hand over the mouthpiece and said, "It's Dennis Kingfield. He said he'd like to talk to his aunt if she is able."

"Oh, yes. I want to talk to Dennis." Elva reached for the phone.

When the nurse hesitated, I said, "It might do her good to talk with him. He's her favorite nephew."

"Dennis, it's so good to hear from you." Elva's voice grew happier as she spoke. "Let me see if my friends mind waiting to visit with me after you and I talk."

I smiled at her and headed out of the room. Blaire followed.

The nurse said, "I'll be just outside if you need me, Mrs. Kingfield."

Elva nodded and turned back to the telephone.

Downstairs, I said, "Blaire, I'm going to look around outside a little. Want to come with me?"

"Sure."

We went out the front door and down the steps. "Why don't we go in different directions and meet in the back?" Blaire suggested.

I nodded. Since I was standing on the left, I went that way. Blaire went to the right, which was the more used path because the porch wrapped farther around in that direction.

As I walked, I looked at the ground and tried to pick up some kind of clue as to what was going on here. Nothing looked strange to me. There were spots in the ground where the grass needed to be reseeded, but there were no distinguishable footprints. I was almost around the back corner of the house when I saw something shining near a downspout. I bent over and picked it up. It was a fork and it hadn't been on the ground for very long. Though it had some dirt on it, it hadn't tarnished. I frowned and turned it over. It was sterling silver, and by the ornate pattern, I figured it was an expensive piece. There was no way anyone would discard a piece of silver like this. It had to have been dropped here by mistake. But how? If it had been on the other side, I'd guess it was dropped by someone who had been eating on the porch, but there was no porch here.

I shook my head and looked around. There was nothing else on the ground in this area. I decided to go on with my walk.

Blaire was waiting when I got to the backyard. "Find anything?" she asked.

"As a matter of fact, I did. Did you?"

"Not a thing."

I handed her the fork. "It was on the ground close to the back corner of the house. This is a good piece of silver. I don't think anyone purposely threw it away."

"Of course not," Blaire said after looking at the fork. "I bet someone dropped it by accident."

"Probably as they were leaving with the set. Let's go inside and see if we can find where Elva keeps her silver."

It wasn't hard to find the silverware drawer in the dining room. It was almost empty.

"Do you think Penny took it?" Blaire asked.

"Probably. She was certainly taking those candlesticks the day I saw her with them. Which, by the way," I added, "they're now missing again."

"She must have come back for them."

"Blaire, I'm going to say goodbye to Elva and then I'm going to talk with Ed. I think we need to get some professional advice."

"You're probably right."

After saying my goodbye, I headed toward my apartment. I wanted to make some phone calls and I needed to use the phone at home. I knew I'd be making notes and the cell wouldn't allow me to do that and drive, too.

I was about to enter Blue Bell Curve, the horseshoe arc in a deserted section of the road. It snaked around an embankment and dropped downward, ending at a small wooden bridge. Many wrecks and several deaths had been blamed on this short piece of road. I thought about Philip's warning almost every time I approached it. But today was different. Today I was thinking about the silver fork and how it may have landed in Elva's yard when, seemingly from out of nowhere, a gray sedan came up behind me. In the rearview mirror, I could see it was getting awfully close. It was as if the driver wanted to ram me in the back. In an instant I knew I was right. I couldn't speed up, but I tried to brace myself. The sedan slammed into the back of my car with full force.

I held it in the road as best I could, and began to pray for help.

It eased back, then came forward and hit me again.

The car was bigger and heavier than my Cavalier and he had no trouble pushing me sideways in the curve. I knew if a car came from the other direction, I would be hit on both sides. I prayed as I tried to straighten my vehicle. It wasn't happening.

The gray car stopped and waited until I was completely crossway in the road. It came at me again and crashed into the passenger side of the car. I felt it push me until my car left the pavement. I knew it was going to turn over, but I tried to keep my wits about me so I could recollect what was happening. As it toppled over the incline, I think I heard the gray car speed away. My face was protected by the airbag, but I felt my head hit the side of the window. I didn't hear anything else after that.

TWENTY-TWO

I CAME TO AND FELT HANDS under my arms. They were pulling me out of the car. "Thanks," I mumbled and went out again.

The next time I opened my eyes, I saw bright lights over the bed where I lay. There were medical personnel standing around me.

"Hello there, young lady," a gray-haired man that reminded me of my father said.

"Hi," I answered. "What's going on?"

"Just checking you over. Do you remember what happened to you?"

"Of course." I returned his smile. "I was headed home when someone decided to run me off the road."

"Looks like they accomplished that goal."

"Why would anyone want to do that to me?"

"I have no way of knowing." He listened to my chest. "Heart sounds good," he said.

"How did I get here?"

"By ambulance."

"But how? Who found me?"

"When we get through running tests, we'll let someone else answer those questions. We only know you were brought in."

I decided I'd just have to wait. I let them prod and twist and check me here and there. I was then sent down the hall for x-rays. I assumed, to see if anything was broken or something on the inside wasn't right. As my bed was being wheeled from one place to another, I tried to remember if I saw the face of the person who had run me off the road. If I did, I didn't recall it. I couldn't even tell if a man or a woman had been driving the car. I did remember that it was a gray sedan, but I wasn't sure of the make or model. I also remembered that it was probably three or four years old.

When I was taken back to the emergency room to wait for the results of the tests, the police were waiting to talk with me. Gary Bumgarner walked in and shook his finger at me. I knew he was teasing because he was laughing when he said, "Reverend Hinshaw, what in the world are we going to do with you? Liverpool was a boring little Southern town and then you show up. Now it seems we have more excitement than New York City."

"I guess it just took me to bring out the undercurrent of crime that was already here," I teased back.

"Well, at least I'm thankful that you weren't hurt any worse than you are."

"I have a terrible headache, but I think that I'm fine otherwise."

"Can you tell me what happened?"

I told him all that I remembered about the accident then I asked, "Who found me?"

"You were lucky there. A couple of bicyclists were coming in the opposite direction. They said a man in a gray car almost ran them off the road because he was speeding and weaving on the road. They were headed for Blue Bell Curve when it happened. When they came into the curve, they were discussing the fact that it would have been awful had they met him there. One of them actually pointed toward the creek and said, 'Hey, we could have ended up down there.' When they looked in that direction, they saw your car. One of them had a cell phone and called 911."

"I see. I hope you have their names so I can thank them."

"I can get them for you."

"Thanks."

"Now, let's get back to the wreck. Do you have any idea who would want to hurt you?"

"No, but I have gotten a couple of threatening notes."

"What kind of notes?"

"Notes warning me to stay away from Elva Kingfield."

"Have you reported them?"

"I gave them to Ed Walsh. He said he'd take care of it for me."

"Then I'm sure he has. I'll check when I get back to the station." He looked at me. "I hope we can find your assailant soon. I don't want you to get hurt any more than you are already."

"Thanks, Officer Bumgarner."

The doctor came in as the policeman was leaving. "Well, Ms. Hinshaw, your tests came back clear. How are you feeling?"

"Other than a headache, I think I'm fine."

"I'd like to keep you overnight so we can be sure you're okay."

"I'd rather go home, unless it's absolutely necessary for me to stay the night."

"It's not mandatory, but as a precaution I recommend it."

"I will go right home and get in bed."

"If you insist, we'll release you, but if you feel at all sick I suggest you call your doctor or come back to the emergency room immediately."

"I will."

A nurse came in after he left. "I'm afraid they had to cut your clothes off. Do you have someone you can call to bring you something to wear home?"

"Yes, thank you."

She took me to a phone and I called Elva's number.

Thirty minutes later, Blaire came to pick me up. "I brought my bathrobe. I hope that's okay."

"It's fine."

They wheeled me out and I got into Blaire's car. Though

I'd told her a little on the phone, I had to go into detail on the way home. She was appalled that someone would do that to me.

It was almost midnight when we got back to my apartment. "Blaire, thank you for coming to get me. I'm sorry I had to call you so late."

"Don't be silly. You know I don't mind." She got out and followed me up the stairs. Inside she said, "Are you sure you're going to be okay?"

"I'll be fine. Wait here a minute." I went into my bedroom and changed into my own robe. I came back into the living room and handed her the one I'd been wearing. "Thanks so much."

"Sure. Do you want me to spend the night with you?"

"No. You need to get back to Elva's before it gets any later. I'll be fine."

"You'll call me if you need anything?"

"Of course."

She left and I took a quick shower, put on a clean soft nightgown and went to bed. I went to sleep almost immediately.

When I woke up the next morning, it took a moment to remember why almost every inch of my body ached as I got out of bed.

TWENTY-THREE

NOBODY AT CHURCH seemed to notice that I moved a little slower than usual. I made the announcements, led the responsive reading, said a prayer and gave my children's sermon. The music was good and I was almost able to forget the accident when the choir rang out with "Victory in Jesus." Though I enjoy many of the new hymns, it seems that some of the old ones touch me more. I guess it's because Mom sang many of them around the house when I was small.

Philip preached a sermon on forgiveness. As usual, there were several points in it that I needed to apply to my life. I asked God to help me do just that.

After the service, I stood at the back door of the sanctuary and greeted the parishioners who left that way. Philip stood at the front. By twelve-twenty, the church was empty and the parking lot had almost cleared.

I had gone to my office to hang up my robe when Philip tapped on my open door. "Got a minute?" he asked.

"Sure." I put the robe on the hanger on the back of the door. "Come in."

"I won't keep you long," he said.

"No problem. I have no plans."

"I just wanted to tell you about last night."

"Oh?" I sat down in my desk chair and motioned for him to sit.

"Myra got out of the house again," he said as he took a seat on the sofa.

"Oh, Philip, I'm so sorry. Where did she go?"

"Actually, I heard the door open and caught her before she could get away."

"That was good."

He nodded and went on. "I can't go on like this, Willa."

I didn't know what to say, so I just nodded and he went on. "I'm going to start checking out nursing homes tomorrow morning. Lord knows, I hate to do it, but I don't really have a choice."

"I know this may sound trite, but I think you're doing the right thing." I truly believed what I was saying to him. "You might find that Myra adjusts well and will even be happier in a place where the routine stays the same."

"That's what I keep telling myself, Willa. It's just that I wanted to look after her as long as I could." He sighed and went on. "But I know if I don't do something, she's going to hurt herself or someone else."

"Surely not."

"Last night she had a big butcher knife with her and when I tried to take it away from her she sliced my arm."

"Are you okay?"

"Yes. I bandaged it and it didn't bleed long. It wasn't a deep cut."

"Philip, I'm sorry."

"You have been very understanding, Willa. I appreciate all the support."

"I've done very little. I wish there was more I could do."

"Just help me get through this. I know I can count on you to do what needs to be done here while I'm away from the church."

"Of course you can."

He stood. "I'd better get home. Myrtle Johnson is sitting with Myra now. I need to let her go home." He smiled at me. "The women's society has been such a help. I know that was part of your doing."

"Not really. Myrtle actually came to me with the idea. I

just suggested they help you with some food and sitting with Myra at times."

"I'll be sure to let her know how much it has meant." He paused at the door. "I'll see you tomorrow."

When he left I said a silent prayer that God would give him all the strength and courage he needed to get through this trying time. I then got my purse and headed home. I was aching all over and I wanted to get into a hot tub and soak my weary bones. It wasn't to be because Ed Walsh was waiting for me when I got there.

"Why didn't you call me last night?" he demanded almost before I got out of the car.

"Ed, it was almost midnight when I got home. I didn't call anybody. How did you find out anyway?"

He was following me up the steps to my door. "Gary Bumgarner called me. He knows I try to keep an eye on you." He took a breath and added, "He also asked me about the notes you got."

"I see." I unlocked my door and he came in behind me. "Have the police found out anything?"

"No, but they're working on it. How are you feeling, anyway?"

"To be honest, Ed, I hurt all over. I'm sure glad I had my seat belt on and the airbag worked. If I got this banged up with it, I'd hate to see how I'd be if I hadn't worn the belt or the bag had failed."

"They do make a difference. Now sit down and tell me what happened."

"First, let me get a sandwich or something. I'm getting hungry. Do you want one?"

"You need more than a sandwich."

"I'm not up to cooking more than that."

"Then you go make yourself comfortable and I'll go pick up something hot."

"That's not necessary."

"Of course it is. Now do like I say. I'll be back in a few minutes and you can tell me all about it."

Before I could argue with him, he was out the door. I shrugged and decided that while he was gone, I'd change. I took off my church dress and slipped into a pair of slacks and a knit top. I did feel better, just to get out of the pantyhose.

In a short time he came back with a box of chicken, potato wedges, coleslaw, green beans and a half-gallon of tea. He ushered me to the kitchen and began putting it on the table. I got plates, napkins and glasses and we sat down to eat. Of course there was enough for four people, but I had to admit, it tasted better than a sandwich would have.

"Now don't let me rush you, but I need you to tell me about last night," he said between bites.

I wiped my mouth and told him everything that I could remember. I added, "There is something that I think is more important to talk about."

"And what would that be?"

I told him about Elva's apparition and about Blaire and I checking around the outside of the house. I ended with finding the fork.

When I finished, he said, "I agree with you that Penny was probably the one stealing from her aunt, but undoubtedly she had help."

I stared at him. It was the first time I had thought about an accomplice. "But who?"

"Maybe I should check out the rest of the family members around here. I'm sure if Penny Saxon was taking things from Elva, someone knows where everything is being kept." He took a drink of tea. "Would you happen to know any of her relatives?"

"Not really. I know there's a niece who has been staying with her, and Trent said she had two sons who came in for the funeral."

"I'll check with Trent. Was that funeral today?"

"Yes. At two o'clock, I think."

He wiped his mouth. "I hate to leave you with this mess, but I think I'll go to that funeral. You'd be surprised what you can pick up around the graveyard."

"But…"

"No buts. I bet your accident and Elva Kingfield's troubles are all tied together. You sit tight and I'll let you know what I find out."

There was nothing much I could say. He was probably right and had I been thinking straight, I'd have gone to the funeral myself. Now it was too late and I was just too tired. I was going to sit tight as he suggested. In fact, I decided it would probably be a good time to get in a short nap. I was sure that would make me feel better. I was asleep almost as soon as my head contacted the pillow.

It was getting dark when the phone woke me. I shook my head to get awake and then said, "Hello."

"Willa, it's Tyrone Wallace. I just wanted to let you know that my aunt is much better today. She asked me to call you."

"Tyrone, that's wonderful. I'm so glad to hear this news. I'm sorry I didn't get in to see her today. I had a little car accident last night and I've been resting this afternoon."

"I hope nothing serious."

"Not at all. I'm just a little sore."

"Is there anything I can do for you?"

"It's nice of you to offer, Tyrone, but I'll be fine."

"I have a light schedule this week. I'll be glad to help you any way I can."

"I appreciate that, but in a day or so I will be as good as new. If you will, please tell Bernice that I'm not sure I'll have my car back in time to come see her tomorrow. It's in the shop and I don't know how long they'll have to keep it."

"I'll tell her. She said you were here yesterday and she wanted me to thank you for coming."

"You know thanks are not necessary."

"I told her that, but she insisted. She also wanted me to check on Ms. Elva."

"Elva is doing well. She has nurses with her and they're taking good care of her. I think I told you that a friend of mine has moved in with her, too. Of course," I added, "nobody can replace Bernice. Elva can't wait for her to get home."

"That will please my aunt."

We talked a little more then hung up. I got off the bed and stretched. It hurt some, but I knew I had to keep myself limber or I'd really ache. I glanced at the clock. It was five-forty-five. The fall days were getting shorter. I knew it wouldn't be long until we went off Daylight Savings Time. Then the daylight hours would really be short.

I went into the kitchen and poured myself a glass of tea. After all the lunch I ate, I was surprised that I felt hungry again. I knew there were plenty of leftovers, but for some reason, I wasn't in the mood for them. I was scratching about in the cabinet I used as a pantry when the phone rang. It was Ed.

He informed me the gray car was reported stolen the same day it ran me off the road and it had now been found in the parking lot at Wal-Mart. There were no clues as to who had stolen it or who had been driving when I encountered it. He promised to keep me informed. I thanked him for the information and hung up.

Back in the kitchen, I made a sandwich and sat at the table with pad and pen. I began listing all the things that had happened since the bomb had exploded in the graveyard. The incidents were jumbled in my head and I thought this would be one way to make them clearer. When I finished, I realized that it all boiled down to Elva's money. Someone wanted it badly enough to attempt to kill her and Bernice. They had succeeded in killing Penny and now they were after me.

But why? I had no control over Elva's finances or her possessions. Then it dawned on me. I was getting too close. Somehow I had uncovered things that could put the finger on the perpetrator. But what had I uncovered? No matter how hard I thought, I couldn't come up with any reasons why I would be a threat to anyone.

I finished off my sandwich and stood. I tossed the list I'd made in my catch-all drawer in the kitchen and went to the living room. I flipped on the television and sat down to get lost in an old movie. That was all I wanted to think about for the rest of the evening.

TWENTY-FOUR

MONDAY MORNING was bright and sunny, but cold. I put on my all weather coat and walked to work. I said a prayer of thanksgiving for the day as I hurried across the street to the back of the church. Philip had said he was going to leave early to check on nursing homes. I knew if it were a cloudy dreary day, it would be harder for him to accomplish his task.

I took care of the work I had at the office and was getting ready to go for an early lunch when there was a rap on my door.

"Come in," I said.

Trent came through the door. He didn't give me time to speak as he said, "Are you all right? Why didn't you call me? You could have been killed."

I held up my hand. "Slow down. I didn't call you because it was almost midnight when I got home."

"You could have called me yesterday."

"I was busy with church, and when I got home I knew you were tied up with the funeral. I went to sleep and slept most of the afternoon." I smiled at him. "I was going to call you today."

"It's almost noon and you haven't called yet."

I glanced at my watch. "So it is. I was going to call and ask you to come take me to lunch since I don't have a car. Now that you're here…"

"Of course we'll go to lunch, but I still want to know all about your accident."

I stood. "If you'll feed me, I'll tell you anything."

He grinned. "Okay. It's a deal. Where do you want to go?"

"I'd like to go by Swanson's Garage and see when they'll have my car ready. Afterward, I hear there's a good Italian restaurant in Kernersville. If it's not too far, could we go there?"

"Yes to both. We'll go by the garage. And the restaurant is Amalfi's. I've been there a few times and it really is good."

"Then, let's go."

When we stopped at the garage, Gaylord Swanson told me that he would try to have my car ready by Tuesday evening or Wednesday morning. After we visited with him for a little while, we said our goodbyes and headed to Kernersville.

Amalfi's was tucked away in the corner of a strip shopping center on the edge of Kernersville. Once we stepped inside, I almost felt we had gone into a small bistro in the heart of Rome. The greenery and paintings on the walls reflected the Italian countryside as did the dark woods of the furniture.

The friendly staff greeted us as if we were their favorite customers and once we were seated in one of the booths, I said, "I think I'll stay here for the rest of the day."

Trent laughed and said, "They do have a way of making you feel special, don't they?"

"I thought it was because they knew you."

"No. I'm sure they have no idea who either of us is. They treat all their customers this way."

"Well, I like the treatment."

We ordered our usual iced tea and studied the menus while the waiter scurried to get the drinks. I decided on the eggplant special and Trent ordered the stuffed shells.

"Now," he said as the waitress again left to turn in our food order, "I'm ready to hear all about the accident. You promised to tell me."

"Trent, I really don't know much of what happened. A gray car ran me off the road and though I wish it had been, it was no accident." I went on to tell him about Elva's sighting of her dead husband and then as much as I could remember about the car, which was very little.

Of course Trent was upset. He began telling me how dangerous some things can be. He had to know if I'd talked to the police and he continued to question me.

"Trent," I said as calmly as I could, "I didn't mean to get anyone all upset by helping Elva. In fact, there is no proof that this had anything to do with her at all."

When I finished, he said, "Of course it does, Willa. I want you to be more careful because I don't want anything to happen to you. You're a minister, not the savior of the world. Sometimes you just have to back off and let people handle some of their own problems. I don't want to see you come as close to losing your life as you did last summer."

"I know that. It's just that I can't let people continue to take advantage of somebody like Elva. If I don't look out for her, who will?"

"Maybe that nephew will take her back to Atlanta with him."

I chuckled. "I'd like to see him try. It would be more reasonable to think that she might persuade him to move back here."

"That could work, too."

"We'll see. He's in California on business, but he says he's coming to see her as soon as he gets back to Atlanta." I changed the subject. "Tell me about Penny's funeral. Did it go okay?"

"It did, though it was a hard one to do. The sons wanted it short and sweet so they could start dividing up her property and be on their way back to their respective homes."

"How sad."

"The niece took it harder than anyone."

"Poor kid. What's she going to do now?"

"Her mother came back to Penny's house after the services and I assumed Jackie went home with her. I was too busy with the sons to think about asking at the time, and when I thought of it, she and her mother had left."

"What were the sons doing?"

"I thought it was unusual, but as soon as the neighbors left they asked me to stay there as they divided up Penny's belongings. They said that anything they didn't take was to be donated to whatever charity I saw fit. They wanted the house cleaned out as quickly as possible so they could put it on the market."

"That is unusual."

"They didn't tarry with the job either. I don't think I was there more than two hours."

"I know this sounds like a crazy question, but did you see any things that looked out of place with Penny's belongings?"

"Nothing that looked like it belonged to Elva Kingfield if that's what you're asking." He smiled at me as he said it.

I smiled back and said, "You're beginning to know me very well."

"I'm trying to know you, but I have to admit, sometimes you keep me guessing."

Our food arrived and we began to chat about other matters. It felt good to tell him about Philip and the problems he was having about putting Myra in a rest home. I began to chat about my family and their busy lives and he talked about his. We discussed the weather and a number of mundane things. In fact, we talked for an hour after we had finished our lunch and finally decided it was time to head back to Liverpool.

When Trent dropped me back at the church it was three-thirty. I checked by Philip's office and he was bent over his desk. I knocked lightly.

He looked up and motioned for me to come in. "I'm glad you're back, Willa."

"I'm sorry I was gone so long," I said.

He shook his head. "Don't be silly. Why are you working today anyway?"

"What do you mean?"

"Willa, I just learned about your wreck. Why hadn't you told me?"

"I'm fine. I didn't see any reason to burden you with anything else."

"You could have told me yesterday, but instead you let me rattle on and didn't say a word."

"Philip, I assure you, I'm fine." I changed the subject. "How did your search for a rest home go?"

"I found one that was nice, and I may go with it, but I still want to look at others so I can make comparisons."

"Of course."

"Really, now. I know you're changing the subject from yourself, but I want to know what happened."

I took a deep breath and told him about the car running me off the road. I didn't tell him about Elva seeing her dead husband or about the things being stolen from her house. I still thought he had enough to worry about.

When I finished talking about my accident, he told me to take the rest of the day off. I protested, but he was insistent. I finally gave up and went home.

The light on my answering machine was blinking when I went into my kitchen. I flipped it on.

"Hi, Willa. It's Blaire. Just checking on you today. If you get this before five, give me a call at work and let me know how it's going." I made a mental note to call her when I listened to the rest of my messages.

The second message was from an overly happy salesperson who wanted to sell me life insurance.

The third was from Jackie Meyer. I could tell she was crying. "I just hope you're happy. You're the reason my aunt Penny is dead. Why couldn't you just keep your nose out of our family business?" She sucked in her breath and added, "And why don't you leave Trent alone. He can do so much better than you." She then slammed down the phone.

I now knew who had made that first call to me about leaving Trent alone. This girl must have a crush on him, and I couldn't help smiling. I knew how teenagers tended to have these feelings for teachers and others in authority. I was sorry that she thought I was responsible for her aunt Penny's death, but I knew that was just misplaced loyalty. And probably some indoctrination from the aunt before her death. I said a quick prayer for the girl and turned on the fourth message.

The deep voice said, "Since you lived through Saturday, you'd better count your blessings and stay out of my way because you won't be that lucky next time."

I shuddered and stepped into the living room to glance at my front door. I know that after the incidents this past summer, I have a habit of locking my door as I come in, but I wanted to be sure. It was locked. I went back in and called Blaire. She was glad that I was feeling better, but I told her that I was going to bed early, so she didn't say anything about coming by. I deleted the message from the insurance salesman and saved the other two. I wanted to let Trent hear the one from Jackie and I wanted to let Ed listen to the threatening one.

I then went into the living room and flipped on the TV. Oprah was on and discussing teenage suicide. It was interesting and I soon found myself completely absorbed in the program. By the time it ended, I had made some notes to discuss with the young people at church. I shook my head at the wonder of how things worked out sometimes. It was such an informative show and if Philip had not sent me home, I would have missed it. It was as if it was meant for me to watch TV at this time. I said a quick "Thank You, Lord."

I got up and went into the kitchen for a glass of tea. After pouring it, I started back to watch the early news. On impulse, I picked up the phone and dialed Trent's office number. The secretary put him on the phone.

"Well, well. What a treat. I get to hear from you twice in one day," he said.

"I thought it might thrill you," I teased.

"More than you know," he said, with a chuckle. He then added, "But I know you had something besides thrilling me in mind."

"I just wanted to ask you a favor."

"What?"

"Would you get me a list of the people in your church who are related to Elva Kingfield? I agree with you that Penny didn't try to pull off the robbery and attempted murder alone."

"You're not going to get more involved, are you?"

"I'm getting things together to give to Ed." I did eventually mean to give them to him.

"In that case, I'll see what I can do. Anything else?"

"If you have time, can you come by? I have another message I want you to hear."

"I'll be leaving here in about thirty minutes. May I come by then?"

"Sure. Do you have dinner plans?" I was in the mood to cook again.

"No. Got any suggestions?"

"I'll think about it and let you know when you get here."

As soon as we hung up I looked in the freezer. There were some chicken breasts and a pack of ground round. I moved them aside and found a package containing three pork chops. I took them out and decided I could do something with them. I continued to look around and found a bag of frozen peas.

In a matter of minutes I had a meal cooking. I sliced the two tomatoes I had bought for sandwiches and put them in a dish of Italian dressing to marinate along with a few slices of cucumber and red onion.

The pork chops were waiting on the indoor grill, the peas were bubbling in a pot, and the potatoes were cooking in another one. I took the half loaf of Italian bread from the refrigerator, buttered it, rubbed it with garlic and added a sprinkling of sea salt.

Thirty minutes later the doorbell rang. I opened it and Trent smiled broadly at me. "Hey, the apron suits you."

I glanced down at the chef's apron that I often wore in the

kitchen. "Thanks," I mumbled. "Come in. Dinner's almost ready."

"What a nice surprise," he said. "I was expecting to take you out to dinner."

"I decided to cook. I hope that's okay."

"It's great. You know I love your cooking." He took off his suit coat and unfastened his tie. "Anything I can do to help?"

"No. Just have a seat and keep me company. Let me get the meat going and I'll let you hear what I wanted you to." I moved to the grill and turned it on to cook the pork chops. Everything else was finished and I turned it all low enough to keep warm.

I then joined him at the table. "This was on my answering machine today. I thought you'd want to hear it." I switched it on.

After the message ended, Trent shook his head. "I appreciate you letting me hear this and I certainly hope you don't take it seriously."

I smiled at him. "Of course not. I know Penny's death wasn't my fault. I also know how teenage girls get these crushes. When I was fifteen, I had a powerful crush on my piano teacher. The fact that he was gay didn't sway me either."

Trent laughed. "So, you've always been headstrong."

"I have," I said as I stood to turn the pork chops.

"Seriously, I've tried very hard to keep the young girls at bay. I know some of the mothers of adult females have pushed them to get close to me, but I've never encouraged it in any way."

I reached over and mussed his hair. "If you weren't so all-fired good-looking, it wouldn't happen."

He grabbed my hand. "You think I'm good-looking?"

"Of course I do. Otherwise, I wouldn't bother with you." I pulled my hand away. "I've got to get the meat off the grill. It's going to burn."

He stood. "I'll help make the plates."

"Okay. There's a tomato salad in the refrigerator. You can get that, too."

When everything was ready, we sat down to a relaxing meal. When we had finished, we decided to drive into Winston-Salem to a movie.

When he brought me home, he gave me a long passionate kiss and then slipped away. As I closed the door, I didn't want to admit, even to myself, how quickly I could get used to sharing evenings with him.

TWENTY-FIVE

A LOUD NOISE WOKE me from a sound sleep. I sat up in bed with a start. I wasn't sure what it was, but I knew it had taken place on my front balcony. I waited for a moment, but I heard nothing further. I glanced at the clock. It was three-forty-five.

My heart was still beating fast when I decided to ease out of bed and go to the living room. The city streetlight on the corner of the parking lot was ample for me to see where I was going. I went to the big window and peeped out through the blinds. There were cars parked in the lot and all the neighbors' lights were off. Nothing seemed to be stirring.

"Maybe I just dreamed it," I mumbled and let the slat of the blind I'd lifted fall back into place. "Sometimes I think I…" Before I could finish my sentence, something banged my front door.

I jumped and swallowed a scream. It didn't sound like a knock. It sounded more like something large hitting the storm door.

I went to the door, but wasn't about to open it. I did flip on the outside light and in an instant I heard feet running down the steps outside. I know I should have opened the door to see who it was, but I was afraid. I went back to the big window and looked out, but whoever had been outside didn't go into the parking lot. I decided they must have gone around the corner and out the back. I was still too afraid to open the door.

I took refuge on the couch and waited for morning. Only when daylight came, did I get up from the sofa and go to the door. I was still hesitant, but opened it slowly.

My breath caught in my throat when I saw the word *murderer* in big red letters on the outside of the door. I realized that when they'd finished, they'd pounded on the door to wake me up.

I closed it slowly and went to the kitchen. I dialed Ed's number.

The doorbell rang just as I finished dressing. There was a police officer with Ed. I told them exactly what had happened. They checked around outside, then came back in to question me again. I had a feeling that Jackie Meyer had been the perpetrator and I let them listen to the message she had left me.

Ed agreed that it was probably her. The officer said they would certainly check her out.

I almost had to laugh out loud when Ed finished his questions with, "It would sure make it easier to clean up if you'd decide to paint your whole front door red."

After they left, I went to work and acted as if nothing had happened. I did call Trent and let him know what was going on. He also thought that Jackie Meyer had done it. We both decided it would be best to let the police handle it.

It was a fairly uneventful morning at church. Philip went to check out another rest home. I did some paperwork and had a call from Blaire. She said she would pick me up for lunch, since I didn't have a car. I let her.

We went to Helen's. I had one of their big hamburgers. Of course Junior piled my plate with enough French fries for the whole church staff. He also slipped us a big slice of cherry pie each. "Mom made this today. I know you're going to like it," he said. Of course, it was delicious.

Blaire insisted that I take her back to work and use her car to visit Bernice in the hospital. It didn't take much to persuade me. Until today, I had never realized how much I relied on my car in my work.

"Just come pick me up at five and then you can come out to visit Elva," she said. "I'll drive you back home later."

"I just want to get home before dark," I said. I then explained to her what had happened.

"You're going to have to move out of there one of these days, Willa," she said. "I love living at Elva's house, even though I know it's temporary."

"I'm so glad. I'm sure she likes having you there, too."

"She says she does." Blaire looked at her watch. "I'd better get back to work, though I'm too full to be very productive."

"I know what you mean." I stood and she followed.

Blaire's office was only a few blocks away. I let her out and headed to the hospital.

I found Bernice sitting in a chair when I got to her room. "Hello," I said.

She greeted me with a warm smile. "It's good to see you, Reverend Willa. How are you?"

"I'm fine, Bernice, and it looks like you're doing better, too."

"I am. They say I might get to go home in a few days." She motioned for me to sit in the chair across from her. "Tyrone told me about your wreck. I'm so glad you weren't hurt real bad."

"The Lord was looking after me." I sat down. "Elva will be excited when I tell her that you're coming home soon."

"I talked to her on the phone today. She says she is doing well and is really enjoying having Blaire with her."

"She is. We're all happy about that. As for Blaire, she's delighted to be staying there and she's looking forward to meeting you." I changed the subject. "Bernice, now that you're feeling better, will you tell me what happened to you?"

She sighed. "I wish I could. The police have talked to me and I've racked my brain over and over trying to remember. All I know is that I was getting ready to come to the hospital to see Elva and I heard a noise in the upstairs hall. I went up there to see what it was, but I couldn't see anything, I started to come back down when something hit my back. I felt like I was on fire. The next thing I knew, I woke up here."

"Whoever it was must have been hiding and attacked you from behind."

"That's what the police are saying." She shook her head. "We may never know who it was."

"Oh, I think we will. It may take a while, but I have confidence in the Liverpool police."

She smiled. "Maybe you're right."

The nurse came in and said it was time for Bernice to get back into bed. I said goodbye and headed for the office. It was just three-thirty. I'd have some time to get some office work done before I picked Blaire up at five.

As soon as I stepped into the front door, Anna motioned that I was wanted on the phone. I nodded and hurried to my office.

"Hello," I said, sitting in my desk chair.

"Reverend Hinshaw, this is Dennis Kingfield."

"Yes, Mr. Kingfield."

"I thought I'd talk with you before I called Aunt Elva. She seems to be doing better but I don't want to get her too excited."

"That's thoughtful. It is hard on her when she gets keyed up."

"I know. The nurse said she gets upset when she has bad dreams." He changed the subject. "I wanted to find out what you think about my coming to visit her?"

I smiled to myself. Didn't he know his aunt thought he could walk on water? To him I said, "I think it would be wonderful. Your aunt loves you very much and I think a visit would be just the thing to make her recovery complete."

"I have a flight out to Atlanta in the morning. I'll stay there a couple of days to let my partner know what I accomplished in California. I should be able to get to Liverpool by the end of the week."

"That's good. Do you want me to mention it to her?"

"I'll give her a call, but I won't tell her an exact date, just in case I run into a snag in Atlanta." He paused a minute. "I'm looking forward to meeting you, Reverend. You have been such a good friend to my aunt. I want to thank you in person."

"I haven't done that much, but I also look forward to meeting you." I paused. "If you let me know when you'll arrive, I'll be happy to pick you up at the airport."

"That would be lovely, but there is no need. I'll rent a car. I want to take Aunt Elva out if she is able and I don't relish driving that big boat of hers."

I chuckled. "I understand. Thank you for letting me know you're coming, Mr. Kingfield."

We hung up and I sat back. I wasn't lying when I said I looked forward to meeting him. I was getting mixed reviews of the man from his aunt and from Bernice. He certainly seemed to be attentive to Elva, and he had made several calls from California to her. I decided I would reserve judgment until I met him myself.

I sat up and picked up the file on my desk. It was time to get to work. I would think about Dennis and Elva later. I only had a couple of hours to get some work done. I didn't want to be late picking up Blaire. I might need to borrow her car again.

At ten minutes to five I put down the project I was working on, and left my office. I waved goodbye to Anna as I went out the door. I got into the car and drove to the insurance office where Blaire worked. I had timed it perfectly. She was coming out the door as I pulled up. I got out and moved to the passenger side.

She slipped under the steering wheel. "You could have driven," she said.

"Why? I like being chauffeured." I laughed.

She chuckled. "You would." She then added, "You're going to see Elva with me, aren't you?"

"If you don't mind bringing me back home."

"I don't mind."

"Should we stop for something for dinner?"

She laughed out loud. "There's food enough at Elva's to feed a dozen people for a week. Those church women just won't let up. They keep bringing it in."

"Maybe I should call Myrtle Johnson and ask her to slow them up a bit."

"That's not a bad idea."

My cell phone rang. I fished it out of my purse.

"Hi, Willa," Trent said. "I was wondering if we could get together tonight. There's a dinner in it for you."

"Sounds good, Trent, but I'm with Blaire. We're going to see Elva, and Blaire assures me there is enough food there for a hungry convention."

Blaire interrupted. "Tell Trent to come eat with us."

I relayed the message.

"How can I resist two such lovely ladies? Besides, I need to visit Mrs. Kingfield. She may want to hear about her niece's funeral."

"Come about six." I glanced at Blaire and she nodded.

"Thanks. I'll see you then."

I hung up and turned to Blaire. "That was nice of you to invite him."

"No problem. I like Trent, and there really is a lot of food. Wait until you see. We could invite several more people and still have food that we will have to throw away."

"I get the point. I'll talk to Myrtle tomorrow. There's no need to throw away good food."

"Thanks," she said as the car approached the curve on Blue Bell Road.

I didn't say anything, but I couldn't stop the shiver that ran through my body. I wanted to scream for her to be careful, but I held my tongue. I don't think I took a breath until we had rounded the curve and were on the straight road again.

I must have let the breath out with a gasp because Blaire asked, "Did I scare you?"

I shook my head. "Not at all. It's just the location. I guess it will be a while before I can take that curve without thinking of that awful feeling as I was being pushed off the road."

"I know it must be terrible."

We didn't say anything else until she pulled into Elva's driveway and parked near one of the large oak trees.

"There are a lot of leaves in Elva's yard. I think I'll mention it at church and see if the youth would like to take on a service project," I said as I opened my door.

"I think that's a swell idea." Blaire came around the back of the car.

We crossed the porch together and she fumbled in her bag for a key. Then rapped with the knocker two times. "That's to let them know it's me coming in. We decided it was best to keep the doors locked while I was at work. The nurses spend a lot of time upstairs with Elva and it would be hard to hear someone coming in down here."

"That's smart."

"Why don't you go on up and say hello to Elva and I'll start pulling out the food."

"I'll help you, Blaire."

"There's no need. I have it organized so I know where everything is. I'm sure Elva will be delighted to see you."

I went up the long carpeted stairway and turned to the right toward Elva's room. For a moment I thought I smelled the faint odor of tobacco. Surely the nurse wasn't smoking in Elva's room. I quickened my steps.

"Hello, ladies," I said as I entered the room. Nobody was smoking.

"Willa!" Elva was all smiles. "I'm so glad to see you. I have wonderful news."

"Oh?" I looked at her. I nodded to the nurse, whose name I didn't know.

"Dennis is coming to see me."

"That is good news."

The nurse stood. "I think I'll go get a glass of tea and let you two visit. Besides…" she looked at Elva and smiled "…I'm sick and tired of her beating me in gin rummy."

"She is kind of crafty," I said as the nurse left the room. I turned to Elva. I was delighted to see her in such a good mood. "So your nephew is coming."

"Yes. He didn't say when, but he said as soon as he could tie up some business he would be here. I hope he comes soon. I can't wait to see him."

"I'm sure he'll come as soon as he can."

"Here." Elva motioned to the chair beside her bed. "Sit beside me." I sat down and she went on. "Dennis told me how you had been keeping him informed about my condition. He also said that you thought his visit to me was a good idea."

"He asked, so I just told him what I thought."

"You're going to like Dennis, Willa." Her eyes sparkled as she said, "He's not married, you know. And you two are about the same age."

I laughed. "Now, don't you start matchmaking."

"I just think if he found a nice young woman here, he might come back to Liverpool to live."

"Maybe he will anyway." I smiled at her and changed the subject. "Elva, you look great today. Are you feeling better?"

"Oh, much better. Michelle, that's the nurse who is here today, got me up and I sat in a chair at the window for a while. It did me a world of good."

"That's wonderful. You'll be up and about before you know it."

There was a knock on the door downstairs and Elva said, "I wonder who that could be?"

"Probably Reverend Trent Freeman. He planned to come by and see you. He wanted to tell you about Penny's funeral."

She nodded. "Knowing her, I bet it was a hard one for him to preach."

I couldn't help smiling, but I said, "Elva, you don't mean that."

"I most certainly do."

About that time, Blaire ushered Trent into the room. As she turned to leave she said, "I'll call when dinner is on the table."

"Thank you," Trent and I said almost at the same time.

I started to get up to give Trent my seat beside the bed, but he said, "Sit still, Willa. I'll just pull up another chair if you don't mind me moving the furniture, Mrs. Kingfield?"

"I don't mind at all, young man."

It wasn't long until Trent and Elva fell into easy conversation. The more they talked, the more I felt my presence wasn't needed. Finally, I stood. "Since you two seem to be on each other's wave length, I think I'll go see what Blaire is getting ready for us all to eat."

"You go right along, dear. I don't mind entertaining this young man at all."

"And I'm delighted to be entertained by you," Trent said. He did turn and wink at me as I left.

When Blaire called everyone to dinner, the nurse came to make a plate for Elva.

"I wish she could come eat with us," Blaire said. "She so loves having people around her."

"I think it would be good for her, too," Michelle said. "But I'm not strong enough to get her down the steps. Maybe she can be brought down in the next few days."

"Well, I think I'm plenty strong enough," Trent said. "After all, she's just a wisp of a woman."

Before anyone could say anything else, Trent headed toward the entryway. I followed.

"Let me go with you. I know Elva. She'll want to make herself presentable."

And she did. It took about ten minutes, but I found her prettiest pink robe and brushed her hair. She put on a touch of lipstick, all the time protesting that this was too much trouble. Nobody listened to her and in a short time, Trent walked into the dining room with her in his arms. He seated her at the head of the table and we all took our seats.

Elva seemed to glow with excitement over the unexpected attention. Though she ate very little, we all knew she was having a wonderful time. Michelle said she didn't need to stay downstairs too long, so in a short time, Trent swooped her up and carried her back to her room.

After helping Blaire clean up, Trent insisted on driving me home so Blaire wouldn't have to go back out. I didn't mind this at all.

TWENTY-SIX

THE NEXT MORNING Philip called me at home. "Willa," he said. His voice sounded sad.

"Yes, Philip."

"I made the decision last night. I'm going to move Myra today."

"Is there anything I can do to help?"

"I thought it might be easier on her if you came to the house and sat with her while I pack some things. She always seems to respond to you and she gets agitated when she sees me doing something different."

"Of course, Philip. I'll be right over."

It only took me a few minutes to walk to the parsonage which was located a block from the church. Philip met me at the front door. "She's in the living room."

Myra was sitting on the yellow and blue striped sofa. She looked at me with a blank stare when I came into the room.

"Good morning, Myra," I said and smiled at her. "How are you feeling today?"

She kind of grinned at me, but didn't say anything. I looked at Philip and said, "Go about your work. Myra and I will sit here and have a nice chat."

I took a seat beside her on the sofa.

She was holding a rolled-up magazine in her hand.

"What have you got there?" I indicated the magazine.

She hugged it to her and muttered something that I didn't understand.

"I'm sure you enjoy looking at it, don't you?"

She began to relax her hands on the magazine and looked at me. "The dead man," she said.

"I see. Where is the dead man, Myra?"

She just looked at me and I was about to say something else when the doorbell rang. "I'll get it, Philip," I called.

"Thanks," his muffled voice said from somewhere upstairs.

I opened the door and Myrtle Johnson stood there with a tray in her hand. "Hello, Reverend Willa. I brought some food for Philip and Myra. I hope you're not here because something is wrong?"

"Oh, no. Come in, Myrtle. I'm just sitting here with Myra. Why don't you put the food in the kitchen and join us?"

"I'll do that."

When she came into the living room she sat across from us. "Now, what's going on?" She looked concerned, not nosy.

"Philip is going to take Myra to a place he's picked out today. I think she's going to like it," I said, hoping that Myrtle would catch on that I didn't want to talk about a rest home in front of Myra.

Myrtle did catch on. "I bet she will like it. There are some supernice places around." She looked at Myra. "How are you doing today?"

Myra nodded.

"She was showing me her magazine," I said.

"The dead man," Myra said. She began flipping through the catalog. In a minute she held it toward me and said, "See the dead man."

I looked at the mummy costume she pointed out to me and nodded. "Yes, it's a dead man," I said.

She nodded. "Yes, Willa knows about the dead man."

Myrtle changed the subject. "Myra, would you like some cookies? I know how much you like the peanut butter ones so I made some for you."

"Cookie. Yes."

We took her to the kitchen table and sat around it having cookies and some coffee that Philip had already made.

Every few minutes Myra would say, "These are good cookies."

Philip came to the kitchen door and paused. He was looking at his wife and I knew his heart must be breaking. She glanced up at him. He smiled and came into the room. "Myra," he said, "I'm going to take you to a place that I hope you will like. You can stay there for a while."

"Okay," she said and stood.

"Good morning, Myrtle," he said.

She nodded and stood. "Is there anything that I can do to help?"

"You've already done a lot and I appreciate it. Thanks for coming."

She went to the door. "I put a meal in the refrigerator." Before he could thank her again, she was out the door.

"Do you want me to come with you, Philip?" I asked.

"This is something I have to do alone, Willa, but I appreciate you offering." He took a deep breath. "Just keep things on an even keel at church if that is possible."

"I'll do my best."

It felt good to walk the block back to church in the cold crisp air. I prayed for Philip and Myra all the way. I silently vowed to help him get through this trying period in any way I could. I knew with his strong faith, he could do it. I also knew that it wasn't going to be easy for him.

I stayed busy all day. I didn't have to talk to many people and for this I was glad.

Blaire called and asked if I wanted to go to lunch, but I declined. For some reason I wanted to be alone. I had a quick chat with Trent in the afternoon. He understood my needing to be by myself. He didn't say anything about coming over and I didn't push.

I went home as soon as the office closed. Because she always cheers me up, I called my aunt Lila to see if she was home from Las Vegas. Her answering machine informed me she was on a bus tour with some friends and wouldn't be home until the week of Thanksgiving.

There was nothing special that I wanted to eat, so I opened a can of tuna and ate it with crackers. I watched a movie on Lifetime Television and then decided to take a hot bath and turn in early.

It took me a while to go to sleep because I couldn't help wondering how Myra was faring in her new surroundings and how lonely Philip was in his familiar ones without her.

TWENTY-SEVEN

THE NEXT MORNING I didn't get to church until almost nine-thirty. I had just hung up my purse when Gaylord Swanson called to tell me my car was ready. He even volunteered to bring it to me. I told him I could come and get it, but he insisted. "Justin is here," he said. "He'll follow me and bring me back to work."

Before I could protest, he hung up the phone. I was putting the receiver of my phone down when Philip knocked on my open door. "Come in," I said and motioned for him to take a seat.

He did and said, "I just wanted to tell you that I visited Myra this morning."

"How is she adjusting?"

"Better than I thought she would. She seemed glad to see me, but she said I couldn't stay long because she had to plan the dinner menu. For some reason, she thought the people in the home were her guests and she had to feed them."

"Probably because she was such a gracious hostess in the church for so many years."

He smiled. "That could be it. I didn't think of that."

"Do you mind if I visit her one day, Philip?"

"Of course not. I think she'd like that. She always liked you and you've helped me so much with her."

"The Swansons are bringing my car back today. Maybe I can get out to see her tomorrow or the next day."

He smiled again. "I'm changing the subject, but I wanted to ask you something else." I nodded and he went on. "They have services at the home on Sundays for the patients that want to attend. They asked if our church would hold a service between now and Christmas."

"Of course."

"I told them what a good speaker you are and that I thought the ladies—their patients are mostly female—would really enjoy hearing you." Before I could say anything, he went on. "Of course, I didn't volunteer you. I told them I'd do it if you couldn't."

"Thank you, Philip. I'd love to do it."

"Good." He stood and handed me a card. "This is the lady who arranges the activities. I told her that we would get in touch."

I took the card. "I'll call and set up a Sunday, then let you know so you won't put me on the program here that day."

"That sounds good."

"Excuse me, Willa." Anna came to the door. "Mr. Swanson is here with your car."

"Send him in, Anna."

As Gaylord came through the door he said, "I'm sorry. I didn't know you were busy. I don't want to interrupt."

"You're not. We've finished our business." He held out his hand. "It's good to see you again, Mr. Swanson."

"Good to see you, too, Reverend Gallaway."

Philip left and I nodded toward the chair that Philip had vacated. "I appreciate you getting my car fixed in such a short time, Gaylord."

"No problem, Willa. With Justin back, it isn't hard to keep up the work."

"I saw LeeAnn at the grocery store the other day. She was planning a meal for you folks and the Pooles. How did it go?"

His eyes lit up. "It was great. Those kids are so much in love it almost makes you sick to watch them." He laughed when he said it. "And to think that it almost didn't happen for them. If you hadn't…" His voice trailed off.

"But it did happen and now they are married and life is as it should be."

"Yep, it sure is. And you'll never guess what we're all going to do to celebrate."

"What's that?"

"We're going to go to Italy. It was the Pooles' idea, but when I saw the look in Portia's eyes, I knew I couldn't say no. I'm almost ashamed of myself for not taking her back home for all these years."

"Gaylord, that's wonderful."

"It's going to take some planning, but both families are going. You ought to go with us."

I laughed. "I'd love to, but on my salary, you'd have to give me at least ten years to save the money."

He smiled. "We were thinking the spring would be the best time. I don't guess that's enough time for you."

"Not hardly, but I think it's great that you're going. And I'm so glad the two families have become so close."

"It took a while, but the tragedy of the summer brought us all together." He chuckled. "Nevis has asked me to take on the fleet of cars at Danforth Industries and Rose is having Portia do some of her women things."

I couldn't help smiling at his choice of words, but I didn't comment. Instead I said, "I know this makes Justin and LeeAnn happy."

"It does. And the boys, Steve and Bently, have become good friends." He shook his head. "Never thought it'd happen."

"Why?" I thought I knew the answer, but I wanted to see if he thought the same thing.

"You know. They're the richest people in town and I'm a mechanic. Not to say that I don't do well by my family, but my job doesn't have the prestige as that of being a CEO of a large corporation. We've always traveled in different circles. I never dreamed that we'd all become such good friends."

"It just goes to show you that people are people, Gaylord.

Money or a prestigious job doesn't make one person any better than any other."

He stood. "You're right about that." He took my keys from his pocket. "I parked your car in front. I hope that is okay."

"I know it's fine, but you don't have to rush. I was enjoying our conversation."

"So was I, but I told Justin to buzz me when he got here to pick me up and my phone just vibrated. I'm sure it's him."

I stood and followed him to the door. "Please just send the bill to my home address. I'll…"

"What bill?"

"For my car, of course."

"Don't be silly, Willa. I'm not charging you for fixing your car after all you've done for us."

"That's not right, Gaylord. I want to pay my debts and I'm sure the parts were expensive."

"The parts are paid for and you've paid your debt to me many times over."

We reached the front of the church and I saw Justin getting out of a company truck. He waved to me and I waved back.

Before I could argue with Gaylord anymore, he opened the door and went outside. I followed.

"Gaylord…"

He went down the front steps and headed for the truck, ignoring me.

Though the truck was running, Justin came up the steps and gave me a hug. "I hope you like the way we fixed your car."

"I'm sure I will, but…"

He turned back around. "Gotta go. We've got a lot of work waiting. LeeAnn said you were coming to see us soon and I'm looking forward to it."

I couldn't answer because he'd already gotten into the truck and was backing out of the parking lot. Justin had parked my car on the other side of Anna's van, but I could see the front of it.

Shaking my head, I turned to go back inside, but stopped. There was something different about my car. Something very different. Yes, it was a white car, but something was wrong.

I went down the steps and around the van expecting to see my little white Cavalier. Instead, sitting where my car should be was a new white Chevrolet Cobalt.

Stunned, I opened the driver's door and the new-car smell hit me. There is no other smell in the world like it. The inside of the car was light blue. It was beautiful and I would love to have one like it, but there was no way I could afford one now. The Swansons had delivered the wrong car to me. I ran my hand over the nice upholstery and bit my lip to keep from breaking one of the Top Ten, as some of the teenagers referred to the Ten Commandments. I was certainly beginning to envy the person that was getting this car.

There was a manila envelope on the front seat with my name on it. I frowned as I opened it. The first thing I pulled out was the title to the car. It was made out to me. Attached to it with a red paper clip was a note. It said, *Dear Willa, the insurance company totaled out your car and we knew you needed one quickly. We hope you enjoy this one. Love from the Pooles and the Swansons.*

I went back to my office without telling anyone what had happened. I couldn't believe it myself. It was wonderful of them and I appreciated it more than they would ever know, but it was just too much. Though I wanted to, I couldn't accept this car.

I gathered my wits about me and spent the next hour on the telephone, first to Gaylord Swanson, and then to Nevis Poole. I was trying to refuse their generous gift. Neither would hear of me not taking the car. To say I was thrilled wasn't close to explaining the feelings that were running through me. I was thankful that God had seen fit to touch their hearts, but I still thought I was unworthy to receive such a wonderful gift.

Betty and Anna took turns coming outside to look at my

new car. They both assured me I should accept it and not try to give it back.

"If they hadn't wanted you to have it, Willa," Anna said, "they wouldn't have given it to you. Besides, they can afford it."

"And I bet they got something for your old car from the insurance company," Betty added.

"But not enough to pay for this car," I said.

Before either could answer, the cordless phone that Betty had brought outside rang. She put it to her ear and said, "Liverpool First United Methodist Church, this is Betty. How can I help you?"

"One moment, please." She turned to me. "It's for you, Willa. Do you want to take it on this phone?"

"I'll go to my desk. You might get another call." She nodded and I went inside ahead of them.

I sat behind my desk and punched line one. "This is Willa Hinshaw."

"Reverend Hinshaw?" the whiney voice said.

I couldn't tell if the caller was male or female. "Yes," I said.

"I know you have a new car, but I won't let that stop me. I'll see you again on Blue Bell Curve and next time I'll make sure you don't get out of the car alive."

TWENTY-EIGHT

WHEN I GOT HOME, I was still shaking. I knew I needed to report the call, but I didn't want to involve the police at this point. I decided I'd call Ed. He wasn't home so I left a message and then dialed the Swansons' phone. I still felt strange about accepting the generous gift and I was going to try once again to give the car back to him.

When Gaylord came on the phone I said, "I can't accept…"

He interrupted me. "Now, Willa, we've already been through this. I'm a busy man. If you only want to complain about the gift you're going to have to forget it. I want you to have it and that's that."

"But…"

"No buts. Just enjoy it and take care of yourself."

I didn't argue much longer because Gaylord wouldn't listen. I finally gave up and called Nevis Poole. I wanted to try one more time with him, but I got the same reaction as I did from Gaylord. He firmly told me if I didn't accept the gift he was going to come get it and give me a more expensive car. I hung up and slumped back in my green chair with a thankful heart. I accepted the fact that these wonderful people really did want me to have this car.

"God, thank You for giving me such wonderful friends," I said aloud and dialed the phone once again.

When there was an answer on the other end I said, "Trent, you're never going to believe what happened today."

"What has happened?" There was some concern in his voice.

I told him about the car and he was delighted for me. He even made me promise to come to take him for a ride soon. I promised him I would.

I was just about to dial Blaire's number when the phone rang. "Hello," I said.

"Reverend Willa, it's Tyrone," he said. "I wanted to let you know that Aunt Bernice may get to come home tomorrow."

"Tyrone, that's wonderful. It's an answer to our prayers."

"Yes, it is. And I feel like it was a sign for me, too."

"What do you mean?"

"You'll probably think I'm silly, but I promised God that if He'd make Aunt Bernice get well, I'd study whatever he wanted me to in school."

"I don't think you're silly, Tyrone."

"I kind of thought I was until I went to my mailbox today. Guess what was there."

"I have no idea."

"I had a note from a friend back home. She said that she knew how much I loved architecture so she sent me a subscription to a new magazine that is coming out. I loved all the drawings in it."

"It does seem that you're getting a sign."

"That's what I thought. I can't help saying, I was thrilled for both reasons."

"I'm sure you are." His enthusiasm was rubbing off on me. "I'm happy for you. And I'm truly thankful for the good news about Bernice. I have a car now and I'll be over to see her tomorrow."

We talked a little longer, then hung up. I was beginning to get hungry after this conversation, so I decided to fix a bite of supper before I called Mom and Dad to tell them my good news. I ate a ham and cheese sandwich and a bag of potato chips.

When I got back on the phone, I called not only my parents, but I also called Blaire. By the time I got off the phone with her, it was time to do my Bible study and go to bed. Ed still hadn't returned my call and I decided I'd talk with him later.

The next morning I checked in the office and found Philip at his desk. I knocked on his open door.

"Good morning, Willa." He shook his finger at me. "When are you going to start taking care of yourself? Today is your day off, you know."

"I'm not going to work long." I changed the subject. "You left yesterday before I got my car. Did you hear what Nevis Poole and Gaylord Swanson did?"

"Betty told me first thing. Congratulations. You deserve it."

"That's just it, Philip. I don't deserve it at all, but I do appreciate it."

He smiled. "There are some good people in this town, aren't there?"

"Absolutely. I'm so glad I came to Liverpool. After living in Charlotte, I wasn't sure I'd be happy in a small town, but I really do love it here."

"I'm glad. I hope you'll be here a long, long time."

I changed the subject. "I know you've been to see Myra again. How's she adjusting, Philip?"

"She seems to be settling down. It hasn't been easy, but I guess that was to be expected. When I was there last night she said she was tired of that hotel and wanted me to take her home. Of course, ten minutes later she was staring at the television and ignoring me."

"I'm sorry."

He nodded his head. "I know you are, Willa. Everyone here has been very supportive. I don't know what I'd have done without our staff and the people in this church."

"You know we're always here for you." I smiled at him. "By the way, Tyrone called me last night. It seems that his aunt is getting much better. I'm going to see her in a little while. She may get to come home today."

"That's wonderful. I've been dropping in and saying a prayer for her whenever I make hospital visits."

"I haven't talked with Elva yet, but I know she'll be delighted." I backed toward the hallway. "I'll probably leave here about ten, unless you think I'll be needed for something."

"Things look pretty clear this morning. I'm going to meet with the pastoral committee. We're meeting at Reverend Nifong's church so if you need me, just call my cell."

"I'll do that."

I went into my office and finished a bit of paperwork. At exactly ten, I stood up and stretched. I was just about to go out the door when the phone buzzed.

It was Ed. "Sorry I didn't get to call you back last night, Willa. I was at my sister's house in High Point until late. I didn't want to disturb you."

"No problem, Ed. I just wanted to tell you about a phone call I had." I explained about the car and how I'd immediately gotten the call.

After saying he'd see what he could do, he warned me about being careful on the road alone at night. I didn't bring up the fact that the first wreck happened in the daylight hours. I just promised him I would be careful. I intended to keep that promise.

I left after our conversation and went to the hospital. I found Bernice sitting in a lounge chair by the window. She smiled broadly as I came in.

"It's great to see you looking so well, Bernice," I said.

She reached for my hand as I sat in a pull-up chair in front of her. "It's because of the prayers of wonderful people like you, Reverend Willa."

"Yes. I believe that, too." I smiled back at her. "How are you really feeling today?"

"I'm much better. At first they thought I could go today, but I had a little fever last night. I'm going home soon, though."

"I'm sorry you can't go today. Tyrone told me that you might get to go."

She smiled again. "He said you and he are friends now."

"That's right. He's a nice young man."

She nodded. "He is a good boy. The whole family is really proud of him. Did you know he's the first one in our family to go to college?"

"I didn't know, but I think that's wonderful."

"I want to thank you for coming to see me so regularly. It's meant a lot to me, Reverend."

"It was my pleasure, Bernice. I'm pleased that you've done so well. Now I hope they catch the person who did this to you."

"I wish I could help the police more. It all happened so fast. I was getting ready to come to the hospital to see Ms. Elva and whoever it was snuck up behind me and I didn't see or hear a thing until I woke up here."

"It's too bad you have no idea who it was that attacked you."

She reached over and took my hand again. "I'm just glad you came by when you did. They told me you were the one who called the ambulance. If you hadn't come when you did I would probably have bled to death. You saved my life."

"I'm glad I came by, too." I patted her hand. "The good Lord knows when to put us in the right place at the right time."

"You can say that again."

I didn't answer because a nurse came in to put Bernice back into the bed. I said a quick goodbye and left with a promise to see her again soon.

Since I had to go by Blue Bell Road to get back to town, I decided to drop by and see Elva. I took a deep breath as I rounded the curve and let it out when I came out safely on the other side.

"I hope I won't always be afraid to drive on this road," I said aloud. "Please, God, help me get over my fear of this curve." I felt better after the short prayer.

There was a green car in Elva's driveway that I didn't

recognize. Wondering who it was, I parked to the side of it and went up the front steps. A woman in her early thirties opened the door when I knocked.

"Hi," I said. "I'm Willa Hinshaw. A friend of Elva's."

"I'm Maggie Thorton. I'm with Daily Maids For You. The service sent me over to clean house for Mrs. Kingfield. Come on in."

"Thank you." I stepped inside and saw another woman dusting the handrail on the stairs.

"That's Ginny Lafaver. She's my helper."

I nodded at the lady on the stairway and said, "I'll just go up to see Mrs. Kingfield now."

"Sure," Maggie Thorton said. Ginny Lafaver didn't speak.

When I got to the room I saw the nurse, Michelle, working on Elva's hands. "Hello," I said. "What are you two up to?"

"Hello, dear Willa," Elva said with a big smile on her face. "Michelle is making me pretty. She's polishing my nails now and we're going to do my hair next. Dennis called me today and he's coming to see me soon. I want to look my best when he gets here."

The nurse smiled. "I thought her nails could use a little pampering." She held up Elva's hand. "What do you think of this color?"

I looked at the pale pink polish she was brushing on the nails and smiled. "I think it's perfect. Pink is Elva's color." I sat down in a chair on the other side of the bed. "When did Dennis say he was coming?" I looked at my happy friend.

"Soon." She almost giggled. "I think he'll probably try to surprise me this weekend."

"Good. I'm looking forward to meeting him."

"He's anxious to meet you, too. I've told him what a wonderful person you are."

"Oh, my. I hope you haven't painted too rosy a picture of me. I can get my dander up now and again."

"Oh, pooh. I can't imagine you upset with anyone."

"You just haven't seen me when I do get upset." I then changed the subject by telling Elva about the wonderful gift I'd received from the Pooles and the Swansons.

She was happy for me, but more happy when I reported on the progress that Bernice had made. "I think she'll be coming home soon," I said.

"I'm thrilled. Will she need a nurse? Should I make arrangements?"

"I don't see why I can't handle two patients," Michelle said with a laugh. "When I worked in the hospital I had as many as ten at one time, and I bet Miss Eaton will feel the same way."

"You wouldn't mind taking care of two frail women?" Elva looked at her.

"If this Bernice is as nice as you, I'll have no problem at all looking after the two of you."

"I think that's a great idea," I said.

"Then it's settled. We'll work it out with the others." Elva closed her eyes.

"Are you tired?" I asked.

"Maybe a little. It's just all the excitement. A lot of good things are happening right now. I'm a happy old lady."

"Don't you dare call yourself old," I scolded in a friendly voice. "I know women in their forties who are older than you are."

"See why I love this girl?" Elva looked at the nurse.

"I do see."

I stood. "Before you make my head swell any larger, I'm going to run. I just wanted to tell you about Bernice and I'm very glad I found out that Dennis was coming soon."

We said goodbyes and I headed back to the office. I'd gotten only a short distance from Elva's house when my cell phone rang. I answered it, though I didn't relish being on the phone as I approached Blue Bell Curve.

After my greeting, the raspy voice I was becoming familiar with said, "I know you'll soon be at our meeting spot. Better watch that curve." The phone went dead.

TWENTY-NINE

MY HAND SHOOK AS I put the phone down on the passenger seat. "How could he know I was headed for the curve?" I asked aloud. "Nobody knew I was going to Elva's house."

The curve was just ahead. "Please, God. Help me," I said and drove as cautiously as I could. In a few seconds I was on the other side of the curve and the road had straightened. Nothing out of the ordinary happened.

He probably knew I'd left the church and figured I was coming out here. Maybe it's a coincidence that he called just as I approached Blue Bell Curve, I thought.

"Thank You, God, for Your protection," I said aloud and then added, "Please help me get over this fear."

I had regained my composure and was almost back to the church when the phone rang again. I hesitated, but did pick it up. I was afraid it was something I needed to take care of. Before I greeted the caller, I glanced at the screen. It said "unknown caller." I took a deep breath and answered it.

"Well, I guess you got around the curve without incident this time. Don't get too brave though. There'll be another time."

"Who is this?" I demanded.

The phone went dead before I got all the words out. I tossed it back into the seat and vowed silently that I wasn't going to answer it if it rang again.

When I got back to the church, Anna handed me several notes from her pink message pad. "These came in while you were gone. One guy seemed anxious to talk with you. I think he was Mrs. Kingfield's nephew."

"Thanks. I'll return the calls now," I said and went into my office.

I was going to call Ed and tell him about the threats, but I decided the other calls should come first.

I recognized Dennis Kingfield's cell number and wondered why he hadn't used his home phone. I didn't have to wonder long. "Hello, Reverend Willa," he said, then chuckled. "I hope you don't mind me calling you that. Aunt Elva always refers to you by your first name and I guess I just think of you as Reverend Willa."

"I don't mind at all. A lot of people address me that way." I changed the subject. "Did you need me for some reason?"

"Not really. I just wanted to let you know that I'm at the airport. I'm leaving Atlanta in a little while and should be in Greensboro shortly. Of course, the flight has been delayed, but I hope to get out of here in the next hour or two. It's only a short flight when we get in the air. So once we take off it will be no time until I land in Greensboro."

"I visited Elva today and she said you were coming soon. She'll be so excited. Shall I tell her you're on your way?"

"I'd rather surprise her unless you think she should be forewarned."

"I think she'd like the surprise." Again I decided the polite thing to do was offer to pick him up at the airport.

He graciously declined. "It's not that I don't want to meet you as soon as possible, but I think I'll need a car. And as I think I told you earlier, I don't care to drive that big boat of Aunt Elva's."

"I do understand."

"The reason I called was to ask if you'd be at Aunt Elva's house when I arrive. I just want to be sure that the surprise isn't too much for her. She tells me how much your presence always calms her down."

I couldn't help thinking that he was a very thoughtful man. "That's very nice of you, Mr. Kingfield. I'd be happy to be there."

"Why don't you call me Dennis? That way we will have the formalities out of the way and we can concentrate on making Aunt Elva feel better."

"I'd like that."

"I'll give you a call when I land in Greensboro. I'm not sure how far the church is from Aunt Elva's house. Will that give you enough time to get there?"

"Oh, yes. Plenty of time. I look forward to meeting you."

"The same here."

We hung up and I couldn't help wondering what Dennis Kingfield looked like. And I still couldn't figure out why Bernice didn't trust him. Maybe I'd know after I met him tonight.

The next call I made was to Trent. He wanted to catch a movie, but I had to decline. "Maybe one night next week," I suggested.

"I'll clear my schedule," he said. "I don't like not seeing you every few days. At least let's get a quick dinner tomorrow night."

"That sounds good because I miss you, too," I almost whispered.

The other calls were church related. Though I didn't like doing it, I had to call a couple of members and tell them the seats for the senior trip to Biltmore House and Gardens were filled, but that I would put them on the waiting list. I then added up how much Sunday-school literature we would need for the coming quarter. It took almost two hours but I finished my list and then placed the order to Cokesbury by phone. I just hung up when the phone rang again.

"Reverend Willa, it's Dennis. I'm at the rent-a-car counter. As soon as I get it rented, I'll be on my way."

"I'll meet you there."

It was time to go home for the day, so I locked my office and said good night to Anna and Betty. Philip was still gone.

I don't know why, but as I drove the few miles to Elva's house, I began to feel a little excited. Though I couldn't explain it, I knew it was because I was going to meet Dennis Kingfield.

THIRTY

I WAITED FOR DENNIS KINGFIELD in the parlor of Elva's house. When he walked in, I was a little surprised at his appearance. He was nothing like I expected. I don't know why I had thought he would be the wimpy computer geek type. Instead he was tall and well built. In fact, he had almost the same physique as Trent. That was where the resemblance ended. Where Trent had dark hair, Dennis had dusty blond. His eyes were a deep brown and his tan gave him the look of a surfer or a lifeguard. I'm sure he had caused many female hearts to beat faster upon meeting him. I knew if Trent didn't already have an unspoken claim on me, mine probably would have been one of them.

"So." He smiled at me. "You're the famous Reverend Willa?"

"Yes, I'm Willa," I said with a chuckle. "I'm not so sure about the famous part."

"Well, according to Aunt Elva, you're more important than any famous person could be. You're at the top of her list."

"Not the top, let me assure you. That spot is reserved for you, her favorite nephew."

"Then, shall we agree that Aunt Elva has good taste?"

"Let's do." I nodded at him and added, "Shall we go upstairs now? I'm sure she'll pout if she knows you're here and didn't rush to her room right away."

He followed me up the winding stairs and down the hall to Elva's room. He paused just before we got to the door. "Why don't you go in first?"

I stuck my head in the door. Elva was propped up in bed

watching the evening news on the television that sat on her dresser. The nurse was sitting beside the bed. "Good evening, ladies," I said.

"Reverend Willa," Elva exclaimed. "It's good to see you. Come in." She clicked off the TV with the remote she held in her hand."

"Hello, Reverend." Miss Eaton stood. "Come on in and visit. It's time for me to get Mrs. Kingfield's dinner prepared."

"Thank you." I entered the room. "Elva," I said to her, "I have brought someone with me whom you'll want to see."

"And just who might that be?" She sat straighter.

Dennis entered the room. "It's me, Aunt Elva. Surprise."

She clapped her hands and her face lit up. "Oh, Dennis. My Dennis. It's so wonderful to see you." She held out her arms. "Come here, my boy."

He hurried to the side of her bed and they wrapped their arms around each other. "You look wonderful, Aunt Elva. They must be taking good care of you."

"They are, but seeing you makes me feel so much better."

He hugged her close to him. "I've been so worried about you. I'm sorry I was at the other end of the country when you became ill. You know I would have been here sooner if I could."

"I know that. I'm just glad you're here now." She began to cry.

"I hope those are happy tears," he teased. "I don't want you getting upset now."

"They are happy tears. I've looked so forward to seeing you."

"I was afraid if I popped in on you, it would upset you so I brought Reverend Willa with me as a buffer."

"Willa is always welcome here, Dennis. Isn't she a jewel?"

"I just met her a little while ago, but from our phone conversations, I tend to agree."

"You two flatter me," I said and began to back out of the room. "While you have a reunion, I think I'll go down and help the nurse."

"We don't mind if you stay, Reverend Willa," Dennis said and looked at his aunt. "Do we, auntie?"

"Of course not."

"I'll be back. You two need to have some time alone together." Before either of them could protest, I left the room and went downstairs.

My feet were almost dancing as I went into the kitchen. "Well, Miss Eaton, I don't think any medicine we have could do your patient any more good than this visit from her nephew. She was so excited about his visit that she had Michelle polish her nails and fix her hair so she'd be ready for him."

She smiled at me and said, "I'm glad Michelle is the other day nurse. She's very good with the elderly patients. And I agree with you, Reverend. Mrs. Kingfield sure does love that boy."

"And he cares about her. He's been so good about calling and checking on her."

Miss Eaton was stirring in a pot. "She told me he was like a son to her."

"I'm so glad she has him." I looked around. "Is there something I can help you do to get dinner ready?"

"It's ready, I just thought I'd give them a little time to visit before dishing it up. Blaire will be here soon. Why don't you have dinner with her? There's plenty. The women from the church keep bringing in food."

"We have a good bunch of women at our church. They are very thoughtful when there is an illness."

"They sure have been good to Mrs. Kingfield."

We fell into general conversation and I learned that Miss Eaton had given up on church several years ago because of the lack of support from her church when her son was caught in a robbery and sent to prison. "Seeing your congregation makes me wonder if I gave up too soon," she said.

"We'd love to have you visit First United Methodist anytime you decide to give it another chance," I said. I didn't want her to think I was pressuring her.

"I might just do that, Reverend Willa."

The back door opened and Blaire came into the kitchen. "Hello, Miss Eaton." She then turned to me. "Is that your new car out there?" she demanded.

"It is," I said with a smile. "Like it?"

"Love it. I bet you do, too."

"Yes, I do."

"Who's driving the green one?"

I told her about Dennis's arrival. When we continued to talk, Miss Eaton said, "I think I'll go see if Miss Elva is ready to eat. She may want to come to the table like she did the other night." She turned at the door. "I invited Reverend Willa to stay, Blaire. I hope you don't mind."

"Of course not." She turned to me. "You are staying, aren't you?"

I did stay and Elva did come down to dinner. As Trent had done, Dennis carried her to the table. We had a good time talking and laughing. Elva told stories about Dennis as a small child and how she and he had always had a special bond. By the time she had to go back to her room I could tell that Blaire was enamored with the handsome man. I thought this was a good sign that her broken heart was beginning to mend.

I left shortly after dinner, and though my heart was pounding, I had no calls on the way home. Neither did I have an incident as I drove around Blue Bell Curve.

THIRTY-ONE

SATURDAY I WAS ABLE TO get my apartment clean and things ready for Sunday morning. Since it isn't a good night for ministers to go out because of preparing for Sunday, Trent and I had our quick dinner at Knife and Fork Café and said good night by nine-thirty.

Sunday was a good day at church and Monday was uneventful. On Tuesday Bernice came home, but I was tied up with the ladies' conference meeting and I didn't get out to see her until the next morning. I found her in her room, propped up on two huge white pillows with heavy lace trim on the cases. She was wearing a blue bed jacket with white lace around the neck and her hair had been styled and pulled into a bun on the top of her head. She wore a touch of makeup and her eyes shone.

"Reverend Willa," she said with a lilt in her voice as she turned off the television that was playing on the table at the foot of her bed. "It's so good to see you."

"It's good to see you looking so wonderful. How are you feeling?"

"I'm really doing good. I was a little tired when I got home yesterday, but a good night's sleep in my own bed made all the difference in the world."

"I can see that."

"Ms. Elva has seen to it that I've been pampered and looked after just as good as they're looking after her." She leaned toward me and whispered, "And to my surprise, so has Dennis."

"Oh?"

"He's treated me like a queen. He said that I was not to turn my hand around here until I was completely well. He even hired a maid and a cook to come in and look after the house and the food. He said the nurse had her hands full with her two patients and needed to concentrate on us." She shook her head. "Maybe I was wrong about him. Knowing Ms. Elva, she probably told him not to pay back the money he borrowed. It wouldn't surprise me if she did."

"She might have. He certainly seems to care about his aunt. He has been very attentive to check on her."

"She told me. He puts her in a wheelchair and brings her to my room a couple of times a day so we can catch up on all that's been going on. I guess I'm going to have to change my mind about that boy."

I nodded and changed the subject. "Has Tyrone been to see you?"

"He was here last night. He and Dennis seemed to hit it off. He said they uncovered Mr. Kingfield's old pool table in the recreation room and played a couple of games."

"I didn't even know there was a recreation room."

"Yes. It's behind the library."

"I was in the library once." I shook my head. "This sure is a big house."

"Yes, it is." Her eyes twinkled. "It's nice to see it come alive again like it was years ago."

"What do you mean?"

"When Mr. Kingfield was here, there was something going on all the time. Besides me there was another maid and a gardener and we all stayed busy. Mrs. Elva was always having people in for tea or bridge or something and Dennis stayed here and played with the Kingfields' grandson a lot. The yard often became full of their school friends playing ball or just horsing around."

"It sounds like those were good times."

"They were, but it all changed when their grandson was killed. They both became kind of quiet and didn't have a lot of company. Then when Mr. Kingfield died, she seemed to give up. Dennis was the only one who could make her smile." She laughed out loud. "Then you came along and things began to change again. I hope it never goes back to the way it was before you came into our lives."

"Thanks, Bernice. But you give me too much credit." I changed the subject back to Elva's family. "I knew she lost a son in war, but she had never told me that she lost a grandson."

"Oh, little Billy was the light of her life. He was just like his father and Ms. Elva loved him dearly. They even stayed close when his family up and moved to Oregon. When he went into the army, Ms. Elva worried day and night. Then when he was killed, she was devastated. Since then, she focused the love she had left on Dennis."

"Well, I'm glad she has him."

"I'm beginning to be glad about it, too."

Miss Eaton came into the room. "Ms. Bernice, it's time for your medicine." She smiled at me. "I'm sorry to interrupt, but the doctor said it had to be given at the same time every day, Reverend Willa."

"No problem. I've got to get on to the hospital. One of our members is there with a heart problem and I want to visit him." I stood. "Again, welcome home, Bernice, and I'll see you soon."

"Thanks for coming, Reverend Willa. It's always good seeing you."

I made the hospital visit and went back to church. As I was going in, I was almost knocked down by Philip running out the door.

"Sorry, Willa. There's a problem with Myra. I have to rush over there."

"I'm sorry. Want me to come with you?"

"No. You take care of things here and I'll talk to you when I get back."

My telling him to be careful was drowned out in the sound of the motor of his Buick as he wheeled out of the driveway.

"What's going on, Betty?" I asked as I went by the reception desk.

"The home called and said that Myra was upset about a dead man looking in her window. I have no idea what really happened."

"Oh, my. Since Philip had her settled there, I hoped she would forget all about the dead man."

"Me, too, but I guess she got it on her mind again. It's strange how the mind of an Alzheimer's patient works, isn't it?"

"Yes, it is," I said and went on to my office.

The rest of the day was uneventful, as was the rest of the week, until Friday. My date with Trent was wonderful. We went to The Chop House in Winston-Salem for dinner and then took in a play at the Little Theater. It was late when we got to my apartment, but he came in and had coffee before going home. It was getting harder and harder to say good night to him, and let him leave. It felt so right when he held me in his arms and kissed me. I was at the point that I never wanted it to end.

I spent most of Saturday at Oak Hollow Mall in High Point with Blaire. We were looking for a few clothes to fill in our winter wardrobes. We ate dinner at Austin's and I was home by eight. I had plenty of time to do my studying for the following day.

On Sunday I did the children's sermon at the eleven-o'clock service and we had a guest speaker from the conference. I was interesting, but in my opinion not as inspiring as Philip's messages. Of course, I'm prejudiced, I know. I dearly love to hear my boss preach.

For lunch I had been invited to the Johnson farm. I was delighted because I love Mabel Johnson's cooking. She didn't disappoint me. We had baked ham, sweet-potato casserole, green beans with corn, potato salad and all kinds of what she called "pick-ups"—sliced tomatoes, cucumbers, three kinds of pickles, cantaloupe, radishes, onions, sweet peppers and celery. She had made yeast rolls and we had three desserts: chocolate cake, lemon pie and blueberry cobbler. I ate until I felt like an overstuffed toy.

Because it was drizzling a cold rain, I played board games with the grandchildren and chatted with the family in the den. Mabel wouldn't hear of me helping clean up the kitchen.

At four I left with a sack of leftovers and another sack full of fall apples and a pumpkin. I knew I was set with good food for the next couple of days if Trent didn't come over and help me eat it up—which I secretly hoped he would do. And on Monday night, he was there just as I expected him to be when I told him what I had to eat. We were in the middle of the meal when the phone rang.

Before I could say anything but hello, Blaire blurted, "Willa, Elva's had a seizure. Miss Eaton came downstairs to get her dinner and when she went back, Elva was having a relapse. I called the doctor then called you because she wanted me to."

"Is Dennis there?"

"No. He's been out this afternoon. I don't know where."

"I'll be right there."

Of course, Trent went with me. He waited in the hall with everyone else when we arrived. "The doctor said to send you right in as soon as you got here," Blaire said.

Elva reached for my hand the minute I entered. She seemed to be calming down, but I wasn't sure. The doctor nodded at me when I asked if she was going to be okay.

"I saw him again, Willa," Elva said. "He came into my room and stood at the foot of my bed and sang the second verse of 'Blessed Assurance' to me. I tried to scream, but he put his finger to his lips and shushed me. I was too stunned to say anything for a minute. When I did call out, he turned and went out into the hall." She lay back on the pillow. "Miss

Eaton and Blaire swear they didn't see or hear anything except my calling them."

"What about Bernice?"

"I don't know. You'll have to ask her." Her voice was becoming slurred.

I looked at the doctor.

"I gave her a shot to help her relax. She'll be asleep in a matter of minutes."

She was.

The doctor walked me to the door. "I think sleep is the best thing for her now," he said.

"Will she have to go to the hospital?"

"I think she'll be better at home this time. Her heart is doing fine and that is my main concern." He shook his head. "If these episodes don't stop, I'm afraid of what might happen."

"What do you mean?"

"Her heart won't continue to stay strong. It is old, as you know, and it is possible for someone to be frightened to death."

"Then maybe the hospital…"

He stopped me. "She made me promise not to send her. She said she wanted to stay here with her nephew and you."

I nodded. I knew she wouldn't want to leave Dennis. I wished he was here now.

As if an answer to my prayer, he came up the stairs. "What's happening?" he asked. I knew by his eyes he was really frightened.

As they were explaining the event to him, I went down the hall and looked in on Bernice. She was asleep. I was sure she hadn't heard anything or she would never have dozed off. I closed her door and turned back.

Trent was behind me. "If you want to stay here a while, Willa," he said, "Dennis and Blaire both volunteered to drive you home later." He shook his head. "I would stay with you but I have a deacon's meeting tonight."

"You don't need to wait for me, Trent. I'll get a ride home

I do feel I need to stay around a while. Elva might wake up and want to talk with me again."

He left and everyone except Miss Eaton moved to the parlor on the first floor. I was seated on a chair and was getting the details of exactly what had happened from Blaire. Dennis was on the sofa and I glanced at him. He smiled and I found myself comparing his charming good looks to those of Trent. I think my conscience was clear when I decided that Trent was the winner.

I glanced away from him and my eyes landed on the picture above the sofa. My heart almost jumped out of my throat. It was the original painting that I saw the first time I was in the house. I stared at it and wondered how long it had been back in its place, but I didn't think that now was the time to bring it up.

After the gathering decided they were going to go into the kitchen and have dinner, I explained that I had already eaten. I said I was going to check on Elva and asked if Blaire or Dennis would drive me home after the meal.

"I'll be happy to take you. In fact, I'll go up with you and check on Aunt Elva and then we'll go before I eat. I had a late lunch in town and I don't mind at all waiting until I get back to eat."

We went up the stairs together. Elva's door was ajar. Miss Eaton looked up when Dennis pushed it open. She smiled, put her magazine down and came to the door. "She seems to be resting well," she whispered.

"Please call me if she wants me to come back," I said. "And of course you know to call if there is any change."

"I sure do, Reverend Willa."

"I'm going to drive Willa home, but I'll be back in a little while. You have my cell number if you need me," he said.

She nodded and we turned to go down, but I saw something out of place on the floor beside the storage-room door. "Wait a minute, Dennis," I said. I walked over to the door and picked up a tattered piece of cloth. "Look at this. I wonder what it is and, more than that, I wonder what it is doing here."

He took it. "I have no idea, but I don't think it's something that belongs here. I'll have to speak to one of the maids about it."

"Yes, do. It could be a piece of one of their cleaning cloths, but I did find a similar one in the yard a short time ago."

He nodded. "We'll get to the bottom of it. I'll leave it in the entry hall so I won't forget about it."

"That's a good idea."

Everyone was in the kitchen when we reached the entry. I left without saying goodbye because I didn't want to disturb their meal.

We were just entering Blue Bell Curve when Dennis said, "I wish they would straighten this road. There have been a lot of accidents on this curve."

"I was told that I actually had one here myself."

"Really, what happened?"

I told him.

He shook his head. "I can't imagine why anyone would want to harm you, Willa. I find that you are nothing but helpful and kind."

I smiled at him. "Thank you."

He took a deep breath. "I would like to ask a favor of you, if it isn't too much."

"I'll try to help out. What do you need?"

"It's really very simple. Of course Blaire will be at work and the maids are off tomorrow. Miss Eaton has her hands full with both Aunt Elva and Bernice and I have to take care of some business for Aunt Elva in the morning. After what happened today, I don't want to leave her alone with only the nurse there. I was hoping you could come out and spend an hour or so with her while I'm gone."

"I don't see why not. Philip has the hospital visits and I was planning to take a little time off anyway. Unless something unforeseen comes up, I'd to happy to visit with Elva and Bernice."

"Thank you so much. That is a big load off my mind."

Dennis walked me to the door and shook my hand. He said, "I know I'm repeating myself, but thank you. You have been a wonderful friend to Aunt Elva."

"I really care for her, Dennis. She is a delightful woman."

He smiled and waited until I unlocked the door and went inside. I heard his footsteps going down the metal stairs. I relocked the door and went into the kitchen. Trent and I had left a mess. I immediately began to clean it up. I knew if I didn't I'd sit down and leave it until the morning.

THIRTY-TWO

It RAINED AGAIN THE NEXT DAY and turned several degrees colder. I called the church office and Anna said that nothing special was happening. I told her where to find me if she needed me and dressed in a turquoise velour warm-up suit. I wished I'd added a top coat when I went down the steps to my car, but I decided not to turn back. It wouldn't take my new Cobalt long to warm up once I turned on the heater.

Dennis was in his aunt's room when I arrived at the house. He said that Miss Eaton was attending Bernice. I nodded and Elva said, "I hear that you're going to babysit me this morning."

"I wouldn't exactly call it that," I said with a laugh.

"Dennis has some things to do for me and he told me he'd recruited you to stay here. I would have put up a fuss had it been anyone but you. He said that was why he asked you. He knew I wouldn't refuse your company."

"I would have come out to visit you today anyway," I said.

"Well, it looks like you're in good hands, Aunt Elva. I'll take my leave now." He stood. "I won't be gone too long, Reverend Willa," he said to me.

"Don't rush. We'll enjoy our visit together. I might find out things about you that you'd rather I didn't know."

He shook his head. "I was afraid of that."

Elva waved at him and he backed out the door.

We spent some time going over what had happened in her room the night before. She insisted that her dead husband had come into her room and stood at the foot of her bed singing the second verse of his favorite hymn, "Blessed Assurance."

When I asked her why the second verse, she told me that he loved the idea of angels bringing echoes of mercy and whispers of love because that was something we all needed. I was beginning to wonder if there was more to her imaginary visitor than we first thought. Elva was convinced that her dead husband was visiting her. I knew that was impossible, but I did wonder if someone was playing mean tricks on her. But who?

I wondered if I should ask Dennis if he'd had a chance to talk to the maids about the rag I found in the hall. Then I remembered it was their day off. It would be tomorrow before he could talk with them. I also knew I wanted to ask Elva or someone about the painting over the sofa, but I didn't think it was yet the time to mention it. Elva was not going downstairs that often and Dennis hadn't been in the house long enough to know anything. I wasn't sure who I needed to discuss this incident with, but I knew it was best to say nothing at this time.

Shortly after eleven, Elva said she was getting a little hungry. I said I would fetch Miss Eaton and see if we could get an early lunch. When I found her in Bernice's room, she said she would make plates for all of us. "I'll get Mrs. Kingfield in the wheelchair and we'll all eat in Bernice's room."

"I think they would like that."

When I told Elva, she was delighted. "I'll go down and help Miss Eaton with the plates. Then we'll wheel you over."

"While you're helping her, I'll watch a little TV."

"Sounds good. I'll close your door because Bernice has her TV on, too. Though her door is closed, I don't want the sounds fighting each other. You may be watching different channels."

I closed her door and started down the hall. I didn't get very far. An arm came around from behind me and a hand clamped over my mouth. My heart raced as I struggled, but the attacker was stronger than me. I felt myself being pulled backward. In a matter of seconds, I caught a glimpse of the doorjamb and knew I was being pulled into the storage closet. It was so dark, I couldn't see a thing. I couldn't help wondering if these were going to be my last minutes on earth.

I then felt tape being slapped across my mouth. I could hardly breathe, and I certainly couldn't cry out. Next a blindfold was put on my eyes and I heard a light switch click on. Still trying to struggle, I expected to be dumped in the closet. Instead I was being pulled farther down a hallway. My mind raced with my heart. Maybe I was wrong about the storage closet. Maybe I am being taken to one of the many rooms on the second floor of this old mansion. Or, heaven forbid, I was in some secret passage that no one knew existed.

It seemed an eternity until I was pushed down on some sort of small bed. I reached to take off my blindfold, but I didn't get to it. My hands were grabbed and forced behind my back. In an instant I felt a rope around my wrists. Then my legs were pulled onto the bed and my feet were bound. There was no escaping now.

Some distance away I heard some whispering. I couldn't understand what was being said. Neither could I understand if the voices were male or female.

Again fear gripped me, but I knew I had to stay calm and try to find out what was happening. Once more the thought crossed my mind that I might not get out of this situation alive. I began to pray.

THIRTY-THREE

THE VOICES CEASED AND I heard a door creak. Then there was silence. I don't know how much time passed as I lay on this uncomfortable bed. I prayed until I could think of nothing else to say. I simply opened my heart to my Lord and asked Him to be with me and know my thoughts.

Sometime later, I must have dozed off because I woke up and didn't know where I was for a few seconds. There was a murmer of voices, but I knew they weren't in the room with me. They seemed to be coming from the wall. I tried to make out what they were saying, but it was only a steady muffled hum.

Hours must have passed, because eventually I dozed off again. This time I was awakened by the squeaking of the door. I tried to sit up as I heard someone approaching me.

"I'm going to take the tape off your mouth so you can eat this sandwich I brought you," a female voice said. "Let me warn you that if you scream, I have a ball bat. If you make a sound, I'll bash your head in with it. I wouldn't mind doing that anyway. I don't like you."

I could tell from the harshness in her voice and the way she ripped the tape from my mouth that she was telling the truth. I kept quiet.

"Now I'm going to untie your hands. The threat still stands."

When my hands were free she pulled me into a sitting position and thrust a sandwich into my left hand. "You better eat. It will probably be a long time before you get something else."

Though I was more frightened than hungry, I did as she commanded.

"Here," she said again and put something in my right hand. "You can wash it down with this."

The drink was some lemon-lime concoction, something I had never liked. I didn't dare say so though.

The sandwich wasn't bad. It was ham and cheese on rye bread. I finished it and mumbled, "I need to go to the bathroom."

"I figured as much." She untied my feet, took hold of my shoulder and pulled me upward. "Come with me."

I was surprised that there was a bathroom in this area. I wondered again if I was being held in one of the upstairs bedrooms. Maybe one of the smaller ones that had been used previously as a nursery or a maid's room.

We returned and she roughly pushed me down on the bed. I tried to engage her in conversation. "Why are you doing this to me?"

"Wouldn't you like to know?"

"Please," I said, "I can't think of anything I've done to deserve this treatment and I certainly don't know why anyone would subject me to it."

She said, "Just shut up. I have nothing to say to you." I could almost see with my third eye that her teeth were clenched.

She tied my hands back and said, "I think we should kill you right off."

I didn't believe what she was saying. "W-why?" I stammered.

"Because I said so, that's why."

I heard her get up and move to the other side of the room. I knew I was not going to get anything out of her and if I was ever going to take a chance, now was the time. I opened my mouth and screamed.

I wish I hadn't because almost instantly I felt a blow to my head. I didn't feel or hear anything else.

It could have been a long time or it could have been minutes when I came to. I only knew that my head was pounding and felt wet where she had struck me. I knew there was some blood. I turned over and realized that my feet were free. I swung them over the side and sat up.

I knew I was alone again when no one challenged my movements. I let my head quit spinning before I tried to stand up.

Once I got to my feet, I moved carefully, feeling with each foot before I made a step. I didn't want to fall before I found something that I thought I could use to pry the rope off my hands. I had gone a few steps when I ran into what felt like a chair or table leg with my foot. I moved more carefully.

It was a table. I turned around and began feeling the top of it as best I could with my bound hands. It was no use. I couldn't reach far enough to find anything that might be placed there.

I then thought that if there was a table, there was probably a chair. I worked my way to the end of the table and sure enough, I felt the seat of a chair with my knee. I backed against it and began feeling for the back with my hands.

When I made contact, I couldn't help smiling a little. It was a chair with a back that had slats between two straight side pieces. I felt to the top of one of the side pieces and was pleased that the top of it was round and smooth. I tried to work it between my wrists, but it didn't help. The rope became tighter.

An idea formed and I turned around. If I could bend over without jabbing the side piece into my eye, I might be able to get it under the blindfold. Then I could at least see what was in the room.

It worked. I got the side of the blindfold over the edge of the chair and began working it upward. All the time I was thinking that in the movies or books this would be the moment that the bad guys would break into the room and thwart my plan.

Fortunately this didn't happen. I was able to get the blindfold off one eye, then the other one. Unfortunately, removing

the blindfold didn't help my situation a lot. The room was still
as dark as coal. I couldn't see a thing.

Disappointed and exhausted, I managed to move around
and sit down in the chair. I wanted to cry, but instead I prayed.
At least, I thought, *I can bombard God with words now. I
haven't run out of them like before.*

My prayer was interrupted when the door opened. A light
clicked on. Before I could get my eyes adjusted she demanded,
"How'd you get to that chair?"

Of course with the tape still on my mouth I couldn't
answer.

I stared at her as she came toward me. She was a teenager
and I knew I had seen her before. I just wasn't sure where.

She ripped the tape off my mouth and asked again, "How'd
you get to the chair without help and how'd you get the blindfold off?"

Instinct told me not to rile her. "I was trying to find the
bathroom," I whispered.

She looked at me and shrugged. Then a sinister smile
crossed her young face. "I sure made a mess of your face. I
wish it had killed you."

"Why do you hate me?"

"If you don't know, I'm not gonna tell you." She took hold
of my shoulder. "Did you find the bathroom?"

"No. This is as far as I got."

"Well, come on then."

When we came back into the room she pushed me to the
bed. "I'm going to blindfold you again. Sit still."

I did as I was told. Since she hadn't taped my mouth, I
asked, "Could I have a drink of water?"

"I reckon." She went into an alcove on the right of the room.
In a minute she returned with a glass of water.

She held it for me to drink. "That's enough," she said before
I had finished.

She moved to the other side of the room and returned with
a roll of electrical tape. Tearing off a six-inch length, she

pressed it on my mouth. She then put the blindfold in place
and stood back.

"There. Now you won't be able to see."

I couldn't say anything. I just hoped she didn't remember
to tie my feet. She didn't.

My mind was racing. As soon as she was gone, I'd try
again to escape. In the meantime I busied my mind trying to
remember where I'd seen her before. I knew it wasn't church.
I knew most of the young people there. Maybe she'd attended
one of the youth meetings with a friend. If she had, I still
couldn't understand what I'd done to make her hate me so.
And hate me she did. It was plastered all over her face.

Instead of leaving I heard her begin to move about the
room. She was moving different objects. By the sounds she
made, I couldn't tell what. The noise continued until I heard
the door squeak again. I waited to see if she left. I knew immediately she hadn't because someone whispered to her. For
some reason, I thought the voice was male. I knew it was when
he whispered loud enough for me to hear, "What do you mean
she got the blindfold off?"

"She was trying to find the bathroom. I took her then put
her back on the bed."

His voice lowered when he said, "Well, I guess there is no
harm done. She saw you, but not me."

"She doesn't know who I am. She wonders, but she doesn't
know."

"That's good. We will keep her in the dark."

After this their voices grew fainter. They were discussing
something else, but I couldn't tell what. I heard another door
open, but it didn't squeak. *There must be another door out of
here,* I thought. *I wonder where it could be?*

I rebuilt the room in my mind. The cot was in the corner
next to a wall. Beside it was a small barrel like table. The rug
beside the cot was a braided one. The table where I sat in the
chair was almost in the middle of the floor. This set was of the
Early American style. The door, the one I thought squeaked,

was directly across from the table. To the right was the alcove where she got water for me. The bathroom was beside it. If there was another door, it was probably on the left wall. I hadn't noticed it, but that was the only place left for it to be.

It dawned on me that this was like a small apartment. A hideaway for something. But for what? I couldn't wrap my mind around the whole concept.

The shuffling and moving lasted for a while longer. Then the door squeaked again and I wondered if they had left. I got my answer when the girl came up to me and said, "Okay, preacher woman. I've got to get some sleep. It's on the floor for you." She took hold of my shoulder and pulled me off the cot. When I hit the floor, I felt cold hard cement. I wanted to ask for a blanket, but I knew she'd just refuse even if I was able to voice it.

I heard the cot give as she lay down. It wasn't long until she began to snore. I don't know how long I lay there before I fell into a restless sleep, too.

THIRTY-FOUR

I woke up when I felt myself being pulled to my feet. "Come on. I'll take you to the bathroom because I know you're going to ask to go."

When we came back into the room, she shoved me down on the cot. "I guess I'll put you here. I don't want him to know I made you sleep on the floor. If you're lying here when he comes in, he'll think you slept there." I felt a cold cloth on my face. "He told me to wash the blood off your face. Not that it matters. He'll probably kill you soon anyway."

I pulled back as she scrubbed the sore place on my temple. She laughed. When she finally finished washing my face and let me lie down, I tried to stretch out my weary frame. I was aching from my head to my toes. I wondered if there was a spot anywhere on my body that didn't hurt. I was also hungry. I wondered if she was going to feed me today. I didn't know if it was morning or night, but at that moment I really wanted a cup of coffee.

In a little while I heard water running. Could it be a shower? Was it here or was it coming from somewhere else in the house? I know I hadn't heard the mumbling from beyond the wall since I was first brought here. Maybe I was in a room that was seldom used or one that was isolated from the rest of the house. I tried to remember how long I had been here. Two days? Three?

My mind raced and I began to speculate about other things. Had I been missed and was anyone looking for me? Then I realized that of course they were. Elva would have missed me right away and she would see that a search was being conducted. I just couldn't understand why nobody had checked this room. Surely Elva knew about it. Maybe she'd just forgotten and would eventually remember. At least this wasn't like last summer when LeeAnn and I had been left in that basement to die. There were people coming in and out here. And they were feeding me enough to stay alive. Though probably small, there was still a chance that I might get away.

The girl spoke. "Ah, a shower makes one feel much better. I bet you wish you could have one." She laughed that mocking laugh of hers. "Of course you're not going to get it. You're going to lie right there until we decide what to do with you." She changed her tone. "I bet you're hungry, too. I am. In fact, I think I'll go get something hot. Maybe ham and eggs or waffles and bacon. Doesn't that sound good?"

It did sound good, but I couldn't tell her so.

A little later I heard the door squeak and I knew I was alone. I wondered if I had the strength to try to get to the door. I wouldn't know unless I tried.

I swung my feet off the bed and sat up. My head was spinning in all directions. I sat very still trying to ward off the dizziness. When it was gone, I tried to stand. My first attempt was a failure. I fell back to the bed. On the third try, I made it. I put one foot in front of the other and was feeling for the chair and table. I had the layout of the room in my mind and I knew it had to be in a straight line from the bed. I stepped forward again and knew it had to be close. I was wrong. The next thing I knew, I stumbled on something and fell hard on the cement floor. When I tried to get up, I couldn't. My ankle gave way and I fell back down. I tried again. It was no use. It wouldn't support my weight. I lay still and wondered if I had broken it.

The door opened and the girl sounded mad when she said, "Not again. When are you going to learn to stay where I put you?" She pulled me upward, but I still couldn't stand on my ankle. "Now you've done it. I think you've broken your foot." She untied my hands and put my right arm around her neck. She half carried, half dragged me to the cot. Dumping me, she said, "You're being a fool, Reverend. Why don't you accept the fact that you've had it? Stop fooling around and hurting yourself." She laughed. "Of course it is pretty funny to see you causing yourself so much pain. It keeps me from having to inflict it on you."

She pulled the tape off my mouth. "Thanks," I muttered.

"Sure. Why not?" She shoved something in my hand. "Here's a biscuit. Eat up."

"Thanks," I said again. "Could I have some water?"

"I guess so." She got the water for me and put it in my other hand. "Now eat so I can get you taped back up before he gets here?"

"Who is he?"

"Don't get your hopes up. It's not the handsome Preacher Freeman. You're never going to see him again."

Then I knew. This young woman was Penny Saxon's niece. Her name was Jackie. I said, "Why did you think I'd hope it was Trent Freeman, Jackie?"

"Hey, how'd you know my name?"

"Trent told me. He's been concerned about you since Ms. Saxon was killed. Are you with your mother?"

"Not on your life. After you got Aunt Penny killed, I ran away."

"But where are you staying?" I didn't want to think that this cramped room was her new home.

She jerked the water glass from my hand, spilling some on my lap. "That's none of your business. Now hurry up and finish that biscuit or I'll take it away, too."

I ate quickly because I knew it would be a while before she brought me anything else. I calmed my voice as much as I could. "Jackie, could I take the blindfold off for a little while? I would love to rest my eyes."

She took a deep breath. "I guess it would be all right."

I pulled it down and after letting my eyes adjust to the light, I looked around the room. Instantly I knew why I didn't find the table I'd sat at before. It had been moved across the room. So that was what all the shuffling around in here had been about. I wondered why they had bothered.

She was still holding the glass. It was half full of water. I reached for it. "Could I have the rest of that?"

She handed it to me without argument.

"Jackie, what am I doing here?"

She shrugged. "I guess you were getting too close to finding out the truth."

"What truth?"

She didn't answer. She simply smiled and said, "Boy, I bet you'd like to know what they're saying about you in town. They're running around like crazy looking for you. Nobody can understand how you could just disappear from the upstairs hall of Elva Kingfield's house. Some people think you ran away. Others think you were kidnapped and still others think crazy old Mrs. Kingfield had you captured and hidden away."

"Where are they looking for me?"

"Everywhere. Ed Walsh seems to be running everything. He's had the pond out back dragged. He's got the state police in on the action. Mrs. Kingfield got so upset between your disappearance and her dead husband's visits that they've put her back in the hospital. Bernice just sits in her room and cries. Your church friends are calling everybody they ever knew looking for you, and Preacher Trent is grieving, too. Of course, he'll get over it. Someday he'll meet a woman that is really good for him. Maybe Blaire would be right for him. She seems to be more his type. At least she's a Baptist. You're sure not his type or a Baptist either."

I ignored her babbling about a woman for Trent. "I'm so sorry about Elva. Is she doing all right now that she's in the hospital?"

"How should I know? And why would it matter? She's a loon. Aunt Penny told me so."

"Your aunt Penny was wrong. Elva is as sharp as she can be. Your aunt only wanted to get her hands on Elva's money."

"That's not so. She just wanted part of it." She got up suddenly. "I won't listen to bad things about Aunt Penny. She was the best friend I ever had. I hate you because you caused her death."

"How did I cause her death?"

"I'm not sure. I just know you did. She asked you for help and you wouldn't help her."

"Jackie, the only help your aunt ever asked of me was to help her get Elva Kingfield declared incompetent. She wanted to control Elva's money."

"I don't believe that."

"Whether you believe it or not, it's true. I couldn't do that to Elva. The lady has a right to control her money any way she wants to. Your aunt didn't have that right."

Jackie took the empty glass out of my hand. I saw tears in her eyes. "I don't believe you and I'm not going to listen to you anymore." She picked up the roll of electrical tape from the small table by the bed. She tore a piece.

"Please don't tape…"

My plea was lost when the tape went across my mouth. In an instant the blindfold went back on my eyes.

When Jackie left me, I lay on the bed going over the things she'd said. I felt sorry for her. Penny Saxon had filled her head with a lot of untruths and the sad part was that the child believed her. Then I thought of Elva. I was so sorry she was back in the hospital. I was sure the so-called visits from her former husband had put her there. I was just sorry my being captured had helped, too.

It struck me. Jackie knew about the visits from her dead husband. Why hadn't I caught that sooner and asked her about them. How were they pulling that off? I thought of the cleaning cloth I'd found in the hallway. Maybe…could it be part of a costume? Dennis didn't seem to think it anything important.

Of course, neither did I at the time. And what about Dennis? Could he possibly be the person Jackie was helping?

Of course not, I thought. *He's only been here a few days. This has been going on for some time. Who could it be? Maybe an old employee. Dennis did tell me that there was a gardener at one time. He could have come back to try to drive Elva crazy. But how would he know Jackie?*

My mind raced from one thought to another. I went on and on concocting scenarios in my mind, pausing only now and then to say prayers for those I love and for myself. That was the way I got through the day.

THIRTY-FIVE

I SLEPT AGAIN. I didn't know if it was night or day when I woke up. I just knew that I was hungry again. Of course all I'd had was that one biscuit. Jackie was not in the room, I didn't think. It was too quiet. I lay there for a few minutes debating with myself about trying again to get to the door. I'm glad I waited.

The door opened. There was laughter as they entered the room. "Boy, that was a good one. It's been so much fun scaring her. I wonder if anyone ever guessed that she was telling the truth about seeing a dead man."

I frowned. The only person I'd heard use that phrase was Myra Gallaway. Surely they weren't referring to her. Nobody would be cruel enough to try to scare a woman suffering with Alzheimer's. How could they anyway? She was safely tucked away in a nursing home.

Jackie's companion whispered something to her.

I had my back to the room and pretended to be asleep. Maybe the second person would then speak and I'd find out who he was.

Jackie came toward the bed. I breathed as steadily as I could. I felt her breath as she leaned over me. "I think she's asleep," she whispered.

"Good," her companion continued to whisper. "I'll get changed and get back out there. There's going to be a search party for Reverend Willa Hinshaw tonight. It wouldn't look right if I didn't join in."

"I understand." I heard Jackie sit down in the chair. "Should I go get her something to eat?"

"Get her a little something, I guess. I want her fed only enough to keep her alive, but I don't want her to build up her strength. She is resourceful. She might just figure a way to get out of here."

"I don't see how."

"You never know what she's capable of. Now scoot, but be careful. Nobody knows you're in town. Don't let anyone see you."

"I won't."

The door opened and shut. I heard the other person cross the room and the rustle of clothes being changed. I continued to stay in my same position.

In a few minutes, I again felt breath on my neck. Then a hand touched my cheek. I tried not to flinch, but I did in spite of myself.

"I didn't think you were asleep," a rough voice whispered. It had to be male. It went on. "As I said, you're resourceful. I have to be very careful that you don't louse things up any more than you have already."

With that, he crossed the room and left, closing the door behind him.

I turned over and sat up. At least now I knew the person Jackie was helping was a man. If he was going to help with a search party for me, then I might have time to escape before she got back. I was about to try to stand when I heard a slight noise on the other side of the room.

So, that's how he wants to play it, I thought. *He pretended to leave the room just to see what I would do with him gone. Okay, I'll put on a show for him.*

First I rotated my neck a few times to indicate I was trying to get the kinks out. I leaned to the right and then to the left several times as if I was trying to exercise some stiffness out of my body. I lifted my legs ten times and then took ten deep breaths through my nose. I sat still for a few minutes then I lay back down and fixed myself so I would be facing the door this time.

I didn't hear any sound from the other side of the room again, but instinct told me that he was still there.

It wasn't long until the door opened and Jackie must have come in. I heard a whisper and then the door closed. I sat up.

"Got you something to eat," she said. She sat down beside me and untied my hands. She pulled the tape from my mouth and said, "I guess you want your eyes uncovered."

I nodded and she took off the blindfold.

"Could I go sit at the table and eat?" I asked.

"I don't care."

I moved to the table and took the chair on the end. She put the food before me and sat down. "Do you like chicken?"

I nodded.

"I got you a two-piece dinner from KFC. I even splurged and got you some tea."

"Thank you. It looks very good." And it tasted good. I wasn't used to only one meal a day and anything would have been good.

"May I ask you something, Jackie?"

"If you want to, but I won't answer if I don't want to."

I smiled a little. "When you said something about frightening someone with the dead man's costume, were you talking about Myra Gallaway?"

"It could be her name. I don't know."

"Where was the lady you scared?"

"In a rest home in Winston-Salem."

My heart sank. It was Myra. "But why would anyone want to scare a sick person like her?"

"She's crazy. It's fun to scare crazy people. Besides, it was to get back at the Methodist preacher."

"What in the world could Philip have done to make you want to get back at him? He's one of the kindest men on earth."

"I don't know what he did, but he did something. I know

that Co—" She stopped herself before she said a name. "It don't matter. Eat your supper."

I took a bite then looked at her. "Jackie, how can you let yourself get caught up in a criminal activity? Don't you know that keeping me here could get you put in jail?"

"I don't think so. Nobody is ever going to know. Now that the lake has been dragged, he said that is probably where he'll dump you."

I shivered. "And the fact that someone plans to murder me doesn't bother you?"

She shrugged. "Maybe a little, but I'll get over it."

"If you don't get caught."

"We won't get caught. He's out there right now searching hard to find you or your body. Whichever shows up..." She laughed. "Or doesn't show up."

"But why? What have I done to you or to him?"

"You got in the way. As I told you before, if you'd helped Aunt Penny, none of this would have happened."

"I know your aunt Penny was stealing from Elva and I know she was trying to get her committed. But she didn't kill anyone, did she?"

"Of course not. Aunt Penny wouldn't do anything like that."

"And do you think she'd be proud of you for taking part in planning to kill someone?"

She stuck her lip out. "She's not here to care one way or the other."

"I know she's not." A thought drifted through my mind. I decided to act on it. "Is the person who plans to kill me the one who killed your aunt Penny?"

She looked as if I'd slapped her. Finally she stammered, "N-no. He couldn't have. He wouldn't have. That's a stupid thing to say." She got up from the table and walked across the room.

"Are you sure, Jackie? If he's the same person who

killed her, what makes you think that you won't be next after me?"

"He wouldn't kill me. I've helped him too much."

"But what will he do when he no longer needs your help? You will just be in his way and someone that could tell everyone what he has done. Someone like your aunt Penny. He probably killed her because she could tell on him. He had to get rid of all witnesses, beginning with her."

"I don't believe you. How would you know anything about it?"

"I must know something. Otherwise, why would he want to kill me?"

"I don't know." She turned back to the chair. "Just hurry up and eat so I can get you tied back up before he comes back."

"Will he come back here?"

"I don't know. Sometimes he checks in. Most of the time he doesn't."

"Are you living here, Jackie?"

"Most of the time."

"It's not a very comfortable place."

"I know, but when we get the money I'll get something nicer or move into the house."

"House? What house, Jackie?"

"That's enough talk." She grabbed the box of chicken from in front of me. "Get back on the bed."

"But what about taking me to the bathroom?"

She looked disgusted. "Come on," she snapped.

I was back on the bed, blindfolded and Jackie was getting ready to tape my mouth. The door opened.

"Did you kill my aunt Penny?" she demanded.

"What are you talking about?" he said in a loud whisper.

"I asked you if you killed my aunt Penny."

"What makes you ask that? Has the good reverend been filling your head with stupid ideas?"

"I don't know if they're stupid or not. I just want a straight answer. Somebody killed her. I want to know if it was you."

"Of course I didn't kill her."

"Do you plan to kill me after you don't need me no more?"

"I will always need you, Jackie."

"What about Reverend Willa? Are you going to kill her like you said?"

"I have no choice."

Jackie stood. "I don't want to kill anybody. Why do we have to do it?"

I saw my chance. She hadn't tied my hands yet. I reached up and jerked off the blindfold.

THIRTY-SIX

I CRIED, "IT IS YOU. But how did you pull all this off?"

Dennis Kingfield strode across the room and glared at me. "Now you've done it." He struck me across the face.

Jackie stared at him. "You don't have to hit her."

"So you're taking up for the enemy now." He turned to her. "Maybe I should give you a lick or two. Teach you how to stay in line."

"I just said you didn't have to hit her. She's not going anywhere. What does it matter that she knows who you are?"

"You're as stupid as Penny was," he snapped at her. "Now I have to kill her. I was trying to think of a plan where I could let her live. You both have ruined that now."

"So you did kill Aunt Penny?" She stared at him.

"What if I did? She was getting too brave. She was carrying out valuables like mad and I knew somebody would catch her. The lovely little reverend here was the one who did."

"But you killed her," Jackie wailed. "You didn't have to do that. I loved her."

"So get over it, kid. We all have to go sometime."

"And just as soon as you have your plan all worked out you're going to kill me and Jackie, aren't you, Dennis?" I spoke for the first time since seeing his face.

"I didn't say anything about killing Jackie."

"But she knows as much or probably a lot more than I do. You can't take the chance that she won't give you away."

He turned to Jackie. "Don't listen to her. She doesn't know what she's talking about. She's just trying to save her own life."

"I'm not so sure. You said once your aunt died and you had everything she owns, you'd give me enough money to leave town. But I would always know what you did to get it. Maybe I would be too much of a threat."

"I think Jackie is right," I said. "You plan to frighten your aunt to death and then you will kill me and then Jackie to hide the facts." I shook my head. "My only question is how you managed it while you were out of town."

"He wasn't out of town. He was right here all the time. He would call everyone on his cell phone and tell them he was in California. He was staying at a hotel."

"Then you must have been the one who ran me off the road," I said.

"Of course I was. It was so easy to fool you. I guess women of the cloth are as trusting as men of the cloth are. At times I got a kick out of seeing how you trusted and helped me."

"But why? Your aunt has left almost everything to you. Why do you have to kill her? She is an old lady. She's not going to live forever."

"But she will probably live longer than I need her to. I'm in deep trouble with my gambling debts. I have to have her money now. I can't wait any longer."

"So that's why you came up with the plan to scare her to death."

"Actually I came up with that plan when the bomb exploded too late to kill her in the graveyard. The fact that the grave was partially opened was a good lead into the plan. Penny helped me make the costume and I showed up on Sunday and stood outside the window and sang to her. I even knew Uncle Leo's favorite hymn. We thought that would do her in, then you showed up and things didn't turn out as we had planned."

"Was it then that Penny decided to get her committed?"

"It was. She got it on her mind and wouldn't let it go. I told her to forget it, but she thought it was the perfect thing to do. When you wouldn't go along with the idea, she decided you were her enemy and she would ruin your name in the town of Liverpool."

Jackie butted in. "So you decided to kill Aunt Penny."

"I had to, Jackie. I needed Willa to keep checking on Aunt Elva and I knew if the town turned against her, she would leave for some other church. I waited until the night that Penny took you to Kernersville for dinner. When she brought you home I called her and told her I needed to meet with her. We met in the parking lot of Willa's apartment. I left her there for Willa to find."

"Aunt Penny was a greedy woman, but she wasn't evil. You're an evil man, Cousin Dennis, and I don't want to help you anymore."

"I'm afraid you have no choice, my dear. You're in it too deep to get out now. You will go to prison, just like me, if we're caught."

"I wouldn't be so sure about that," I said. "She didn't have anything to do with killing her aunt. She might have to pay for some of the things she's done, but she won't be in prison for life like you will."

"Reverend Willa is right. I don't want to kill anybody."

"What about Bernice? I will tell everyone you stabbed her," he said.

"But I didn't. You did. I saw you do it."

"Do you think they'll take the word of a teenager over that of a man?" He sneered.

"I think they will," I said. "Especially when they find out he is a confessed murderer."

"I don't plan to confess."

"But you already have. Jackie and I both have heard your confession."

"Well, neither one of you is going to live to tell anyone about it."

I glanced at Jackie. I knew from the look in her eye that she had decided to side with me against her cousin. I judged the distance between me and the door. It would be hard, but maybe if I got him distracted enough Jackie could make a run for it.

"Dennis, I feel sorry for you," I said.

He laughed. "Why? I'm about to become a very rich man."

While he had his eyes on me I lunged for him. At the same time I shouted, "Get help, Jackie."

She ran for the door yelling at the top of her lungs. He reached out to stop her, but I grabbed the cup of iced tea that was still sitting on the table and aimed it directly for his eyes. I then lunged at him again. Though I was no match for him, while he was off balance, Jackie made it out the door. The next instant he came up with a right hook to my jaw and sent me across the room and I sprawled half on the bed and half on the hard floor. He turned to run after Jackie.

When I got my balance and began to clear my head, I headed out the door as fast as my sore ankle would let me.

Arms grabbed me as I came out in an old garage area. I struggled until I heard a gentle voice say, "Take it easy, Preacher Willa. You're okay now."

My dear friend Ed Walsh had never sounded so good.

He carried me out of the garage into the backyard. A police officer was putting cuffs on Dennis Kingfield.

Jackie ran to me. "Are you okay? I was afraid he was going to kill you."

"I'm fine, Jackie. And you?"

"I'll be okay." She smiled at me. "Will you help me get everything straightened out?"

"Yes. I will."

Trent raced to me. "Thank God they found you." Ed let me go and Trent folded his arms around me. "I'm so glad you're all right."

"It's all thanks to Jackie." I smiled at her. "She saved my life, Trent."

Trent looked at her and smiled. "I always knew you were special, Jackie."

"Thank you, Preacher Freeman. Now I realize how special Reverend Willa is."

Another police officer came up and told Jackie she would have to come with him. "Don't worry," I said. "I'll do everything I can to help you."

"I know you will," she said and walked toward the waiting police car.

Trent looked down at me. "I think I need to take you to the hospital."

"Yes. I want to be there to tell Elva what happened. She's going to be devastated when she learns her beloved Dennis is behind all this turmoil."

He chuckled. "I meant I wanted to get you checked out, but it's just like you to be thinking of someone else."

"I just can't help it. It will be some time before it's all sorted out. I want to be there for Elva."

"Then let's go to the hospital. I insist that you get checked out first then I will escort you to Mrs. Kingfield's room myself."

"Wait a minute. I have one question." I looked at them. "Where were they keeping me?"

"It was a room that Mrs. Kingfield had forgotten about and nobody else knew existed. There is a closet on the second floor that has a false back. It leads to a secret passageway that ends in the room where you were kept. It was built as a safe passage during the civil war."

"So that was how they were getting into and out of the house." I looked at Ed.

"Yes and the exit to the outside was well hidden in this old garage. If Jackie hadn't shown it to us, we'd have never found it," Ed said.

"And we were standing right here in this garage looking for you the first night that you disappeared," Trent said. "We never dreamed we were so close."

"I heard voices, but I didn't know where they were coming from. There was no light in the room except when they switched it on." I felt myself getting a little woozy. "I think I'd better go now. You'll have to fill me in on everything else a little later."

Trent put his arm around me and led me to his car.

"Call me and let me know how she's doing," Ed said as Trent helped me into his SUV.

"I will."

I put my head back on the seat and tried to relax. I had decided to let Trent handle everything from here on.

THIRTY-SEVEN

IT DIDN'T TAKE AS LONG to straighten things out as I thought it would. Jesse Snow agreed to take Jackie's case. I knew there wasn't a lawyer in the area that could do any more for her than he could. He had her out on bail the next day and everyone expected her to get probation with a lot of community work instead of jail time. Her mother was getting better and was going to move to Liverpool so Jackie could be near her friends. Rose and Nevis Poole had agreed to let them live rent free in one of their properties until the mother was able to work again. Nevis even said he'd find a job for her. Trent had arranged for them to get counseling.

Elva was heartbroken at first, but ended up taking the news about Dennis much better than I expected. She was happy to know that her husband hadn't come back from the dead, and she was also glad that now everyone believed that she had seen a walking corpse—even if it was a made-up one. She was home from the hospital in two days and said that she would provide the money for a lawyer for her nephew, if we could find an attorney who wouldn't call her to testify.

Bernice didn't brag about the fact that she'd never trusted Dennis. She just smiled at me when I told her what had happened. "I thought I might be wrong about him, but I guess I wasn't," was all she said.

Blaire decided to continue living with Elva and Bernice as soon as Elva asked her to remain. She loves it there. I don't see her quite as much as before because she is interested in a new insurance salesman who has come to work in her company. He seems like a nice guy. The two of them went to dinner with Trent and me the other night. I'm keeping my fingers crossed for her.

The saddest part of the ordeal was the fact that Dennis had been creeping up to Myra's window at the rest home in his death costume just to scare her. He confessed that he did it because Philip had once told the Kingfields that he was a troubled boy and needed to be seen by professionals. He also confessed that he'd slipped the Halloween costume book to Myra when he caught her alone in the backyard of the parsonage. It had a picture of a mummy and that was how he had dressed. He told her that the dead man would come and get her one day. After the time she ran across the street naked, it became a game with him. He wanted to see what he could make a troubled person like her do. Philip was livid about the whole thing, but said he was trying to pray his way through it. At least we knew that Myra would never have to worry about the dead man again.

I learned that Dennis thought I was beginning to figure out his scheme the night he saw that I had noticed the original art was back over Elva's sofa. He felt he had to do something to stop me from giving away his entire scheme. I had been right about Penny Saxon stealing things from the house. She had kept them in a storage unit and little by little, Dennis had been taking them back inside. He'd hoped no one would notice they had been gone. He'd wanted everything to be in place when he inherited the estate.

As for me, when Trent took me to the hospital, they discovered that I was anemic. My bumps and bruises would heal, but I needed a supplement for my blood. Not only did I get the medicine, but Trent has insisted on feeding me liver, broccoli and anything else he can think of that has iron in it. I am beginning to get sick of it and craving a big hunk of chocolate cake.

I'm still not sure what is happening between Trent and me. It is getting harder and harder for us to deny the physical attraction we have for each other. We both know we have to do something about it soon. I know we care for each other deeply. In fact, I wouldn't be afraid to say that I'm in love with him. I'm pretty sure he feels the same way about me. We made a date to talk about our situation tonight. I have cooked his favorite meal and I have put on soft music and lit candles. We are not going to answer the phone or anything else.

The doorbell and the phone rang at the same time. I ignored the phone and answered the door. Trent stood there looking very handsome in his khaki pants and peach sweater.

"Hi," he said as he held a dozen pink roses out to me.

"They're beautiful," I said and stood aside for him to come in. "I'll put them in water and we can decorate the table with them."

He nodded and followed me into the kitchen. "You look lovely tonight."

"Thanks," I said. I didn't tell him I'd spent two hours bathing and primping and getting ready to see him. "Dinner is going to be a few minutes. Would you like some tea while we wait?"

"Not really." He smiled at me. "Why don't you take a chair and we'll just talk a bit."

I sat down. Looking at the twinkle in his eyes, I knew he had something on his mind. "Sure," I said. "What do you want to talk about?"

"This," he said holding a small velvet box toward me.

I stared at it. "T-Trent…" I stammered. "Are you asking…?"

"Yes, I'm asking. I love you, Willa. Will you marry me?"

* * * * *

REQUEST YOUR FREE BOOKS!

2 FREE NOVELS
PLUS 2 FREE GIFTS!

WORLDWIDE LIBRARY®

MYSTERY™

Your Partner in Crime

YES! Please send me 2 FREE novels from the Worldwide Library® series and my 2 FREE gifts (gifts are worth about $10). After receiving them, if I don't wish to receive any more books, I can return the shipping statement marked "cancel." If I don't cancel, I will receive 4 brand-new novels every month and be billed just $4.99 per book in the U.S. or $5.99 per book in Canada. That's a saving of at least 25% off the cover price. It's quite a bargain! Shipping and handling is just 50¢ per book in the U.S. and 75¢ per book in Canada.* I understand that accepting the 2 free books and gifts places me under no obligation to buy anything. I can always return a shipment and cancel at any time. Even if I never buy another book, the two free books and gifts are mine to keep forever.

414/424 WDN FDDT

Name	(PLEASE PRINT)	
Address		Apt. #
City	State/Prov.	Zip/Postal Code

Signature (if under 18, a parent or guardian must sign)

Mail to the **Reader Service:**
IN U.S.A.: P.O. Box 1867, Buffalo, NY 14240-1867
IN CANADA: P.O. Box 609, Fort Erie, Ontario L2A 5X3

Not valid for current subscribers to the Worldwide Library series.

Want to try two free books from another line?
Call 1-800-873-8635 or visit www.ReaderService.com.

* Terms and prices subject to change without notice. Prices do not include applicable taxes. Sales tax applicable in N.Y. Canadian residents will be charged applicable taxes. Offer not valid in Quebec. This offer is limited to one order per household. All orders subject to credit approval. Credit or debit balances in a customer's account(s) may be offset by any other outstanding balance owed by or to the customer. Please allow 4 to 6 weeks for delivery. Offer available while quantities last.

Your Privacy—The Reader Service is committed to protecting your privacy. Our Privacy Policy is available online at www.ReaderService.com or upon request from the Reader Service.

We make a portion of our mailing list available to reputable third parties that offer products we believe may interest you. If you prefer that we not exchange your name with third parties, or if you wish to clarify or modify your communication preferences, please visit us at www.ReaderService.com/consumerschoice or write to us at Reader Service Preference Service, P.O. Box 9062, Buffalo, NY 14269. Include your complete name and address.

WWLI1